Praise for Denise A. Agnew's
Before the Dawn

"Breathtaking, exquisite, bold, romantic, and suspenseful are only a handful of words that describe *Before the Dawn...* I highly recommend *Before the Dawn* to anyone that is a diehard romantic longing for a book that is packed full of romance, suspense and two people destined to find the love and redemption that they were looking for. I look forward to reading more from Denise Agnew..."

~ *The Romance Studio*

Look for these titles by
Denise A. Agnew

Now Available:

Hot Zone
Male Call
Unconditional Surrender
Private Maneuvers
Close Quarters
Hot Pursuit

Marshall's Law
Dark, Deadly Love
For A Roman's Heart

Print Anthology
Intimate Alliance

Before the Dawn

Denise A. Agnew

Samhain Publishing, Ltd.
11821 Mason Montgomery Road, 4B
Cincinnati, OH 45249
www.samhainpublishing.com

Before the Dawn
Print ISBN: 978-1-60928-596-8
Digital ISBN: 978-1-60928-493-0

Cover by Kim Killion

First Samhain Publishing, Ltd. electronic publication: June 2011
First Samhain Publishing, Ltd. print publication: May 2012

Dedication

To my husband, Terry, whose faith in me gives my heart wings and is a true blessing.

Acknowledgements

A book like this can't be written without significant research. Along with the research there are helping hands. Many thanks to: author Diane Whiteside for her generous help. I drew from her extensive knowledge of the railroads on more than one occasion. To my husband, Terry, for listening to me go on about this book and suggesting numerous ways to create railroad mayhem. To Park Ranger Douglas J. Richardson of the Allegheny Portage Railroad Museum for his excellent knowledge of the area and invaluable information. Thank you for your generosity and kindness indulging this author.

Author's Note

During my research on Eastern State Penitentiary, I was lucky enough to find many documents that gave me the flavor of what living there in the 1840s and '50s would have been like for a prisoner. Because this story is fiction, I have taken liberties with some details. I've tried to retain the flavor and kept most of the details as accurate as possible.

Chapter One

"...he is like a man buried alive; to be dug out in a slow round of years; and in the meantime dead to everything but torturing anxieties and horrible despair."

Charles Dickens commenting on Eastern State Penitentiary

Eastern State Penitentiary
Philadelphia, Pennsylvania
June, 1850

Elijah Jonas McKinnon would never forget the day he left the penitentiary the revenge in his soul the only reason for living.

But the day he learned he'd soon be free...now that day came in a close second for perfect memories.

"You're out, McKinnon. Don't ask me how, but you're one lucky son-of-a-bitch."

Elijah stared at the rail-thin jailer while disbelief chewed at his mind like a rat on an old leather boot. Elijah dropped his bible on the stone floor, and the thump echoed around the cell and probably the whole damned penitentiary. He opened his mouth but not a syllable emerged. He'd gone insane. Finally, God had granted his wish, the one he prayed for at night after the lights were extinguished and the huge structure taunted him with phantom whispers he knew couldn't issue from any living human being. Often, all the gables, the buttresses, the arches of this prison came alive in his nightmares. Perhaps they were truly animated. Became the horrible dream from which he expected to remain for a goodly portion of his life.

Elijah gazed upward at the skylight in the barrel-vaulted ceiling, the meager illumination at this time of day bathing his face. He closed his eyes as a mix of relief and fear battled for supremacy within him. He returned his attention to the jailer.

Elijah tried his voice, something he used only for furtive whispers late at night, when he resorted to kneeling on hard stone and holding his rosary close to his heart. "What did you say?"

The sound was rusty and aching with disbelief.

The jailer's arrow-sharp nose tilted upward as he stood at the open cell door. Lank, dark, greasy hair fell over the man's forehead. His grin held an eerie delight and showed in his ice-cold blue eyes. "You got a reprieve. 'Parently your brother found evidence you didn't do it. Your brother Amos done killed your woman."

Elijah's jaw tightened as a thousand emotions crawled up his throat, threatening to erupt in a cry one part agony and one part relief. What did he feel? He should shout with joy, pump his fist in the air with victory that he'd been vindicated. After all, hadn't he vowed to leave jail and find Amos because he knew his brother was guilty? The heavens had granted Elijah another chance. One he wouldn't squander.

"That all you got to say, McKinnon?" His jailer's sour expression turned to an almost friendly façade. "Damn, but if it was my worn hide, I'd be pissing myself with happiness."

Elijah ambled towards the man, throat still tight, body coiled with a sudden desire to run. The jailer took a tentative shift back on his heels, eyes caught between wariness and cool bravado.

Elijah swallowed hard. "Jesus, Mary and Joseph. If you're lying to me, Mouse, I'll leave here, find a knife, then come back and cut your throat."

Mouse's eyes widened, his long face almost as dirty and greasy as his hair. "So that's what you sound like when you're angry. You really are a Mick."

"Yes, I really am."

"If you was a smart boy you wouldn't talk yet. What if I was trying to trick you into talkin', then clapped you in the iron tongue?"

Elijah allowed a smile to wander across his face, the first he'd attempted in months. "You're my jailer, but you're not as bad as half the men in here." Elijah coughed. "You've never treated me unfairly before. Why would you start now?"

The men halted conversation when another voice echoed nearby. "Ought to be a law against a bastard like McKinnon leaving this place."

Elijah's muscles tightened at the sound of the rough, hateful voice of Tobias Varney. Tobias wandered into view at the doorway, edging Mouse out of the way.

Mouse threw a vile frown at Varney. "Get outta here."

Varney took a step forward into the cell, his thick, blond hair as luxurious as a woman's but his pock-marked face almost as frightening as a specter. He slapped a stick against his thigh in a rhythmic stroke. "Nah, I don't think so. I think they should keep this murdering son-of-a-whore here. What do you think, you stupid Mick?"

Elijah's temper surged high, threatening eruption. He understood the man, who had tried to provoke him many times over five years. He knew what this ass wanted. Damned if he'd give the man satisfaction of creating a scene that would result in more incarceration.

Throat still aching and raw with emotion and lack of use, Elijah said the one thing least likely to cause retribution. "Feck you, Varney."

Varney threw back his head and laughed, his face contorted with cruel merriment. Varney strode forward, and

11

Elijah's fists clenched, his whole body stiffening in anticipation. "I ought to take you down with this stick." Varney drew the stick over his head. "Ought to show you what bastards like you deserve."

Mouse hurried forward and stood next to Elijah. Though the smaller man didn't possess a stick, Gulliver "Mouse" O'Toole had guts. "Back away, Varney. You know it ain't right. The Mick hasn't done anything."

Varney tilted his head and gazed at the other guard as if he'd lost his head somewhere along the way. "You're only takin' his side because you're Irish like him."

Mouse gave his fellow guard a cold smile. "I'm a nativist like you, man, and a Protestant. I despise his filthy hide as much as the next. My family has been here since 1785. This here Mick...well, I don't think ten years is near long enough to make him a real native. Do you?"

Varney's mouth twisted as he continued to slap the stick against his leg. "Nope. So, why are you helpin' him?"

Elijah hoped the men would leave soon. Leave him so that he could enjoy his upcoming freedom within the confines of his cell.

Jerking his head to the left, Mouse said, "Come on. I hear tell the warden is makin' his rounds soon. We're almost off our shift. I'll buy you a drink, Varney. Get outta here, and I'll meet you later."

Licking his lips with a bizarre anticipation, Varney gave Elijah one last glance, and then headed out the door.

After the man's footsteps echoed down the hall and disappeared, Mouse cleared his throat. "So...what you gonna do when you get outta here? Find Amos? Beat the stuffin' outta him?"

Pure relief and hatred mingled inside Elijah's battered soul. His body and mind ached with a desire to leave this hellhole, to find Amos, the man who'd taken sweet Maureen's life. At the same time, he wanted to run home to his Ma and his other brother Zeke. Grief rose up inside for all the months...the years lost in this god-forsaken place. His throat tightened again.

"No." Elijah struggled for the next words, strangled by a force inside him he didn't recognize and that scared him to the roots of his aching soul. "I'm going to kill him."

Dear Ma,

I apologize for not writing to you before, but as you no doubt know, I was not allowed to send or receive letters until now. I guess since they know I am an innocent man, they think I deserve the opportunity to send post to my loved ones. Zeke wrote me and said you still live in Kensington. I would like to come see you the day I get out of prison. Before I go to see Zeke at his new home. There is so much I want to discuss, dear Ma. I missed you so much while I was in this hellhole. You cannot imagine the surprise and joy I have felt upon learning the governor had pardoned me, and I am about to taste freedom. Please write me.

Love,

Your obedient son, Elijah.

Dear son,

My new husband, George, suggested I write this letter. Did Zeke tell you I had married again? Just a month ago. He is a fine man with lovely manners, money and a good job. He owns a dry goods and sundries store in Kensington that does very well. I do not have to work in the sweatshop anymore, which suits me fine since my bones are getting old.

I am sorry to say that George doesn't want you to come see us. I cannot say I blame him. He says that even though Zeke proved you innocent, that we cannot be seen associating with someone who has been in prison. At first I was angry, but I understand how he feels. It would not do. Our lives are complicated because he has a son who is a minister at the Presbyterian Church. I hope you have been praying every day,

13

son, for the redemption of your soul. Maybe we can meet someday when George forgets where you have been and what you have seen. I think if you converted to Protestantism, like I have, life here might go easier for you.

As ever, your mother.

Ten days later

Elijah stared at the row house in front of him and admired Zeke's abode. "Well, I'll be damned."

The brownstone didn't have the shabbiness Elijah associated with living in his old Kensington neighborhood. Envy played a part in his feelings, and he understood that. While his life once filled with despair and heartache, Elijah's brother had made something of his life.

But Elijah had no time to wonder about Zeke's life. Hunting down Amos meant he needed to hurry.

Elijah wiped his palms on his trousers. Straightened the worn and not exactly crisp white jabot. He tugged on the bottom of his waistcoat and tried the doorknocker. He half expected a maid to answer, but the door swung open and revealed Zeke. An older, sharper version of Zeke, but Zeke nonetheless. With light brown hair neatly combed back with oil, expressive brown eyes, and craggy features, Zeke resembled their Ma more than Amos or Elijah. Shorter than Elijah by a couple of inches, he still commanded respect with his muscular frame.

"Brother." Elijah's heart and mind roiled with a thousand words, a million platitudes to express thankfulness.

Zeke smiled and clapped a hand on his shoulder. "Good to see you. Sorry I couldn't come to the penitentiary but my wife is indisposed." He glanced over his shoulder and lowered his voice. "We need to keep our voices down. She's sleeping."

The tight grip on Elijah's shoulder almost hurt, but he would take that brotherly sign of affection anytime after five years.

"Come in, come in." Zeke motioned for him to follow. Zeke

closed the door and led the way to the left and a large parlor.

Elijah took in the interior of the row house. Though well furnished, it was middle-class. The frippery Elijah associated with a female presence seemed muted, as if the lady of the house didn't like to overdo. He doubted his brother could afford extravagances on his pay as a reporter for a new paper in town.

"This is a fine house, Zeke."

Zeke winked. "You'd think so wouldn't you? If it wasn't for my wife's money, we wouldn't have this much. Her father owns a mill on the other side of the city."

"And how did an Irishman like you manage to marry into money?"

Zeke must have heard the sardonic tone, for his smile grew wider and rueful. "By being the luckiest damn bastard there is."

"*No*, I'm the luckiest damn bastard there is."

Zeke's gaze narrowed. "You might be. Care for a drink?"

Elijah's mouth watered as his brother wandered over to a table holding a decanter filled with amber liquid. "Haven't had a drop in five years, but I don't have time for neighborly visit. I have things I need to do."

Zeke sighed and nodded. "You hungry?"

"Can't waste a minute on my stomach. I'll eat later."

"You'll want money, I suppose."

"You know I'll pay you back."

Zeke led the way into the parlor and opened a drawer in a small desk near the door and pulled out some bills and coin.

A loud snapping noise from the wood stove made Elijah tense and jerk, every muscle coiled for—he didn't know what.

Zeke's brows lowered. "You all right, brother?"

Elijah frowned. "Five years of solitary...well, you'd think a big prison holding that many men would have mighty noise. Once in a long while I'd hear some madman yell, but most of the time you'd think I was in a tomb. Loud noises startle me. Haven't figured out how to stop reacting that way."

Zeke gripped Elijah's shoulder. "You don't have to explain. I know how hard it must have been for you."

Anger lifted from deep within Elijah, boiling and frothing like the pool at the bottom of a waterfall. He pulled away from under his brother's grip. "No, you don't know. Until you've had to keep your mouth closed for five years except to answer a jailer's question...well, then you'll know."

"I'm sorry. Again." Zeke handed him the bills, his eyes troubled. He loosened the cravat at his throat and unbuttoned his waistcoat. "That's all I can spare."

Elijah nodded as he shoved the money in his pants pocket. "You've been most generous with me." Emotions tumbled inside him, chaotic and remorseful, indefinable. He swallowed hard, and his accent thickened. "Sure, and you know if it hadn't been for you, I would've rotted in that cell for many more years."

Zeke's jovial expression returned. "Take ease, Elijah. You see, I know if it had been Amos or me...neither one of us would have survived that prison." A shiver passed over his frame. "That our own brother..."

Zeke shook his head.

A long silence ensued. What could either of them say when five years had separated so much, when words seemed insufficient to recover what they'd lost...Elijah didn't know. The hollowness inside yawned like a dark, dank cave with no end in sight. Again his emotions scrambled.

"I know what you're planning to do," Zeke said.

Elijah's head jerked up. "What?"

"I know what you're planning. You aren't going to just find a place to lie low until you find a job. You're planning something. What is it?"

Elijah couldn't deny his brother's accuracy. He dangled between telling his innermost thoughts and lying vehemently. "Who says I want to do blacksmithing again? I worked hard in the penitentiary and didn't keep a plugged nickel."

Zeke's eyes darkened, as if he had a million questions but

decided not to ask. "You walk all the way here?"

"Needed the fresh air. Fresh air was on short supply in my cell. The facilities there weren't flushed every day. At least not the first year I was there. The stench sure wasn't like a lady's finest perfume. The venting in the skylight...it didn't always work well. And the sun...damn if it didn't feel good on my face today."

"You got a hat?"

"Didn't buy one."

"Best you get one."

"It'll feel good to have the wind in my hair for a while."

"You've got a long time now to feel the sun."

"I won't if my plans work out."

Zeke's gaze centered on him, hard with questions. "What do you mean?"

Elijah would let him have a safe illusion. "Like you said...finding a job. Just not as a blacksmith. Maybe I'll go back to being newspaper boy on a street corner or head out west and become a mail order cowboy. A minor thing for a murderer."

Zeke grunted and put his hands on his hips. "Jesus, Mary and Joseph, little brother. You aren't a murderer. I proved that."

"And now Maureen's real murderer is gone, and I'll be a murderer once I find him."

Zeke's eyes widened with apprehension. "You what? Now get that idea right outta your head. The law will find him."

Seeing his brother's disapproval didn't chill the fire burning in Elijah's gut. "There's nothing for me here anyway."

Zeke closed his eyes and threw his head back. Elijah remembered he used to do that when they were kids when he wanted to show disapproval or disbelief. Looked like he'd never lost the habit.

"Save us, St. Patrick," Zeke said. "Amos will be punished. The law will catch up to him."

17

Though Elijah wanted to say he didn't give a tinker's damn about the law, he knew it wouldn't sit well. Better to let this subject curl up and die before it caused bad blood.

Elijah pondered his options. He could try and find a room for the night, but his body protested the idea and so did his mind. Only one day out of prison, and he felt so tired he didn't know which way was up. "I need to find some people in Kensington."

"Who?"

"Old friends of Amos."

Elijah gave that weary, older brother sigh. "Dad blame it Elijah, if you go there and start asking questions, your life won't be worth half a cent."

Elijah's temper started to boil, but he drew a deep breath and held back. "If I can find one of Amos's friends to tell me where he is, I'll be in luck. You really think I'm afraid of asking?"

Zeke rubbed both hands over his face. "You're not afraid of anything. You never were, even when you should've been. It's me that's afraid, little brother. Your damn fearlessness helped get your arse thrown into that penitentiary in the first place."

Elijah grunted. "Maybe. I've made many mistakes in my life already. What's one more?"

"Then you'll forget this ridiculous idea of going after Amos, right?"

"I can't promise that."

"Then I won't give you any more money if you ask. I won't finance my own brother's murder."

Elijah's body stiffened. "Who's? Mine or Amos's?"

"Either. Because I know if you go after him, he'll try and kill you."

"Try he might. He'll fail."

"But you wouldn't fail to kill him, would you?"

Silence dropped between them, and Elijah knew he'd

arrived at a crucial junction in his relationship with Zeke. His insides twisted. If he agreed to abandon his search for revenge, Zeke would be happy. Yet if he truly dropped this need for revenge, he would have nothing left to strive for in this world. How did a man deal with that? What else did he have left?

"I can see your mind working." Zeke walked towards him until he could clap a brotherly hand on his shoulder again. "Why don't you sleep on it? Give your mind a rest and make a decision in the morning."

Elijah didn't acknowledge at first whether he would comply. He vacillated from wanting to say "go to hell" and remaining humble because of his brother's generosity. "I need to do something now. Can't wait."

Zeke released him and tucked his fingers into his vest. "If you're all-fired determined, then I have information for you. I didn't want to tell you this, but I figure it's better than you tearing through Kensington. Amos fled to Pittsburgh."

Anger tightened the muscles in Elijah's jaw until it ached. "And when did you plan to tell me this? Or were you going to tell me at all?"

"I found out from the authorities that they did an investigation in Kensington while cleaning up another nativist riot there two weeks ago."

"There was another one? I figured them bastards would have packed up and moved away a long time ago."

"Hell, no. Fact is they still have way too much pull in Philadelphia and beyond. The authorities discovered Amos is off to Pittsburgh. They've alerted the sheriff to be on the lookout for him."

"I see."

"Do you? Are you satisfied now that they will bring him to justice? You're free and clear of the criminal life. Start your life over today. Forget about Amos."

Elijah made a sound of disbelief. "Sure, and I'd be Judas if I forgot what he did to Maureen and to myself."

19

"Maybe being Judas in this case is the right thing to do."

Confusion didn't enter into the picture. Elijah saw clearly what must be done. "Not this time, Zeke." He reached out and took his brother's hand. "Thank you again for the money." He started towards the door and as he opened it, he paused long enough to take one more look at Zeke. "If I don't see you again, have a good life."

With a heavy weight tightening around his neck like a hangman's noose, Elijah left.

Chapter Two

Philadelphia & Columbia Railroad
Philadelphia to Lancaster
Two days later

Mary Jane Lawson felt the man staring at her from across the train, and everything inside her screamed that he was dangerous. She had noted the man's presence since she boarded the train in Philadelphia. He never seemed far away, always keeping her within viewing distance. She tried ignoring him, but it rarely worked. She always knew when his gaze rested upon her.

When she dared swing her gaze in his direction, everything inside her froze. His observance, so rude and intent, should have brought on moral indignation. The fact she could not find fault with his staring disturbed her. Mary Jane tightened her grip on her skirts, her gloved hands too warm in the black leather.

She noted his thickly lashed, dark green eyes. His attention swept over her in more thorough assessment, as if he had never seen a woman. She had never witnessed eyes that intense, and something within them scared her in a way she could not understand. Light flickered over him as clouds parted outside the train window. His mahogany hair, full and thick, curled in an unruly toss around his collar. Macassar oil or bear grease didn't tame his hair as it did most men's locks. The side part was a little imprecise. While he wore no beard or mustache, his sideburns were long.

She sniffed, lifted her nose and looked away. There. He *deserved* a cut, a refusal of acknowledgement, for not following common manners.

Since when has a man's direct attention ever bothered me?

Her mother's indignant voice rang in her head. *Good heavens, you do not ask a man to dance. You wait for him to ask you. And stop staring. It is rude and implies you are a loose...well...loose with your attentions and affections. Do you want to garner a reputation?*

Drawn to the green-eyed man's presence, Mary Jane glanced over at him and saw he still stared at her, as she might be the most fascinating thing he had ever seen. Most civilized man were too...well...civilized to make interest so obvious. This man didn't seem to care what she thought.

Hmm. Now that was another thing she was not used to. She started to smile at him and stifled her inclination. Now was not the time to allow it free rein.

Mary Jane opened her reticule and extracted a handkerchief. The wood stove at the far end of the car behind her generated too much heat, even for an unusually crisp June day. She dabbed at her cheeks and the cloth came away slightly sooty. *Awful.* See if she ever took another train.

On the other hand, the lure of adventure drew her into excitement, and if it were not for the terrible reason behind her train trip, she would almost enjoy the soot and grit and the loud hustle bustle.

She did not know whether to feel exhilaration or amazement at what she accomplished so far on this excursion. After the train had left Vine Street in the center of Philadelphia, they had crossed the Schuylkill River on a huge viaduct. All along the way she had marveled at the beauty displayed to the north where farmhouses and stone barns dappled the land. Their railway coach was hauled up a high area called the Belmont Plane. After that, coupled to steam locomotives, they made their way to the canal basin where they'd soon traverse the Susquehanna River near Columbia.

The speed was terrifying, the noise deafening, the entire ride uncomfortable. The rattle, rattle, rattle of the car over rails irritated her. From what she had gleaned at their last stop, they would try to make it all the way to the town of Columbia. If bad weather dictated, they would finish their trip for tonight at Lancaster around three o'clock. A stagecoach would not have proved much better for comfort and certainly not for speed, and transporting Father relied on the train. Returning to her mother and sisters would prove a trial as well, but in the meantime she could take some comfort in the hours it would take to reach home.

Home. She should not feel eager to return to the one place she longed to escape. She closed her eyes and sighed, glad for the relative emptiness of the railcar. As she sighed, she still felt the green-eyed man's attention. It made her want to squirm. Weariness dragged at Mary Jane's eyelids. Heat threatened to choke every drop of air from the compartment. Her neck itched. Her palms sweated. She swallowed back the lump in her throat that threatened to grow with every hour. Tears prickled and she drew a tight breath. No, she would not. She could not lose control. Staying strong was more important than purging feelings. She tugged at the ruffled lace neckline. She unfastened two buttons. More than once she'd wished she'd forgone wearing a crinoline. But no, that wouldn't do. Simply wouldn't do.

Thank goodness her chaperone Prudence could not see her opening the blouse. Her long nose would tilt high with pure disapproval. On the other hand, when her mother and sisters discovered she had left Prudence in Philadelphia, well, she would never hear the end of it. She sighed. Soon, this would all be over. Father would find his eternal place in Pittsburgh—his body laid to rest near his ancestors.

Movement to her left started her out of her reverie. The mysterious man stared at her again. Seconds slowed as their gazes locked, and that look seared awareness into her brain and all through her. Her lips parted in soundless amazement as his eyes warmed with interest...and if she dared think it, a nameless heat. Then he looked away and she wondered if she imagined that brief moment of connection. She straightened, stiffening her back as if it would deny the outrageous sensation that she'd stepped into danger. Her heartbeat quickened. Good thing Prudence wasn't with her. The lady would have vapors for certain.

Two men Mary Jane had seen earlier in the day wandered past to sit in the seat in front of her. Her gaze tangled momentarily with one of the men, but something...something felt different. With blond hair, sharp nose, tight mouth and pale skin, he took her in with cold eyes so washed out she could not tell if they were ice blue or chilly green. Hairs on the back of her neck prickled despite the insidious heat. A horrible chill, soul-deep and profound shivered through her.

She yanked her gaze away from the man as he slid into the seat and scooted over for the other man. His companion, a skinny man with frayed trousers and frayed waistcoat, was far friendlier in appearance. Seedy, but without the cold eyes. As he reached his seat, he tipped his hat, nodded, and said with a raspy voice, "Ma'am."

With reluctance, she nodded in acknowledgement. His gaze took in her black silk traveling dress and hat. She returned his bold stare with one of her own. No. This man's stare did not make her feel anything like the green-eyed man across the aisle. Her mother's nagging voice followed her in the same indignant voice.

You have been disgraced. No fine Pittsburgh man will be the least bit interested in marrying you.

Mary Jane sighed. She could not allow indiscretions in her past to ruin her future. Not when her bold nature had created havoc in her life up to this point.

The blond man made a sound in his throat, and she

realized he had aimed and missed the spittoon near his feet. Her stomach roiled. *Honestly, some men are perfect swine.*

The skinny man turned around in his seat and gazed at her point blank. Then his blond friend did the same.

"Ma'am." The skinny man lifted one eyebrow as his insolent attention swept over her. "You a widow?"

Startled at the question, she did not speak right away.

The skinny man wiped his nose on his sleeve. "Seems a bit strange you travelin' by yourself."

Repulsed, she did not know what to say.

"She isn't traveling by herself," said the deep, Irish-accented voice to her immediate left. "She's with me."

Both men in front of her glanced over at the green-eyed Irishman. Startled, she did the same.

The Irishman's expression stayed neutral, but his eyes held a warning. "She's my wife. Her mother died recently."

Stunned by the man's declaration, she could only think he meant to save her from the other travelers' attentions. She did not know whether to be frightened, angry or both.

"That true, Mrs...?" the blond man asked.

"Mrs. McKinnon." The Irishman man didn't miss stride.

She opened her mouth, and the words flowed naturally. "Please, sirs, I would like to remain quiet. My father—my mother's death has been difficult." Her voice broke. "Let me mourn in peace."

Tears filled her eyes. Before she could catch her emotions, they ran away with her. She fumbled inside her reticule for the handkerchief. When she located it and held it to her eyes, a shuddering sob slipped out.

A big, warm grip clasped over her gloved left hand. She quickly glanced over at the Irishman. His gaze filled with genuine concern and a caring she had not expected from the hard glances he had bestowed on her before.

Irishman squeezed her hand gently. "You all right?"

25

Mary Jane didn't resist his grip. "Yes, I am fine."

Skinny man nodded. "We're sorry, ma'am."

After the skinny man and his friend turned around, a heavy sigh left her. Good.

For a second she thought the Irishman would leave his touch on her hand forever, but he slowly released her. As she looked at him, his intense perusal raked over her one more time before he turned his attention forward. Not one smile. Just hard, cool dismissal.

Well. What should she think about the bizarre episode? Why would he take such lengths to help her? If he had simply told the blackguards to leave her alone, they might have picked a fight. Instead, he concocted a story she would have to stick to until skinny man and blond head departed for good. Which she hoped would be soon. Bemused by the event, she remained tensed, ready for anything. Certainly the need for a chaperone presented itself now. Her mother would never let her hear the end of this. She sighed and dabbed at an errant tear that remained on her cheek. Her heart ached with not only sorrow for her father, but a profound loneliness she did not understand. Once secretly thrilled to the idea of traveling alone, now she experienced it, she recognized the perils all too well. What if the Irishman thought she owed him...well, she would not even dare to think that far.

The steady motion and clack, clack of the train lulled her into a trance. She watched the scenery, recalling the trip to Philadelphia after they received word that her father had died most horribly. She cringed inside. Somehow, in the back of her mind, she had known he would come to this. Now her family must mourn. Heaviness weighed down her eyelids and soon they drooped. *So tired.*

Time floated until she sank into a dream. A man chased her, cloaked and hooded, his evil certain, and his laugh as hideous as a hound from hell. Behind the man chasing her stood the warm, welcoming protection of the Irishman with the intense eyes.

A horrendous screech sliced through her dreams, and a gasp escaped as she awoke with a start. As predicted, the train had stopped at Lancaster because rainstorms between Lancaster and Columbia demanded they shorten the trip.

Frustrated by the slow progression, she took a deep breath and glanced at the Irishman. She expected him to stare, but this time he maintained cool distance.

She noted the bustling station with people walking to and fro with energy. The conductor asked the Irishman and Mary Jane to disembark. They would make the remainder of the trip to Columbia in the morning.

As she stood, the Irishman caught her gaze once more. "Come on, darlin'."

The mysterious man urged her to move into the aisle in front of him. Men around them heard his accent. Some looked at him with distain, others polite indifference. Two red-haired twins, handsome and stoic, left the carriage ahead of them.

She played along as his wife, an anticipatory shiver adding to the adventure. The devil on one shoulder found this thrilling while the angel on the other berated. Soon they alighted from the car, and the man in front of Mary Jane waited at the steps and held his hand out to her.

"Thank you, sir," she said out of habit for a gentleman's chivalry.

As he helped her down to the platform, she took in the sights and sounds with curiosity. The town certainly did not boast the size of Philadelphia or Pittsburgh, but it hummed with activity. On the outskirts, one-story buildings dominated, but she could see a square populated with three-story brick buildings. Various transports lumbered down the streets, from omnibus, curricle and numerous freight wagons.

To her surprise the Irishman took her upper arm in a possessive grip. Though his touch in no way bruised, he urged her along. "This way, darlin'."

The Irishman stopped in a secluded section of the station. Before she could squeak a protest, he slipped his arm around her waist and drew her into his body. They pressed chest to chest. Hip to hip. The intimate contact filled her face with heat.

Indignant, her hands landed on his chest as she started to push away. "What on earth are you doing?"

He held tight and leaned close, his mouth hovering near hers. His breath was refreshingly clean, his voice low. "Those men from the train are watching. Play the part or those scoundrels will know you're not my wife."

Caught in his embrace, her senses took in the hard, long length of his body, his wide shoulders and chest evident even through his worn waistcoat. Without hat and with wild hair, he seemed more the rounder than upstanding citizen. He looked thoroughly capable of debauching a naïve woman. But the last thing Mary Jane considered herself was naïve.

"I do not know who you think you are, sir, but I will not be treated like a piece of meat to haul around. You will release me immediately."

"After I know you're safe and not before." His declaration rumbled deep, his voice filled with a husky flavor she found maddening. It infuriated and fascinated her. "While we're on this trip you'll need to play along, or I guarantee those men will see you as fair game. I don't trust them, and my instincts about these things are straight and true, darlin'."

Darlin'. The endearment whispered against her ears with an intimacy that started warm, treacherous tingles low in her stomach. How dare he make her feel...she could not identify the dangerous feeling.

"How do I know you are not one of them?" she asked.

One corner of his mouth lifted, and a wicked twinkle entered his eyes. "Think a moment with your heart and not your head. What do your instincts tell you?"

Astonished, she almost shoved at his chest again. Instead, that enticing gaze gathered her almost as closely as his grip. His powerful body and secure hold let her know she could not escape. She could scream and someone would come to her rescue. But who? She glanced around and saw the two blackguards watched from a distance.

"Those men *are* watching us," she said with apprehension.

"As I said." He cupped her cheek. "Trust me."

His mouth closed over hers, and pure, sensual pleasure engulfed her. Her eyes closed as his mouth tasted with a ruthless but tender exploration. All her senses pinpointed to the moment, caught in a whirlwind. The strength of his fingers as they slid away from her cheek to cradle the back of her neck, his clean scent of soap and some unknown spice, the cautious yet strong grip of a powerful arm around her waist. The crinoline proved no barrier to this man. She felt surrounded, cherished, utterly disarmed.

Surprise and dismay slammed her. *Absolutely not.* She would not allow this.

The last time she had let a man kiss her like this...well, disaster had ensued.

But this man...oh, his kiss was different. Delicious. So beguiling that she felt her inhibitions crumbling, rolling down a rocky slope.

Before she could pull away, he lifted his head. He assessed her, his gaze hot and hungry. He looked as if he wanted more. Much more.

"Release me." Her throat felt tight. "Release me or I will scream."

His gaze still simmered, but now she saw anger there as well.

Ashamed that she stood like a placid child, she pulled out of his arms. "That, sir, is just the reason why I should not trust you."

"Take my protection. Those other men will do far more than kiss you, and I guarantee you won't like it."

She gasped in indignation. "I knew you were not honorable. Why, I do not even know your name."

"McKinnon, darlin', just as I said on the train. Elijah Jonas McKinnon. And your name?"

Half tempted not to give it to him, she said, "Mary Jane Lawson."

"A proper name, indeed."

"You are Irish."

"Dirty Irishman, darlin'?" His voice held sarcasm, his accent more pronounced, his eyes hard.

Nervous, she reached up and adjusted her hat. She started to turn away. "I do not need to explain myself to you."

She headed for the conductor, and after pulling out a few coins to pay for her Saratoga trunk to be delivered to the Rittenbocker House, she asked, "I understand the Rittenbocker is a short walk. Is there anywhere else to eat?" She smiled at the short, gray-haired man. "I confess to being quite tired of inn food."

"Certainly." The man smiled. "The Brown Restaurant is only a block away." He gestured north. "One block north of the Rittenbocker. It's a very nice place. I should know. My sister is the cook."

"Thank you so much. Have a good day."

She scanned the surrounding area and noted that McKinnon leaned against a pillar, his arms folded and his attention pinned upon her. She shivered in reaction. How dare he ask her to trust him? A perfect stranger? Her cheeks heated again as she thought about how his lips had felt on hers.

Better than Professor Ricker's?

Oh, no. Do not think about *that* now. The past would stay in the past. Her new, solid, respectable life started from the moment she'd heard her father had died. And she'd keep on that path come flood or famine.

She tugged down her jacket bodice, hooked her reticule

over her wrist, and sucked in a breath. Her corset and crinoline pinched, but her new short boots felt comfortable. A short walk would not only loosen the knots in her back, but allow fresh air into her lungs. She headed out of the station. Thankfully the rain had subsided and the temperature, though crisp, was not intolerable. After a break in the conveyances trundling down the dirt road, she lifted her voluminous skirts to cross the somewhat muddy street. She glanced about, her gaze sweeping over the busy station and then the town all around her. No sign of the disreputable men, and that included the Irishman. Good.

Triumphant, she continued without care, confident she had handled the earlier disruption. As she walked, she paid little attention to her surroundings and more to her inner thoughts. While she knew the perils a woman alone could face, she also knew a woman's attitude could often deflect the most persistent blackguard. She would do fine. Her mother and sisters depended on her to bring father home.

Ahead she noticed the two-story building the conductor had mentioned, and she hurried towards it. Her stomach growled. She had almost reached the building when two men stepped from the alley in front of her. She gasped and stepped back.

Skinny man tilted his tall hat in a mockery of polite society. Presented with his body odor and dirty clothes, Mary Jane wrinkled her nose in disgust.

Skinny man pursed his lips and started to circle her. "Why there you are, Mrs. McKinnon. We thought we'd lost you."

She glared at them, composing her face though her heartbeat galloped in her chest.

The blond man also tipped his hat. "We don't think you're really Mrs. McKinnon. Thought maybe that stinkin' Irishman might be tryin' to take advantage of a young, pretty miss."

"Gentleman, if you will excuse me, I do not have time for this. My husband will join me shortly."

She started past them. Skinny man grabbed her right

upper arm. "Now wait a minute, missy."

"Leave me be." She jerked against his grip, but his fingers tightened. She gasped as pain radiated up her arm. She stomped his foot.

Skinny man's faux charm disappeared in an instant as he released her arm with a howl.

The blond man laughed. "We know you aren't married to that—"

"I am a married woman, sir. If you know what is good for you, you will leave me be."

His voice cut off as his glance snagged on something behind her.

Blond man poked the skinny man in the side with his elbow. "I thought you said that Mick wasn't anywhere to be found?"

The ruffians both escaped down the alley at a run. Trembling, she turned and saw the Irishman running towards her, his stride brisk and no nonsense. She rubbed at her arm and tried to soothe her abused flesh. As McKinnon reached her, he glanced down the alley and measured the retreating figures of the two men.

Relief spilled through her body. She had never been gladder to see someone in her life.

"By the blessed virgin, are you trying to get killed, woman?" His voice lashed with stern disapproval, his accent more pronounced. Then, just as amazing, his gaze softened with concern. He cupped her shoulders. "Did they hurt you?"

Her indignation lost steam. "I...no. I mean, that one awful man with the stovepipe hat...the skinny one grabbed my arm and that hurt. But I taught him a lesson."

He squeezed her shoulder in a comforting caress. "You're fortunate that I saw you before they had a chance to drag you into the alley."

Mary Jane's insides jumbled, her stomach rolling in

disapproval. "I do not need your help."

His brow lowered in a fierce frown. "Don't need my help? Are you deliberately being ignorant, or do you really believe those men don't want to take you down a back alley and assault you?" He crossed his arms. "You may have stomped his foot, but if they really wanted to hurt you, you wouldn't have escaped so easily."

She huffed. "I have dealt with men like him before."

The Irishman's eyebrows rose. "I find that hard to believe."

An urge to allow the old Mary Jane freedom boiled in her blood. "I have learned a few things about defending myself against men up to no good. If you know what is good for you, sir, you will heed my warning."

He went silent for a second, then completely ignored her earlier tirade by saying, "I heard you say you're a married woman."

His rough tone broke through disbelief. "What difference does it make if you come running to my rescue? They have guessed I am not your wife."

He leaned in close once again, towering over her—six feet of bristling male intimidation. "And whose fault is that? You ran away from me at the station and the gig is up. Now there's only one way to keep you safe." He reached into his pocket and drew out a small red box. "This is one of my few possessions. My brother kept it for me."

She glanced at the diminutive box and wondered if the man might have escaped from a lunatic asylum. "What is that?" He flipped open the box, and she gasped. "Surely, sir, you have lost all faculties of reason."

"Take it. You'll need it if you're going to pretend to be my wife for the remainder of this trip to Pittsburgh, *Mrs.* McKinnon."

Chapter Three

Mary Jane sat across from Mr. McKinnon and could not believe she had agreed to participate in such a ridiculous ruse.

By all that was holy, she should have learned her lesson by now. Dangerous situations were best left to the imagination. On the other hand, she burned for excitement, some semblance of a life that did not include corsets and crinolines.

Her mother's disappointed voice rang in her head again. *I am afraid your habits have ruined everything for you now and into the foreseeable future.*

Mary Jane gritted her teeth and tried to forget her mother's admonishments.

The restaurant sparked with activity. As the conductor promised, the food so far proved excellent. Patrons thronged to the large, pleasantly furnished dining room. Conversation murmured in low, reasonable tones, and a cool breeze ruffled lace curtains at the far end of the room. She enjoyed a lovely glass of red wine, something she could never indulge in at home. She needed it after her encounter not only with the blackguards in the street, but the unnerving Mr. McKinnon. They had consumed a dinner of Boston brown bread, tea, beef stew and pan-dowdy. She half expected the man to indulge in gin-sling or other liquor, but he did not. She found his soberness, if not his brashness, refreshing.

"You did not drink any wine, sir," she said into the silence at their small round table.

His dark eyebrows winged upward. "No. Why should I?"

"The men in my family have always had a glass of port at night after dinner at the very least."

"The men in your family?" Unidentifiable emotion flashed over his face. He lifted his teacup for a sip, then set it down on the saucer with a rattle. "Are you married?"

She sat up straighter. "Certainly not. I would not be on this trip alone if that was so. I was thinking about my father and late uncle."

He nodded but did not speak for quite some time. Finally, he said, "You're dressed in mourning."

"Those ruffians think my mother has passed on based on what you told them."

"You'll have to keep your counsel on that. My sympathies, though, on your father."

"Thank you."

She sighed, marveling at her situation. This adventure...and that was the only way she could think of it without wondering at her own sanity, became more bizarre by the hour. She glanced down at the ring on her left hand.

"Like the ring?" he asked.

"It is beautiful. I have never seen anything like it."

"Belonged to my maternal grandmother."

She held up her hand and observed the intricate twining of gold knots and twirls. Though she had a small hand it fit her almost perfectly and the gold band was wide. The jewelry gleamed with such splendor she wondered how much it must have cost.

"Why did you have it in your pocket?" she asked.

His eyes stayed intense, so brooding most of the time that she had to look away or fall into them. "Like I said, it's one of my few possessions."

Her lips tightened as a horrible thought leap to her mind. "Is it for your wife or betrothed?"

"It was for my betrothed."

Her heartbeat thudded, a disappointment settling in her stomach. "Was?"

Mr. McKinnon nodded, his expression guarded. "She...she died five years ago."

Sympathy swallowed her up quicker than she expected. Without thought, she reached across the table and covered his large, well-shaped hand. Heat swirled and tingled as bare flesh touched bare flesh. Warm and hard, his hand represented power and masculinity. Just as quickly she snatched her hand back, embarrassment filling her face with heat.

"I am so sorry. It seems we have both suffered loss. What happened?" she asked.

The Irishman gazed across the table, his concentration centered on her with disconcerting attention.

His mouth twisted in a spasm. "She was murdered."

"Oh my." Her rasp of surprise sounded hollow, without enough substance to describe the horror. "I cannot imagine..."

"Most people can't. On another subject, what are you doing traveling alone at a time like this? Or traveling alone at any time, for that matter?"

"My chaperone Prudence took ill in Philadelphia. She begged me to go on without her. She is an older woman with many health complaints, most of them doubtful."

"Ah, one of those. I had a spinster aunt back in Ireland like that."

"Yes, well, she insisted I should not hold up the urgency to take my father back to Pittsburgh. So here I am."

"You weren't afraid to travel alone?"

"Of course not."

"Then you're an unusual woman, Mrs. McKinnon."

"I am *not* Mrs. McKinnon."

"You are if you know what's good for you. Don't fret, darlin', it won't be that difficult to pretend. Unless the idea of playing my wife repulses you."

Did it? Her gaze danced over his tall body, his thick, waving hair, the handsome cut of his jaw and mouth. Though his attire was a bit shabby, a woman could hardly fail to notice his extraordinary looks.

Her mother's voice came back to haunt her. *Mary Jane, a man's handsomeness, as you discovered, has nothing to do with his character. You should know that by now.*

But no, Mary Jane had not listened to her mother that one time...not at all...

Rebellion and shame, disappointment and guilt twisted in her gut.

She would make it up to her family if it were the last thing she ever did.

She lifted her napkin and dabbed at her lips. "Why would you go to all this trouble for a woman you do not know?"

For the first time, Elijah McKinnon bestowed a full-fledged smile upon Mary Jane, and it unsettled her to the core. His smile came and went like a lightning bolt, filled with as much sarcasm as genuine amusement. Still, the smile did not unnerve her so much in a frightening way, but in a disturbing, delicious extravagance that tantalized her.

"Because I realized you were alone, just like every man on the train realized it. I saw the way those jacksnipes sitting in front of you looked at you."

"How did they look at me?"

"As if you were a pretty prize. A woman vulnerable and available."

"How would you know they were thinking that?"

Once more his face transformed, all strength and hardness giving way to a glorious smile fit for the gods. "Because I'm a man, darlin'. I was thinking the same thing."

She drew back in her chair as the implication struck. "You were...you were not thinking of me as a prize."

He reached for her left hand and brought her naked flesh to his lips in a gentle kiss. "Do you want to know what I honestly thought?"

Did she? He hand tingled where his lips had brushed. "Curiosity and daring always result in a lady's downfall, or so my mother always says."

Those intriguing eyes, full of challenge, dared her in ways she had not even imagined yet. "And what do you say?"

Mary Jane left her hand in his, and McKinnon's thumb swept over her skin in a caress. She shivered all over with pleasure and forced words passed her lips. "I say the same."

His gaze tangled with hers, and the boldness she felt both energized and frightened her. "I don't believe you."

"It is true, sir. Why would I lie?"

"I don't know why. But I can tell when a man or woman is lying to me, and you *are* lying through those pretty lips."

Heat did another sweep through her, a mingling of indignation and frustration. "I never lie, even when the truth hurts."

"I don't believe that either. You see, most women I know tell untruths all the time. Not because they want to so much, but because they have to."

Connection flared inside her. She wanted to shout that she agreed more than she could possibly say.

The old Mary Jane would. She pressed her lips firmly together.

"But since you won't be honest with me this time, then I won't tell you what I was thinking...at least not yet," he said.

Disappointment mingled with relief. He pressed another sweet kiss to her hand and released her.

Mary Jane's body acted in the wickedest fashion. Heat flushed her face, her breasts felt heavy, and a strange ache between her thighs pulsed with matching warmth. Despite her newly caged heart, this man caused fluttering and feelings she recognized and should reject. *Take care, Mary Jane. You know nothing about this man.*

His commanding glare brooked no argument. "From now on I'll call you Mary Jane, and you'll call me Elijah. We can't refer to each other as Mr. McKinnon and Miss Lawson, now can we?"

Still a bit flummoxed, she hesitated to answer.

"Mrs. McKinnon?" he asked, his features deadpan.

"I suppose it cannot be helped."

She should not be curious about this man. She resisted her desire to know more, clamped her lips shut on the questions that wanted to escape. Anything he wanted her to know, he would reveal.

She sipped water and gazed outside into gathering clouds. "Oh my."

His attention turned to weather, his expression nonchalant. "Looks like the bad weather farther west is drifting our way. We need to be on our way to the hotel."

"About that...we need two rooms at the hotel."

He shook his head, eyes hard. "No."

She bristled, too tired from her day's travels to endure poppycock. "Sir, this is not negotiable."

"You don't think it's going to look mighty strange if you have a room separate from mine?"

She tilted her chin higher. "I do not care what other people think. There are plenty of couples who have separate rooms."

"Uh-huh." He pushed his chair back a foot. "I see what concerns you, Mrs. McKinnon."

"Is it necessary for you to call me that? My name is Mary Jane Lawson. I told you that before we sat down to eat."

Deadpan, he said, "I'm practicing."

She rolled her gaze. "Honestly, you have the most irritating way of saying things sometimes."

"So do you."

His refusal to defer to a lady the way so many men would,

kept her stumbling around for a response. Irritation nagged at her like an itch.

She sat back and rummaged in her reticule for her money. "If we want to make it to the hotel before it rains, I suggest we leave."

"You're not paying for my meal."

She sighed. "I did not assume that I would. But I am certainly paying for my own."

"If you insist, Mrs. McKinnon."

Annoyed with his insistence on emphasizing the fake name, she signaled for the waiter. Not long after, they paid the bill and headed for the door.

As they walked west towards Rittenbocker House, Mary Jane's nerves started to jump and jolt. The Irishman walked alongside her, his casual walk conveying strength and a coiled readiness that comforted and disconcerted. She had no doubt the blond man and skinny guy wouldn't stand a chance against him. At the same time, all McKinnon's power could hurt a woman. Something predatory and hard encased him, giving him the air of a warrior. She wondered if he had served in the military or if a hard life had simply given him this invincible, cool façade.

She adjusted her hat upon her head. "Sir—"

"Please call me Elijah. Even if I wasn't playing your husband, I wouldn't want you to call me Mr. McKinnon."

"Elijah." His name tasted intimate and forbidden in her mouth. "Elijah, you cannot possibly think any proper woman would agree with you staying in her room." She perused his threadbare clothes. "If you need money for a room, I will give it to you."

He shifted his shoulders like a horse shrugging off an unpleasant rider. "I don't need your money."

"Fine."

"Fine."

"It would not only be unseemly for you to stay with me, you cannot expect me to trust a man I have met on short notice on a train."

"You're right."

She stopped on the walkway. "What?"

He halted and crossed his arms. "I'll admit that you shouldn't normally trust a man you've just met. I could be a cretin of the first order. A thief. A rapist. A murderer."

"Are you trying to frighten me?"

"I'm telling the truth. Just as you are. But I'm not any of those things." He stepped towards her, his hands palm up. "All I want is for you to be safe and make it to Pittsburgh as you planned." He took her arm gently. "Make haste, Mrs. McKinnon. It's starting to rain."

"I'm soaked." Mary Jane stood just inside the single room they had claimed at the Rittenbocker House. "And *of course* they only had one room left."

She knew she sounded childish. She did not like it. Any of it.

Was she destined to keep falling into situations that would get her into trouble?

Elijah's mouth twitched and for a moment she almost...almost thought she saw humor sparkling in his eyes and emerging on his mouth. But no. He sobered before she could blink.

Mary Jane also did not care for getting soaked to the skin. Especially not if it meant standing in front of this man while resembling a wet rug. Lightning flashed and thunder rolled. She reached for her sagging hat and worked to unpin it from her hair.

His gaze flicked over her. "You're shivering. Better get undressed and into bed."

As he removed his waistcoat and revealed a shirt that had

seen better days, she also saw the dark wood end of a weapon peeking from one pocket inside the coat. He went to a basin, poured water into it and splashed his face. He used a small towel to dry off.

Fear rose inside her. "You have a weapon?"

"A Colt revolver."

All of her muscles seemed to stiffen. She tilted her chin upward ever so slightly. "Whatever for?"

He put the waistcoat over the back of a chair and worked on undoing his cravat. "Obviously, for protection."

Well, she could not deny the practicality of it, even if she hated guns. She decided to ignore the weapon, even if it made her nervous to know he possessed it. "Turn around while I undress."

"Whatever you've got, I've seen it all before, honey."

Anger filled Mary Jane as she remained still, paralyzed by sudden self-consciousness and apprehension. She sneezed. "Why I have never heard such—"

"Don't worry your head about it, darlin'." He put his hands on his hips. "I'm going down to the bar and have that port." His eyes held impatience, as if he regretted their need to stay in one room. As if she was a troublesome and recalcitrant child that needed a keeper. He reached into his pocket and drew out the key. He handed it to her. "Lock the door after I leave. Don't open the door to anyone but me."

Her face heated. "Um...I need someone to undo the buttons on the back of my dress."

His eyebrows went up, but he did not mock her with a smile. "Turn around then."

She did, but when his fingers touched the back of her dress, all she could feel was his heat behind her. A blush worked its way up her throat and into her face again as he performed the intimate task. He worked quickly, thank goodness.

His voice sounded rougher when he finished the last button. "There. All finished."

After he put his waistcoat back on and left, she locked the door and put the key on the table. Still nervous, she took a deep breath. The last thing she enjoyed was feeling out of her depth. She hurried to her trunk and unlocked it. She tossed out dry clothes and came to her nightgown. She hurried, stripped off her sodden garments and hung them on a chair by the fireplace. Not an easy thing to do considering the plethora of layers. Thank the heavens she could loosen and remove her corset without his assistance. Lacing into it then next morning would be a different problem altogether.

Half expecting him to return immediately, she rushed to towel dry and slip into her nightgown. She hurried into bed. She did not expect to sleep, but tiredness came with amazing swiftness. Before long she drifted into slumber.

A thump awoke her. She gasped and sat straight up.

"Darlin', it's me."

She would recognize that voice anywhere, even on short acquaintance. She jumped out of the bed and snatched the key from the bedside table.

Once her hand touched the cold doorknob, she hesitated. "Mr. McKinnon?"

"It's me."

She sighed and opened the door. After he entered, she locked the door again. His gaze trailed over her, but in the voluminous folds of her ecru nightrail, she still felt vulnerable.

"You all right?" he asked.

"I fell asleep. What time is it?"

"About two in the morning."

"Oh my goodness." She yawned. "Why did you stay out so late?"

He unfastened his waistcoat and worked on loosening his tie. "Now that is a question a wife *would* ask."

43

"Humph." Mary Jane examined the ring on her finger. "How would you know?"

She watched his movements with a mixture of fascination and trepidation. He didn't answer, his expression grim and purposeful.

Curiosity strangled her, but she heard her mother's admonishment in her head. *Ladies are not inordinately nosy.* "All right, you do not wish to talk. I see."

"Let's get some sleep." He tossed his waistcoat and cravat on the end of the bed. "We have to rise in a couple of hours to make the trip over the canal." He pulled off his old Hessian style boots. "Don't worry, I'm sleeping in the chair."

"Of course you are." She settled into bed again after he sat in the chair.

"Keep the lamp on if it makes you feel safe."

"You can sleep with a lamp on?"

"I can sleep anywhere except where it's noisy."

She squirmed under the sheets, trying to find a comfortable spot. "Why were you downstairs so long?"

"I was thinking. Planning."

"Oh?"

"Personal business."

"Oh."

"Goodnight, Mrs. McKinnon."

"You said you would call me Mary Jane from now on."

"Mary Jane, then."

Outrageous feelings disconcerted her. What did she make of her odd reaction to him? Elijah McKinnon did not belong in her same social circle, a poor man without any prospects. Attraction to him on any level for any reason could not result in a good outcome. She did not want this intense draw. Did not want it, and she would do about anything to forget it.

Her mind continued to whirl and would not let her sleep. She wished her diary were not secured away in her trunk. She knew exactly what she would tell the pages. The secret pages no one else would ever see.

Dear Diary,

I met the most extraordinary man today. No, not extraordinary. Irritating. Annoying. Frightening. His name is Elijah McKinnon, and he has a bit of an Irish accent. With his threadbare clothing and lack of hat, he is clearly not of the upper classes. Mother would advise me to stay as far away from him as possible, just as she warned me away from Professor Ricker. McKinnon is tall, with very dark hair, brooding countenance...some would call him cruel-looking or perhaps handsome in a most disturbing fashion.

He reminds me a tad of Thaddeus Ricker. That worries me.

What if I am being led astray again?

Surely that would be disastrous.

The professor had power and influence and money. Elijah has little money, but his power is from another source. From something within him. It draws me towards him almost against my will.

I thought I had erected a wall against men like him so they could not influence me ever again.

Mary Jane pondered that realization, then imagined what else she would say in her diary.

Mr. McKinnon insists on an intimacy. He calls me darlin' off and on. Highly improper.

I refuse to feel anything but contempt for his manners, even though he did try to rescue me from some dangerous men earlier in the day. Not that I needed rescuing. At this point I am not sure whether he is to be feared or admired.

No. Not admiration. Therein lies danger. After all, I admired the professor at first and, well...he was not good for me, was he?

Moreover, I betrayed myself with him.

Mary Jane frowned. Anyone reading her diary would imagine her a muddle-headed twit. She could not seem to formulate what she would say with any intelligence.

She only knew one thing. A man would not cause her to lose her way again.

Before she could ruminate further, she fell asleep.

Chapter Four

"No. No."

Mary Jane woke with a start at the hoarse cry. The anguished voice did not come from her dreams, but from Elijah across the room. The lamp still burned, and she could see him clearly. He slumped in the chair with his head tilted to the side, arms propped on the armrests and legs spread apart. He sprawled like a lazy, powerful animal with not a care in the world. But his dreams told a different story.

"No." The hoarse word left his lips, pleading as his mouth twisted in what resembled pain.

He shifted and a lock of inky hair fell lower on his forehead. His shirt was open part of the way, and her attention snagged on the dusting of black hair along sculpted muscles. The sight of so much masculinity, blatantly exposed, froze her in place. She pulled her attention back to his distress.

"Maureen. Oh God. Please forgive me. Please forgive me." His breathing went harsh, and though his eyes stayed closed, the torment in his words couldn't be mistaken. "Please, Maureen."

Concerned, she left the bed and walked to him. She leaned over him as he thrashed in his chair. "Maureen. Damn it, Maureen."

She took a tentative step nearer and grasped his shoulder. "Elijah, wake up." He jerked awake, eyes wild, sad, furious. He reached for her and jerked her down into his arms. She squealed in surprise and alarm. "Mr. McKinnon, have you lost your senses?"

With one arm around her back and the other hand clasping her waist, he held her securely. His eyes focused and the dream faded from his eyes.

"I'm sorry," he gasped the apology, his eyes filled with alarm. "Did I hurt you?"

She did not hurt anywhere. Acknowledging what she felt, though, went beyond words. His hard thighs bunched beneath her buttocks, his breath feathered her mouth, his strong chest beneath her fingers...oh, all of it held her in thrall. A dangerous, amazing thrall.

When his thumb passed over her chin, his gaze dropped to her mouth. "Answer me, Mary Jane."

"No...I mean, no, you did not hurt me. You were having a horrible dream."

"Yes. Same one I have every night. I'm sorry. I should have warned you it might happen."

"You have dreams like this every night?"

A cloud darkened his eyes. "The last five years."

While she longed to ask why dreams plagued him, she became aware of his arms tightening around her. "Release me, please."

Something stirred beneath her, a hardness that pressed against her buttocks.

His hips shifted and a muscle in his jaw worked. White-hot fire leapt across her body as his eyes met hers. Nothing prepared her for the sweeping intensity of a man's arms holding her like she was precious to him. All that hardness and strength combined with gentleness shook her to the core. Her breath hitched, and his masculine scent warmed her clear through.

His touch slipped over her cheek in a tender caress that belied his tough appearance. "Has anyone ever told you, darlin', what a beauty you are?"

Pleasure mixed with apprehension. "No."

"In Ireland the men would turn wild for you." He heaved a deep breath, his lips parting. "Quick, Mary Jane. Get off my lap before I do something I shouldn't."

She pushed away, and Elijah helped her rise to her feet. Affronted and relieved at the same time, she stiffened her spine and marched back to bed.

Once she drew the covers up to her chin again, she slanted a cautious look his way. "Why did you hold me like that?"

He leaned his head back and closed his eyes, his posture once more the abandon of a lazy cat. "Just what you feared would happen. I let my baser nature take hold." His voice went husky, a drawl mixed with Irish magic. "But don't worry. I won't hurt you."

She lay in bed staring at him, astonishment and female gratification warring for supremacy within. A secret part of her enjoyed that she had shaken him. Made him lose control.

A question came to mind that would not stay contained. "Elijah, who is Maureen? Your betrothed?"

He visibly stiffened, his back straighter in the chair. He looked ready for flight. "Where did you hear that name?"

"You said her name several times while you were dreaming."

He scrubbed a hand over his face and sighed. "Don't ask me about her again."

Elijah's prickliness assured her whoever Maureen was that talking about the woman was off limits. When he didn't say another word, she closed her eyes. This time she didn't fall asleep right away.

Lancaster to Hollidaysburg

They left Lancaster around five in the morning and not a moment too soon for Elijah.

Elijah's "wife" kept a distance from him. Not enough to cause conjecture by anyone around them, but not near enough to appear affectionate. She stayed stubbornly silent and so did he. When they reached Columbia on the eastern bank of the Susquehanna after a twelve-mile jaunt, they had breakfast at Mr. Donley's Red Hotel. Once more she talked little. The noise in the dining room gave them ample excuse not to converse.

As he stood on the platform with Mary Jane waiting to board the canal boats that also served as rail cars, he noticed the two bastards that bothered her yesterday boarding ahead. He glanced over at Mary Jane and watched her, conscious that he spent too much time staring at her petite nose, the fine line of her jaw, and the glossy lighter hues in her dark hair. Her startling pewter gray gaze often met his in a direct fashion, then skittered away when he returned her look for too long. From the first moment he saw her yesterday, he found his senses, his mind drawn towards her. He shouldn't think about her so deeply, shouldn't trouble his thoughts with how she'd felt in his arms two times yesterday...how her lips molded to his with a fire that mocked innocence.

And damn her sweet hide, when she greeted him at two in the morning last night with those almond-shaped, intelligent eyes, those full red lips and willowy body, Elijah knew he'd stumbled upon something special. Whether she realized it or not, men looked at her with lust, him included. Skinny arse and that blond bastard had designs on her person. Without a chaperone or husband she was more vulnerable than she might admit.

He didn't want to give a damn, and resolved that other than offering her temporary status as his wife as a form of protection, he couldn't afford to care. After all, he needed to get on with his most pressing business. Finding Amos and sending him to his maker.

Anger stabbed like a white-hot poker to the gut. *Amos. Damn him all to hell and the devil.*

Yeah, and maybe the devil will come for me when I rid the

earth of Amos.

So be it.

Conflicting emotions battered him. Maureen had suffered a man's savage needs, to Amos's murderous hands. Elijah glanced at Mary Jane. She might be an upper class woman with a prickly side that irritated him no end, but her defenselessness made her fair game for any man with half a mind to mischief. In his experience, women with fine clothes, highbrow manners and soft leather gloves displayed little sense and needed a man to take care of them. Not like a woman who toiled her whole life. Not like his ma.

Elijah glared at Mary Jane, resentful. He hadn't taken this trip to act as protector for a woman more interested in frippery and finery than common sense. Still, Mary Jane had defied him in ways a true milquetoast woman wouldn't dream of, and she'd shown fighting spirit when skinny and that blond bastard had accosted her.

No matter. He didn't have time to worry or wonder about her. He ought to leave her to her own devices.

Yeah, but your Ma taught you better than that, Elijah. Taught you respect for women.

That was before Amos destroyed the only woman I'll ever love. Nothing else matters but finding my brother and putting him in his grave.

He would keep an eye on Mary Jane, but maintain a distance. A woman tagging along would slow him on the path to revenge.

Assured that he *did* understand his own mind on the subject, he turned his attention back to the next cog in the wheel. The canal boat held quite a few people, and when they entered, he selected a bench at the back. Once more Mary Jane took up all of one bench seat with that flimflam crinoline. A goodly portion of the boat, at least thirty-six feet or so, served as cabin in the day and sleeping quarters at night. A section of the night dormitory area served as ladies' quarters. The dormitory had berths where people could sleep, but Elijah didn't think he'd use one. Hell, he practically slept with one eye open these days.

Something more pressing took control of his thoughts. He didn't like this place, not one bit.

It felt...tight. Confined.

Easy, man. Take it easy. You're not in prison anymore.

He'd never seen anything like this odd boat. At least eighty feet long and eleven wide, it gave him a closed-in feeling that reminded him of the prison. He drew in deep breaths, his heart racing too fast, his need for air almost sending him to his feet. He closed his eyes and tried something that used to work when his cell closed in around him. He resolved to take deep breaths, to steady himself with images of the beautiful green shores of Ireland.

This leg of the trip would take some time to complete, so he leaned his head back to catch some shuteye. Elijah's dreams, though, held sway over him. He dreamed of Mary Jane nestled in his arms, her rounded bottom teasing his cock. Last night when she'd awakened him from that horrible dream, he'd wanted her in his arms for comfort. His comfort, admittedly, not hers. More than anything Elijah wanted to tell her what he felt when he held her. To ease his iron-hard spike into her warm body, to feel the plump fullness of her breasts against his chest. If he'd been a rake of the first degree he could have seduced her...perhaps. But then he'd be no better than the cretins who had eyeballed her on the train. One more complication he couldn't afford.

Now, as his dreams intensified and flooded him with visions of Mary Jane's sweet mouth trailing a sinful path down his body, he relaxed. *Oh, yeah.*

Then he felt it. Someone stared at him. He could feel it. He opened his eyes and glanced in Mary Jane's direction. He caught her perusing him. She jerked her gaze away and sat all prim and proper, eyes forward, her black leather gloved hands folded on her lap, black skirts flowing around her. Many women looked sickly in mourning black. He doubted she could ever appear anything but beautiful. His mind flashed back to her warm weight in his arms. Tall and slim, but not rail thin, he liked how she felt. Strong but feminine, womanly but not so fragile he felt as if she might break in his grip.

Right, McKinnon. After five years solitary you appreciate the feel of any woman in your arms. You should have found a prostitute last night and banged out your frustration. Sure, and he would have thought of Mary Jane the whole time. Damn he wanted to find his first pleasure in five years enjoying the tight, hot clasp of her body around his aching cock. He wanted to howl. Growl his disapproval of his own thoughts. Disgusted with himself, he started to look away again when her gaze snagged him and wouldn't let go. He fell right in. Trapped. *Son-of-a-bitch.*

He tore his gaze away from hers once more and retreated into the newspaper he'd bought that morning. Reading would keep his mind off how damned small the space around him felt.

"Do you read often?" Mary Jane's soft voice carried, but mingled with the other passenger's voices.

He kept his attention on the words in front of him. "Where I've been we didn't get anything to read at first. Later on all we got was religious reading material." He smirked. "I didn't even know who the president was during my time in there. The world could have been going to all-fired Joe, and I wouldn't have known it."

A gentle smile touched her lips along with a hint of confusion. "Where were you? A monastery?"

"Might as well have been."

There you go, McKinnon. Since you almost released your secret to the world, allow her to think what she wants. Better she knew as little about him as possible. If she discovered he'd been in prison, she'd run from him like a hare, and that would prove dangerous. He didn't want her taking chances with any other bastards on this route.

After he read the paper, an irresistible urge for sleep overcame him despite voices humming around him. He clasped his hands over his stomach and leaned his head back. Slumber came swiftly.

Elijah heard the whistling wind from a bitter cold winter as a snowstorm barreled down on the penitentiary. Cold air filtered in from the small vent in the skylight above. His bunk was cold and hard, the single woolen blanket barely enough to chase away the cold. He knew better than to undress in the winter other than to take his once a week perfunctory shower. No, it was too damned cold all winter to do otherwise. Still, what he wouldn't give to feel sheets against his skin. What he wouldn't give to taste Ma's fine soda bread and rest easy in his own soft bed with clean sheets and coverings. The smelly blanket covering him now hadn't been washed in two years, if that. He opened his eyes, desperation suddenly gripping his throat with sharp talons.

Jesus, Mary and Joseph.

No. It can't be true. I'm out of prison. I'm free.

Unless I'm mad and never left prison. Unless the whole train trip, Mary Jane, the feeling of fresh air in my lungs was but a cruel joke.

Oh, sweet Jesus—no.

No!

Elijah jerked awake, a cry ripping from his lips. A cry resembling a desperate animal bent on escape. "No!"

Breath rasping heavily from his throat, he stood up.

He couldn't stay here. *I must get out.*

Passengers stared at him, men with pity-filled expressions, and some with undeniable disgust. Elijah didn't care. He couldn't breathe. He couldn't breathe—

"I say there." The steward came down the aisle, expression mixed with annoyance and concern. "Sir, we can't have commotions like this."

"Elijah?" Mary Jane's gentle voice cut through Elijah's panic. Her small hand clasped his bicep. "Elijah, sit down. You're safe here."

As he glanced over at Mary Jane, he saw something in her eyes he would never expect. Confusion, yes, but more than that...compassion and concern. Her hand tightened on his bicep.

The steward planted his hands on his hips. "We can't have any trouble. If you're trouble, we tie you up in the back until we reach our next stop."

Tie him up? Elijah wanted to laugh. That would surely be the last nail in his coffin. If the steward thought him a wild man now, wait until they tried to restrain him.

He bristled. "I'll be damned if—"

"Elijah, please." Mary Jane's grip on his arm tightened, and she threw a pleading gaze at the steward. "Please, sir, we are quite sorry to disturb everyone. My husband just had a nightmare, nothing more. It will not happen again."

Again Elijah wanted to toss a mocking grin her way. If she thought that nightmare was nothing, she should see what other demons haunted him in the night.

"Sir?" The steward gave Elijah an implacable glare, backed up by the disapproving stares of the other passengers.

Elijah glanced down at Mary Jane again and the plea in her eyes. Something inside him softened a little. "Yeah. I'm fine. My wife was right. It was just an unfortunate nightmare."

The steward eyeballed him a tad longer, then returned to his work on the other side of the boat. Conscious of stares, including Mary Jane's continued curious examination, he pulled out of her grip and sat down. Embarrassment mingled with self-loathing. How much longer would these nightmares plague him? By God, he would conquer these devil-spun dreams.

The other passengers returned to their books, papers and naps.

Elijah's heart had barely returned to normal when Mary Jane reached across the aisle and touched his arm again. "Elijah, are you all right?"

He flinched and jerked back. "Don't touch me, darlin'. Not now."

Hurt flashed over her face, then haughty dismissal.

That's good, darlin'. Learn right now that you shouldn't care about me.

As if a woman of her level in society ever would?

Mary Jane kept her own counsel and once more had almost nothing to say to him. Later, the steward and helpers set up berths to accommodate everyone on board, including the two ladies. Realizing he'd have to move his place, he decided sleeping in a berth would make his distaste for tight places even worse. Mary Jane retreated to the back nearby the other woman, sectioned by an opaque curtain to maintain feminine modesty.

Elijah made peace with the steward by admitting he couldn't abide small spaces and that's what caused his nightmare. The steward allowed him to keep one bench open and not arranged into a berth. Maybe the man figured that was better than risking another full on nightmare from Elijah.

Finally, the announcement for Harrisburg brought him to full attention. He thought he heard rain drumming on the top of the boat.

"All disembark at Harrisburg," came the announcement. "There's heavy rain outside, and we'll not be traveling all the way through tonight as we first thought."

After the berths were refolded and everyone returned to normal seating, Mary Jane sat on the bench next to him. Mary Jane's soft voice almost didn't reach his ears. "I was hoping we would make it to Duncan's Island this evening."

He almost reached across the expanse and clasped her hand, but stopped himself. Frowning, he said, "Such is life near the Allegheny Mountains."

She sighed. "I will admit this trip to Philadelphia was my first across the mountains. I have never been much of anywhere outside of Pittsburgh." She frowned. "Well, there was that time after the fire."

"The fire?"

"In 1845, when the city center burned to a crisp. Father was worried he had lost his manufacturing building. But it was far enough outside the fire area and survived. It was a horrible few days." She shook her head. "Father was worried, and we left town for my Aunt Claurice's outside the city."

He nodded. "Then there are fires that aren't caused by an accident."

She must have heard the change in his voice, the bitterness he knew remained whenever he thought of one particular fire. Her eyes narrowed. "Which fire?"

"Come on." He stood and held his arm out to her. "Let's rustle up some accommodation and dinner."

She threw a curious glance at him, but didn't ask anything more about his statement.

An omnibus took passengers from the quay to hotels or eateries. They stopped at a small restaurant that served food in the public room. Elijah and Mary Jane sat at a table and ordered tea and small beef pies.

"Tell me about the fires not caused by accident," she said as they waited for their food.

He wouldn't pretend he didn't know what she meant. "Back in '44, my mother worked in a sweatshop near where we lived in an area of Philadelphia called Kensington. We'd only lived in the United States four years by that time." He caught an almost imperceptible shift in her expression. He continued the story. "The nativists in the area decided it was a good time to riot and protest against the Catholics and the Irish in particular."

Dismay drew small lines between her eyebrows. "I cannot deny that I have heard of the nativists or the riots. They are a political party that believes Catholics are trying to take over the

United States?"

He nodded.

They cut off conversation as the waiter brought their pot of tea and informed them the meat pies would take longer. When he left, Mary Jane said softly, "My family is Episcopalian."

His gut clenched. He hated religious discussion. "And? Does your family believe the Catholics are trying to take over the United States?"

She sighed. "That is a complicated question."

"Is it?"

Her gaze, so bright and pretty, almost distracted him from her answer. "Yes, it is. Let me see if I can explain. My mother went along with whatever my father said in public. My sisters are quite the same way. The few times they even considered disagreeing with him, he was very sharp and critical. In my house there is always disagreement about what is right. My father had an old copy of *Awful Disclosures of Maria Monk* and *Further Disclosures*. Have you heard of those books?"

He nodded. "Unfortunately."

"Well, he put them in the library in a drawer he usually locked. I tried opening the door once and it surprised me when it unlatched. I took a peek at the books and read what they said. I thought them ridiculous. The things these books said about priests corrupting nuns...it was scandalous and awful. I did not believe it."

"Do you think I'll corrupt you because I'm Catholic?"

She didn't miss stride. "You could not corrupt me unless I wanted you to."

Heat gathered in his loins and hardened him to stone. What he wouldn't give to introduce her to carnal love. Thank God there was a napkin over his lap.

She continued. "Father said women should take a man's lead regardless of her own feelings and that includes religion."

He made a disbelieving snort. "Do you believe that?"

She stared at him as if he'd lost his senses somewhere back on the water. "You do not think he was right?"

He poured the tea for them, an action his mother would have admonished him for doing. After all, a woman poured tea, not a man. "Does it look like I'm a conventional man?"

"You do not act like many men I have known. But I suppose you are conventional in many things."

He leaned on the table and looked into her eyes, wanting her to know his true beliefs. "I'm a Catholic, Mary Jane. But I'm not interested in taking over the world or converting anyone else into believing what I believe. I figure each man and woman has to find their own way to their own God."

Her plump lips parted, and once more her delicate beauty halted his breath and scrambled his thinking. "That is very unusual. My father definitely believed everyone *should* be protestant. I am sure he would not have liked you much."

"I'm certain I wouldn't have liked him."

She licked her lips. "He told my mother and sisters they were improper even when they kept such a tight rein on themselves. He told them..."

"Yes?"

"That I was the only one going to heaven when the time came."

Elijah swallowed back his distaste. "Because you believe what he believed?"

She smiled, but there was no humor in her eyes. "Because at one time he thought he understood me."

"Darlin', I'm confused here. Do you think a man should have dominion over a woman or not?"

He'd rarely witnessed a woman as expressive, as revealing as Mary Jane. Right now she looked a might confused. "My inner self, the one I kept hidden from father says a woman should have far more autonomy than society says."

He nodded. "I can see that in you. And I can also see you're not telling me everything about yourself."

She smiled. "That is true. When I was younger I thought Father was right because every child believes their parents are gods. Then, something happens sometimes that changes that belief. A child's eyes can open wide to the truth."

"Did yours?"

"Far more than I wanted. Sometimes I wish I still had my illusions. You see, my sisters are very proper, no matter what my father said, and so is my mother. But I was not as virtuous as he believed. I have done things my sisters would not dream of doing."

"Such as? Not wearing a crinoline?"

She flushed a bright pink, and he liked how it livened her skin and gave her a flustered innocence that stirred his body and mind. All that fire wrapped up in false purity drove him mad. Was she still a virgin? Was she trying to tell him in her offhand way that she wouldn't mind a roll in the sack with him? His cock hardened even more.

"Sir, you should not..." She glanced around. "It is certainly not done to speak of unmentionables."

"I'm sorry." He wasn't. Eager to understand her mind, he poured more tea in her cup and refilled his. "So tell me, what makes you so improper?"

She licked her bottom lip, and his body reacted traitorously to that innocent movement. He wanted to groan.

She took a sip of tea, then placed the cup in the saucer with such a delicate touch it barely made a sound. "I was more proper when I was younger."

His eyebrows went up. "Younger? You can't be that old now."

Mary Jane's gaze flicked up at him, edged with annoyance. "Old enough to know how the world works, sir. I am cured of my ignorance about my situation in life." She took a deep, shuddering breath. "It seems there is no place but hearth and home for a woman."

He could tell by the hard line of her mouth he wouldn't get much more of an explanation than this. Elijah saw something more flickering deep in her pretty eyes, a core of stubbornness and pride a man would have a damned difficult time breaking. Yet she acted as if she'd already been rode hard and put up wet. As if life had dealt her a blow that smothered her desires as sure as water over fire.

He wasn't sure he liked that. "Tell me more about your family."

Pain thinned that delicious mouth, and she looked down at her hands folded in her lap. "My father had interest in other women and mother looked the other way. He could be so unapproachable."

"Why?"

Her eyes, a little exotic and mysterious, met his. "I do not know for certain. He was in Philadelphia when the riots happened. He wrote mother a letter and complained that the..." She lowered her voice. "He started spouting nativist rhetoric and said he was helping their party pass out fliers. So you see, I have read all about the Catholics and the Irish."

Disappointment welled inside him. "Do you believe what they say about us?" He heard the crisp, cutting tone and didn't temper it. "Tell me what you think."

As if tired of dealing with her gloves, she slipped them off her fingers and placed them in her lap. A rebellious move for a virtuous woman, but he appreciated it. Her long, beautiful fingers caressed her teacup. He swallowed hard as his groin tightened. He imagined too damned well what it would feel like if her fingers caressed his body.

The waiter delivered the meat pies and stalled the conversation.

Soon after the man left, she said, "I did not want my father to be wrong, you understand. So I believed his ramblings and the pamphlets for quite a long time. My mother and sisters always believed it. Eventually I realized he was being alarmist."

Surprise made Elijah silent for several seconds. Maybe some highbrow women did have guts. "You are a strong woman."

An equal astonishment flared in her eyes. "Most men would say it is a weakness for a woman to speak her own mind. I often envy my mother and sisters."

"Why?"

She swallowed hard. She dallied with her teacup, turning it around on the saucer and lifting it with her left hand. "Because I do not think an outward show of unladylike turmoil should replace decorum. To go against what convention says only harms a woman. I have learned my lesson."

Amusement managed to crack through the shell around his heart, but he didn't smile. "You're traveling without a chaperone, darlin'. Isn't that a little form of rebellion?"

She nodded. "Perhaps. In another way my sisters and mother are horribly weak. They claim to think for themselves, but they are just as prideful and certain about other people. Judge not least ye be judged is something they spout, yet they judge at every opportunity." She shook her head. "My father's ramblings about a woman's place felt pernicious to say the least, but what sort of outlet does a woman have when society will bruise her severely for showing any outward sign of strength? I realized that I did not believe a word of what I read in those hateful pamphlets about Catholics and Irish."

Elijah felt an awakening straight down to his gut. Maybe he'd judged this woman as more shallow, less interesting than he should have. "Few people I've known in my twenty-six years have admitted to any weakness big or small. It's right admirable that you have."

Her glorious smile returned, if a bit tarnished around the edges. "Thank you."

"Not all Catholics are like me." He tried a smile, but it died before it could start. "Some of the ones I know are just as bad as the nativists."

Perhaps he imagined the understanding within her expression. He couldn't say for certain.

"You are not telling me everything that happened in Kensington in '44. I have a keen mind for telling when a man is holding something back. That is another trait my father did not admire."

Though her voice was pure femininity and formality, there was a sensual huskiness within it that brushed over his skin like a physical touch. He bit into his meat pie for distraction. He chewed and swallowed. "A curious woman is always in trouble...like you said."

She smiled. "Not *I*, sir. Like my *mother* said."

"I think I should meet this mother of yours. She sounds similar to my mother. Proper and guarded." He placed his meat pie on the plate when he saw she used a fork. "Sometimes like you."

Her mouth twitched. "Always like me."

"You're a contradiction, wife. It's enough to make a man wild."

Her eyebrows shot up, and the small feather in her hat quivered. "I am not. I mean...improper."

"Then why were you talking with me about religion? Especially a man you just met yesterday. A man you slept in the same room with, too."

This time a delicate pink flush covered her cheekbones. Glory be to St. Patrick, but he'd like to feel that soft skin under his lips and experience her hidden heat.

"Ah, I've embarrassed you," he said. "Or is that anger I see?"

"Anger, sir. Pure anger."

"Elijah, remember?"

She took a healthy bite of meat pie. "Well, you slip a Mrs. McKinnon in there from time to time. Besides, my mother called my father sir in public. It is natural."

Her feisty response pushed him and fueled a heated response in his cock as well. He shifted on the hard chair. "Nothing natural about it." He lowered his voice. "There are other things I'd call my wife if I had a real one."

She kept her gaze on her plate. "Religion and marriage are serious subjects for anyone. We should restrict our conversation to more prosaic discussion."

"Sure, and there's always a lot of swill in politeness."

Disapproval tightened her features. "True. But polite swill is better than rudeness any day."

He laughed, and he didn't care how loud or obnoxious it sounded. Her bright eyes widened as she glanced around, obviously concerned. He didn't give two figs. The laugh caught him by surprise, too. It felt good. Freeing.

He squelched the chuckle and reached for her left hand across the table. "Thank you."

Her hand curled naturally into his, her voice a bit breathless in response. "For what?"

"That's the first good laugh I've had in five years."

She withdrew her hand from under his. "Well, that is a compliment. I did not think what I said was that funny."

He kept smiling. "It is to a man who—"

No.

He shut down his amusement like water tossed on a flame. He shook his head. "Never you mind."

She stared at him with disconcerting attention until she finally asked, "Your nightmares are quite intense, sir. I thought for certain the steward would make good his threat and have you hogtied in the back of the boat. Why are you plagued by such dreams?"

Elijah took a deep breath, an ache starting in his throat. "I never talk about my dreams. *Never.*"

"But—"

A white hot flash outside the window and an instant

explosion jolted the inn. Elijah startled, his heart banging a hundred miles a minute. Mary Jane yelped and threw her hand over her mouth.

It was her turn to smile as the heavens opened. "My goodness, that lightning was right outside."

She observed the light and noise show with an almost childlike fascination. He leaned back in his chair and watched people scramble from one side of the street to the other as they tried to escape the storm.

Her eyebrows pinched together. "I do not want to be stuck here for the night."

"Stuck in a room tonight with me, you mean. There's no avoiding that. Even if we made it all the way to Duncan's Island, you'll still have to stay overnight again."

"I know that." Impatience colored her tone. She sighed. "I hope we do not meet anyone we know during this trip."

He tilted his head to the side. "Since you'll be seen in the company of an Irishman?"

She huffed in annoyance. "Truly, you do put words in my mouth. Despite your gallantry in protecting me, if word gets to my mother and sisters that I slept with a man..." She gulped.

Once more he leaned close over the table and kept his tone for her ears only. "Sure, and I can tell you that you didn't sleep with me. I would have remembered that and so would you."

"Oh, why you..." She huffed again, eyes stormy as she stood and started to walk away.

He didn't follow. She wouldn't go far.

Chapter Five

Lemon House

Summit of the Allegheny Portage Railroad

Amos McKinnon walked towards Tobias Varney and knew this man could help him with his goal. One of his goals, anyway. Amos took in his surroundings at the same time he observed the man sitting at the small table in the dining room. Varney's long legs sprawled open and swallowed all the space under the table. His worn gray and bottle-green waistcoat had seen better days, patched at the elbows and threadbare. His battered stovepipe hat was set on the table next to a pewter tankard. Varney wore a nasty expression the way he wore scuffed Hessians...with a broken-in and at ease look.

Amos didn't give much credence to *knowing* like so many seers claimed back on the old sod. Yet Amos knew Varney stirred strange sensations inside most people, something that would grab an ordinary man by the gut and gave him the shits. Reluctant admiration struck Amos. Yeah, it didn't take much to see Varney would prove the right man for deeds that needed accomplishing in a quick, efficient and violent manner. The first time Amos had met him, back several months ago when it looked like Zeke might prove Elijah innocent, Amos knew Varney wouldn't hesitate to kill under the right incentive. He liked that.

"Don't just stand there." Varney's gravelly voice echoed across the room. He ran a hand through the remainder of his sparse, greasy blond hair. He gestured to the seat across from him. "Sit."

Amos spied a broad-hipped barmaid in the corner cleaning two tables. He waved her over. "You. Bring me a whiskey. Best you have."

The plump, round-faced woman threw a glance at Varney, her eyes wary. She nodded and scurried out of the room as if hellhounds nipped at her heels.

Amos ignored an uncomfortable sensation in his gut that made him feel like he hung by a frayed rope over a huge gorge. "This isn't a good place to meet."

Varney snickered. "Well, is anyone lookin' for you in here? I don't think so. This is a long way from Philadelphia. Don't think anyone here would know your face."

Amos glanced around. "Keep your voice down."

"Ain't nobody in here." Varney's ridiculous grin split his already disadvantaged face. Pock-marked and thin, he resembled a cadaver that had already started to decompose. His thin, high-bridged nose gave the man a regal and yet shrewish look that belonged on the statue of a despot king.

Amos sank slowly into the chair and reconnoitered the room. It smelled of cigar smoke and the outdoors. Someone had left a window cracked at the far side of the room, and rain slashing at the building threatened to enter. He couldn't take it. Damned untidy situation. He stood and walked across the room, slammed the window closed and returned to his table.

Varney chewed on a fag, then he lit it. Acrid smoke drifted upward. "What the Sam Hill was that all about?"

"Now that I have money, I don't like untidy places."

Varney sneered and took a drag off his smelly cigarette. "You never tell a man like me that you got money. Bad idea."

Amos sat up straighter, aware he outweighed the thin man by quite a bit and his strength more than equaled him. Varney tried to test a man's weaknesses like a stubborn horse trying a fence to locate a flaw. "You know I have money already or I couldn't pay your price, now could I?"

Varney stubbed out the fag on the table. "That be true. You're a damned strange man, McKinnon. What does your mother think about what you're doing?"

Amos set his hat on the table. "My Ma?" He laughed. "Ma is mad. She married some Englishman and said she'd converted to a protestant."

Varney's thick eyebrows rose and his forehead wrinkled. "Oh, yeah? Thought that's what you planned to do. Turn protestant."

The barmaid rushed into the room, whiskey glass in hand. She placed it on the table in front of Amos, then glanced back and forth between him and Varney. Her blue eyes held a wide, startled, stupid look Amos found irksome. She better not stand too close again.

After she left, Amos glared at Varney. "I already turned away from the bloody papists. Did that five years ago after Elijah went into the penitentiary. But Ma—she's not mad because she's thinking of turning protestant. It's that she married an Englishman. He's a feckin' Englishman." He felt the blood rising up in his face, his heart pounding faster as he thought about it. "There isn't any excuse for that. She's an Irishwoman."

Varney nodded. "Well, then, you got yourself another problem, eh? You want me and the boys to take care of her good-for-nothing Englishman? If you do, it'll be more money."

Amos's heartbeat didn't slow as excitement gathered. He licked his lips. "I'll do it myself. Uphold Ma's honor since she made a mistake marrying that man."

Varney tipped his chair back, and the Sheraton chair creaked in protest. "Yeah? I could kill your stinkin' brother just fine."

"No. I can do that myself."

"Yeah, but you can't track worth a damn."

Amos twitched, his thoughts gathering momentum until

they bounced in chaotic madness. He lifted his whiskey glass and slammed the liquid back, enjoying the hot glow. "I haven't done that kind of work in a long time."

Varney let his chair thump back onto all fours, creating a bang Amos figured would bring someone running. "I know how you are, McKinnon. You got an awful thirst for killin'. And you don't lie well."

Tired of the idiot's insolence, Amos glared. "I lie better than anyone else I know."

"I seen guys like you before. I'm forty years old, boy. Damn near old enough to be your father. I seen things you wouldn't dream of seein'. But wait. Maybe I'm wrong about that since you kill because you like to. I just kill to make money."

Amos felt a strange panic well in his throat. The man's words said too much, revealed too much. Amos didn't like this naked sensation, as if his Ma had walked in the room and found him pleasuring himself. Insanity lay in that direction, or so his Ma once said. He heard her voice in his head. *Boy, don't let me ever catch you doin' that again. Sure, and the devil will come to take you if you do.*

That was damn reason enough to kill her when he got the chance.

Varney waved a hand in front of Amos's face, and Amos slammed back to attention. "Feck off, Varney."

"I know it when I see it."

"It?"

"The blood, man. You don't dare taste it, but you want to. Each time you kill it gets easier and easier and feels better and better, don't it?"

Amos's stomach twisted and gurgled but he ignored it. He knew what Varney meant. "So?"

Varney's wide grin stretched his face from ear to ear in a macabre clownish look that would scare women and children. Hell, would scare most men. Everyone but Amos.

Varney leaned on the table, his elbows an affront to polite society. His gaze traveled over Amos's clothes with devil-may-care insolence. "You really don't understand it, do you? You think I'm a piece of shit on the bottom of your boot, but tripe knows tripe." Varney's lips curled into a cruel smile. "You think gettin' all prettied up makes you a different man. But it don't. There's evil men in the fanciest clothes."

Amos's blood boiled, but he drew in deep breath and corralled the desire to reach across the table and strangle the rounder. "Is there a point to this, Varney?"

"What I mean is you killed that Maureen girl...the one that was your pisswad brother's girl. You know it, your brothers know it and now your English-marrying, mad Ma knows it. Hell's bells, the whole world knows it now. But you dress nice 'cause you got a little money, and you think that makes you less a cold killer than me. Well, it don't." Once more he leaned back in the chair and it creaked again. "You think fancy pomade and shined boots and a new opera hat is guarantee people will think you're somethin' special. Well, you ain't. You know why? I'll bet Maureen weren't your first kill. You messed around with a woman or maybe a girl when you was just a pint-sized pee waddin'. Found you liked hurtin' her and doin' her whether she wanted it or not. She probably didn't even tell her folks because you said she'd be branded a whore."

Amos took a deep, shuddering breath and reined in the desire to prove Varney right. As clear as day, he imagined knocking the table aside, placing his hands around Varney's neck and strangling the life out of him. Just like he had Maureen.

Any other time and place and he would have.

"You walk a thin line, Varney."

Varney shrugged. Once more his chair hit the floor with a thump and creak. "I just tell it like I sees it. Here's the way I sees it. You got some weird need to kill 'cause you can't resist it. I've known your kind—"

"So you said. Get on with it."

"You and your whole damned family put on airs. You see, it don't mean a tinker's damn to me whether you are protestant or papist or some other damned religion. I ain't got use for any of it. I just know you Irish come into my country and start tryin' to change things. And most of you is poor and not worth a half penny. So I ain't interested in whether you got a twisted mind and like to kill little girls or diddle men. Don't matter to me. All I want is what you owe me, and I'll do what I'm paid to do. You, though, you kill 'cause it tastes good in your mouth. You'd do it whether your boss paid you or not."

A new, dark place opened inside Amos, and he wished he didn't need this miscreant to rid the world of Elijah. "Boss?"

"Yeah. You work for that nativist, don't you?"

Amos could have denied it. Wanted to lie. He almost tried. "You say nativist like it's a bad thing. You just got through telling me that you hate immigrants."

"Nah, I don't hate nativists. I'm just sayin' you'd kill even if you didn't work for Leonard Fenwick. That's his name, right?"

"Yes."

"You one of his men?"

"You know I work for him."

Varney's self-satisfied grin returned. "What do you do for him?"

"None of your feckin' business. He's the leader of the nativist party around these parts."

Varney laughed, this time a barking caterwaul sure to bring attention.

Irritated more than he'd been in a long time, Amos growled out his next words. "Shut up. I don't pay you to know anything about me. You just do as you're told."

"Yes, sir." Varney's accent changed to a slow drawl laced with condescension. "Whatever you say. So I got my first portion of money, and everything is in order."

Amos's pulse lowered, his anxiety and anger slowing. "You have your men in place?"

"They're in place. Don't you worry. By the time your brother gets to the western side of these mountains, you'll be able to make a dead man outta him sure as I'm sittin' here."

Amos liked the certainty, the sound of it. He'd spent too much time running or preparing to run. The law, such as it was, intended to find him. Fenwick's other men, men with influence, had promised to stall the law for him. Yet he'd heard the sheriff had sent secret men after him. Whatever the Sam Hill secret men were.

"You know what I can't figure?" Varney asked as thunder rolled outside. "I can't figure why you didn't kill Zeke before he could prove you was the one that killed that little whore Elijah planned to marry."

Amos's mouth twisted. "Because I never believed Zeke could figure it out. Never prove it."

"Fooled you."

"Once I'm done with Elijah, I'm going after Zeke and that pretty wife of his."

Varney chuckled. "You want his wife for yourself? Or you just goin' to take your pleasure on her?"

Amos grunted. "Women like me." Amos felt his heart thumping in his chest, his muscles tightening. Words rushed from him like a dam break. "Especially Maureen."

Varney leaned forward again, eyes gleaming with a sick fascination. "Yeah?"

"I planted my seed in her. I figured Elijah would disown her." He poked at his chest with his index finger. "He didn't, and that's when she had to pay."

Varney shook his head and took a sip from his tankard. "You're a madman, McKinnon, but I like that in a person. Keeps things interestin'." He raised his drink. "A toast then. To makin' those papists stew in their own blood, no matter who they are or where they come from."

Though Amos hated Varney's guts, he could agree with two things. Papists needed to leave the country, and Amos needed to kill Elijah.

Thunder rattled the building, and Mary Jane jumped. The sky darkened as more rain pummeled the earth. A glance at the parlor wall clock verified the late hour. Elijah stood with her at the window.

A conversation ensued between several well-dressed men about the state of the weather, the pique on their faces consistent with displeasure. Mary Jane decided to ignore their ranting. It was not as if anything could be done about the weather. She returned to staring out the window, and remembered Elijah's words earlier in the day about sleeping with her.

I would have remembered that.

Elijah's intensity as he had said those words echoed in Mary Jane's mind over and over. His eyes had burned into her, filled with two emotions she was not sure could be combined in one man at one time. Lust and exasperation. Oh, yes, she had seen both in his eyes. He confused her. After all, how could he find her bothersome and yet still appear interested in her carnally?

She almost longed to see him laugh again. She tried to imagine what could have kept him from laughing for five years. Had Maureen, whoever she was, caused his sadness? His secrets were many and truly none of her business. She should stay away from questioning the Irishman. But, oh, his smile had channeled raw, sweet need deep into secret places she didn't know she possessed until she'd met him. His eyes, so vivid, had sparked with a fire enticing and thrilling. Not even Thaddeus had made her yearn for things the way the Irishman did.

You almost confessed your entire past to him, Mary Jane. Do not be so foolish.

For if he knew her past, would he think her easy to give out her affections? Would he see her as a light foot he could trifle with regardless of all decency?

"How did your father die, Mary Jane?" Elijah asked.

She didn't expect that question. "In a riot."

"What?"

Perhaps she had revealed too much about her family. "A riot. The small one that started around Kensington last week." She turned to face him once more. "It was a freak accident, from what I'm told. At first the authorities said he had been murdered."

His eyebrows pinched together. "What made them change their minds?"

An ache settled inside her. "I do not think we'll ever know the complete truth. My father had gone to a nativist rally in Kensington after he checked progress at his factory. From what the police say, the nativists were standing on the podium doing a speech. My father was in the crowd watching with two supervisors from his warehouse. Those men said an Irishman started hurling insults at the men on the podium. Moments later, a small riot erupted and fights broke out among the nativists in the crowd and Irishmen. In the scuffle my father suffered a broken skull and a knife wound."

Elijah's eyes stayed almost cold, but she saw the anger emerging from those cool green depths. "That's horrible."

She sniffed. "If he had not gone to that ridiculous rally, he would still be alive."

Mary Jane fumbled with her reticule and pulled out her handkerchief. She dabbed at her eyes and fought to keep tears from escaping.

"As much as you had difficulties with your father, you still loved him."

She nodded. "A strange thing, really, because I know I did not respect him. He was esteemed by so many, but now that he is gone, the real man he was is more clear to me."

"Why didn't your mother come with you to Philadelphia?"

She shrugged. "She is quite inconsolable. They had many quarrels, so I did not think she would be devastated. My Aunt Claurice went to stay with her and my sisters. She is a good...steady sort."

"You almost sound as if you wish she was your mother."

His insinuation fired her indignation. "Of course not. I do not feel comfortable with Aunt Claurice."

"She's a spinster?"

She reached up and adjusted her hat, which did not feel secure on her hair. "Her husband and two boys were killed in a carriage accident many years ago."

She heaved a sigh to relieve the tightness that drew the muscles along her shoulders into sharp pain.

Before Mary Jane knew it, Elijah's face altered. The indifferent mien slipped, a flash of sadness reaching his eyes. Suddenly, he twined his arms around her and drew her to his chest. One solid arm anchored her back, while his other hand clasped hot and comforting at the back of her neck. As surprise held her immobile, she pressed her cheek to his shoulder and gave herself up to comfort. His body was solid and strong when she needed it. But she only allowed a momentary respite before she remembered who she was and where she was. Without looking him in the eye, she disengaged from his arms. She turned back to the window. She had to halt this insidious need for his sheltering touch. It would not do to continue relying on him. It would not do.

The boat captain walked in and glanced around the room. "Anything I can do for you folks?"

Elijah nodded. "We'd be obliged if you could give us directions to the lodge or inn, please."

"Of course. There are both about five blocks away, though, and since it's raining like all tarnation, I don't recommend walking."

"My wife isn't walking in this. We'll hire a cabriolet."

The boat captain gave them a clever, warm smile. "If you can find a cab that is out in this weather. I haven't seen it rain this heavily in a long time. Maybe you should have taken the omnibus straight to a hotel."

As if to confirm his statement, thunder rumbled louder, and lightning flashed across the windows. A resounding crash followed, and Mary Jane started.

"We'll find one." Elijah's statement sounded confident. Mary Jane hoped he proved right.

Several other men took directions from the captain on where to find accommodations and left the room.

A petite, stiff-faced woman of about forty and an equally small man about the same age strode into the parlor. The haughty woman floated across the room, the size of her crinoline beating Mary Jane's by at least six inches. With sharp-nosed importance, features pinched into displeasure, she comported herself like an indignant queen. The lady's violent red hair was parted down the middle, ringlets bouncing at each step. She lacked a hat, and her clothes spoke of clear wealth.

"Ah, there you are Captain Hargrove," the woman said. "When do we depart?"

Drawing himself up to his full height, the captain said, "As we announced before, we can't leave here tonight, ma'am. The weather has obviously taken a turn for the worst."

The woman halted in front of the man, irritation written on every inch of her dour face. "Do you have any idea who I am?"

Tall and sapling thin, the official didn't flinch. "I know who everyone is on board the Philadelphia and Columbia. You're Delilah Montgomery."

She drew herself up to a total height of perhaps five feet. "Mrs. Montgomery." She gestured behind her. "That is Mr. Fritz Montgomery of the Philadelphia Montgomerys. If you want to keep your job, you will return to the station and tell them we demand this trip proceed."

"The weather *demands* we halt for the day, Mrs.

Montgomery. We're giving everyone directions to the Cedar Lodge and the Cambrian Inn. They are lovely places just built within the last year."

"Unacceptable." The woman snapped the word, her face growing red, eyes flashing with indignation.

Before anyone else could speak, skinny man and blond man walked into the room. Mary Jane was surprised. She thought they had disappeared for good—she had not spied them since departing the canal boat earlier that day. Mary Jane's stomach cramped as the filthy pair walked into the room with the air of rats searching for cheese.

"This is not to be tolerated," the exasperated woman said. "We cannot stay in this town tonight. We were scheduled to reach Duncan's Island today."

The captain nodded. "Yes, we were, ma'am, but with the weather like it is, there is a threat of flood. I would be happy to give you the name of a stagecoach that might leave tonight, but that's not a given. You will also have to forfeit your ticket on the train if you do that."

Sighing dramatically, the woman threw a glower around the room. "Then I hope you have suitable accommodations at the Cedar...." She waved one hand in dismissal. "Cedar Inn did you call it?"

"The Cedar Lodge, ma'am. And the Cambrian Inn. But I wouldn't say the rooms are expensive, Mrs. Montgomery. This is a simple town with simple choices," the captain said.

The haughty woman planted her hands on her hips. "Honestly, I have never heard of anything more ridiculous."

Tired of the woman's rant, Mary Jane stepped forward. "Surely it is not wise to continue traveling until the rain stops. I am..." Mary Jane stumbled over her fake last name. "Mary Jane McKinnon."

Mrs. Montgomery gave Mary Jane an insulting up and down inspection.

When the shrew said nothing, Mary Jane gestured to

Elijah. "This is my husband, Elijah McKinnon."

The woman's husband walked up before Elijah could speak. He looked as frazzled as the woman and as put out. He held a tall hat in one hand and retrieved a pocket watch from his waistcoat. His long, dark mustache was speckled with gray. "Are you *that* Elijah McKinnon? The one who was just released from Eastern State Penitentiary?"

All the air seemed to leave the room. Mary Jane's mouth opened in shock at the announcement, but she could not form a single word.

Chapter Six

Mary Jane stood in stunned disbelief as she tried to keep surprise off of her face. Several men, including the skinny man and blond man, turned towards the conversation. Along with astonishment came humiliation and anger. And, in an odd way, a sense of betrayal. Of course he would hide the fact that he was a criminal. Disappointment piled on to her fear. She had known there was something different about him but never suspected she kept company with a rogue.

Elijah's normally secretive expression cracked and clear anger flashed over his features. "This is a misunderstanding."

Fritz tucked his thumbs into his waistcoat pockets. "I recognized your name. There were articles about you in the newspaper after you were released."

One of the red-headed twins she had seen earlier on the trip walked up. "What was he in for?"

Fritz's nose tilted upward. "Murder."

Fritz's wife gasped and put her hand to her throat. "My God. A murderer in our midst."

The other red-headed twin bristled and stepped forward, coiled to spring. "An escaped prisoner?"

Fritz waved a hand. "No, no. *Released* from prison."

Mary Jane's throat felt as if someone had twisted a rope around it. She could barely suck in the next breath.

"Well, don't that beat all?" the skinny man said.

Elijah's face hardened to granite. "Come on, Mary Jane."

Before she could utter a protest, Elijah took her elbow and marched out of the room. She heard voices behind them and looked back. The red-headed men walked fast to catch up, the blond man and skinny man behind them.

"Wait," one of the redheads said. "Unhand that woman."

Elijah released Mary Jane, but he put her behind him and confronted the men. He held his hands up in a conciliatory fashion. "Gentlemen, this is a misunderstanding. My wife and I just want to be left alone."

All four men glared at Elijah. She recognized if things turned ugly, Elijah wouldn't stand a chance. He was certainly strong, but how did any man take on four others and survive? The well-dressed, red-headed gentlemen were powerful looking and determined in appearance. Of course, the skinny man and blond man appeared as mean as ever, and she did not trust them.

One of the redheads spoke. "Mrs. McKinnon, just give us the word, and if this man is in any way causing you harm—"

"My wife doesn't need your help." Elijah's voice deepened, his accent turning thicker. "Now, if you'll just let us be on our way."

"Gentlemen." The captain came around the corner. "If I have to, to I'll send for the sheriff. No crime has been committed here. Yet."

Blond man's smile didn't fit the gravity of the situation. "We think this man is holding this woman against her will."

"She's my wife." Elijah's definitive statement came out strong and clear.

"Let the lady speak," the captain said.

Elijah's fists clenched, his body tight with tension.

"You don't need help, ma'am?" One of red-headed brothers stepped closer. Sincere concern etched his features, his voice going soft as if he feared frightening a doe. "We don't mind escorting you to the hotel if you need it."

She did not wish to create a scene, and she knew if she balked and told the truth, something awful might happen. She took the path of least resistance. "We are all exhausted and the rain has put everyone in a bad sort. There is no need to create trouble."

One of the red-headed men took a single step forward and Elijah tensed. "Ma'am, if this criminal is holding you against your will—"

"I'm not holding her against her will." Elijah's voice rose and the redhead's eyes went bright with suspicion and anger.

Mary Jane realized mayhem would erupt if she did not do something. *Bother.* How did she get into these situations? "Please, sirs. Your concern does you credit, but there is no need for worry. My husband and I want to retire for the evening."

After a long, tension-filled moment, Elijah took her arm again and led her away. She glanced back, but the men did not follow.

Elijah walked so fast that she almost had to trot to match his long stride. They advanced on the doors leading to the street and the large overhang porch. Rain came down in heavy sheets, the air redolent with moisture. Water threatened to rise over wooden walkways along the buildings. The ire on Elijah's face threatened more than the storm.

"Slow down." She tugged against his hold. "Mr. McKinnon."

He ignored her, hardness etched into his eyes and features. Under the low light coming from windows along the street, he looked every inch the lawbreaker. Fear rose higher. She must escape him.

Irritated, she snatched her arm from his grip. "Let me go."

As they stopped, he towered over her, all muscle and authoritative male. Intimidating seemed too light a word to describe him. "We don't have time for this. There's a single cabriolet down there—" Just then two men jumped into the cab and it rolled down the street in the opposite direction. "Damn it."

"I'd ask you not to curse, sir."

He planted his hands on his hips. "You could ask, but it won't do you much good. We'll have to walk."

They hurried to the Cambrian Inn, which was closer than the lodge. All along the trip, she tried to think what to say. Her mind skittered from point to point. She knew one thing for certain. She refused to stay another night with him. They hurried as rain pummeled the earth. Lightning and thunder flashed nearby with an ear-splitting crack. Mary Jane felt like a player in a macabre tale of terror she had read as a young girl.

She pointed at a sign, just visible through the torrent across the street. "There is the Cambrian."

Elijah lifted her in his arms with rippling strength. She gasped in protest, but he ran into the rain and across the street. The way he dashed across the street, holding her as if it caused no effort, amazed her. Rain sluiced across her face, drenching her immediately.

Before she knew it, he set her on her feet under the crude awning in front of the hotel. "Here we are, darlin'."

She swiped water from her face with her gloved hand. "Do *not* call me darlin'."

Exasperation crossed his features. "Mrs. McKinnon."

"Do not call me that, either. I am tired of the deception." She wanted to scream. Her body ached. Her scalp itched under her hat. Water trickled down her neck. His display of masculine force sent quivers of reaction straight to her midsection. She was angry and yet...something about him still captivated her attention.

"I am not your darling or your wife, so you can stop pretending."

His eyes flashed with answering indignation. "I know why you're angry, but you'll have to let it go. Now isn't the time—"

"Let it go? I do not think so." She poked one gloved finger

into his midsection. "I am not staying in this hotel with you in the same room. We are getting separate rooms."

"We *are* staying in the same room."

"We are not." She gritted out each word with emphasis. "You are not my husband, and I certainly have not taken any vows to obey you. And even if I had, it would not matter."

"Listen to me—"

"I am through listening to you." She poked him in the chest again for emphasis. "You lied to me."

Thunder rumbled across the heavens, and he glanced up as the heavy clouds turned the day into early dusk.

His gaze snapped back to her, filled with as much fury as the heavens. "I have never lied to you."

"By omission."

"Mary Jane, I never lied. But you're not interested in hearing what really happened to me, are you?"

"Not in the slightest."

Lightning splintered the sky, jumping from cloud to cloud in an eerie dance.

"Then I guess I was wrong about you."

"Me?" She huffed. "What have I done?"

He stepped closer. His gaze clashed with hers, eyes intense, burning with a firm desire to explain, to tell her secrets she did not know if she wished to hear. "When I first met you I thought you were a prissy, uppity snippet of a woman."

She gasped. "What?"

"Then I thought maybe I was wrong. But the way you acted just now tells me my first impression was right."

Almost trembling with a combination of anger, cold and even fear, she asked, "How so?"

"By convicting me before you know the facts of the matter. I've never given you any reason to think you couldn't trust me."

She made a scoffing sound. "Oh? You could have told me right up front you had been in prison."

He laughed, but the sound held no mirth. "And you would have run screaming immediately and straight into the arms of those two creeps."

More resentment piled high. "What? That is absurd. I am not an imbecile, Elijah McKinnon. I do not run screaming to anyone. I would ask you not to insult me."

"Darlin'," his lilting accent filled with biting, unmistakable Irish charm, "I never insult a lady."

Her fists clenched at her sides. "Then why did you practically drag me down here and haul me across the road like a package?"

He pointed down the street, his gaze flashing almost as quickly as the lightning. "Because those cretins that accosted you are waiting for a chance to catch you alone like they did the other day."

"I think you were simply embarrassed because that man recognized your name."

"Lady, you're something else. I was beginning to think you were different than some of the high society prigs I've run into in my life, but I guess you're not."

Her voice rose to unladylike proportions. "How dare you?"

"I dare because it's the truth."

Once more he edged closer, and she realized they were almost chest-to-chest. Apparently he thought bullying would make her cower. She would show him.

One last time she poked him in the chest. "I do not know why I am bothering having this conversation with you."

"Sure, darlin', and that wouldn't be proper decorum now, would it? Waiting long enough to calm down and listen just wouldn't do."

The sarcasm in his voice fueled her desire to have the last word. "That is also your fault."

"What?"

"Only a man with a questionable background would spend

his time outside a hotel in the middle of a horrible storm arguing with a woman."

His eyes turned smoldering, dangerous, and warning her to back away from the challenge. "I could've made some assumptions about you at the beginning. That even though you're in mourning dress you're a weak, insipid, defenseless woman in need of a man."

"That is what you did. You decided you needed to rescue me. Well, I do not need rescuing."

A raw, consuming heat entered his eyes. "Listen, if I was the rounder you're accusing me of being, I could've hurt you before now. Really hurt you in ways you can't even imagine. And there's a good chance, if you don't keep on your guard, that some other man on this trip will try just that."

Something hot and exciting moved between them, and her chest rose and fell with her quicker breathing. Conflicting emotions tumbled and swirled within her, demanding notice. Anger, certainly, but something more worrisome took its place. Despite the fact Elijah infuriated her, she wanted more from him. More of his touch. More of his arms around her.

Fear stalked her, but not that Elijah would harm her. Trepidation that she would do or say something even more outrageous than she already had.

All her past failings rose up and threatened to overwhelm her. To remind her how weak she really was.

"If those men approach and try to hurt you, what are you going to do? Scream?" he asked.

"Of course. And fight back."

Once more his gaze trailed over her from head to toe, and she felt his attention caress her like a touch. "That dress keeps you hobbled, not capable of fighting a man as well as you could. I suggest you remove the crinoline. At least without that you have some chance."

"I cannot leave behind my crinoline."

He smirked. "Didn't think you would."

Rain dripped from his drenched hair and splattered onto his nose. Mary Jane ripped her gaze from his, unable to withstand the emotions she saw there. Her attention landed on his proud nose, then the interesting line of his mouth. In a bizarre, unexpected way, she wanted that mouth on hers. Needed his taste. She remembered the heat as his mouth had molded and tasted and learned. The incredible sensations that had bombarded her. Mary Jane knew there was more pleasure to experience under his touch. Recklessness threatened to sweep her up, demand more adventures, more forbidden exploration.

"The last thing I need is to take protection from a criminal," she said in defense.

Unmistakable perturbation cut through his face. She stormed past him and into the hotel. She paused as she took stock of the entryway. Wingback chairs graced the area, as well as a large settee next to a roaring fireplace. Gleaming copper, pewter and wood finishing, dark green velvet and red drapes covered windows and blocked out lightning darting across the heavens. A few rough and tumble men stood by the windows watching the storm toss the branches of gigantic trees. They glanced at her but quickly lost interest. Satisfied, she hurried to the front desk. Well aware she probably looked a sight, she resurrected the smile she used for difficult moments.

The dignified, mustached man at the counter smiled in return. "Good afternoon, ma'am. Horrible storm."

"Indeed."

Mary Jane half expected Elijah to stride into the hotel any minute. She glanced around, but another man and woman dashed in the front door, sputtering as rain continued to lash the area. She saw no sign of Elijah.

"Is anything wrong, ma'am?" the front deskman asked.

"Well, there is actually. My husband and I had a bit of an argument. I would like a room to myself, and he will require a separate room."

The older gentlemen's caterpillar thick eyebrows rose high on his forehead. "I see, madam. I have just the room. I doubt your trunks will make it over from the station in this weather, though."

"I will not need it this evening."

"Well, then, we have room eight for you. There's only two more rooms even left for tonight, so you just made it."

After writing her name as Mary Jane McKinnon in the register and paying for her room, she headed to the second floor via the staircase off to the right. Room eight, as she quickly discovered, was at the top of the stairs and to the right. Likely to be a noisy pathway, but what could she do?

Once she settled in her room, she unpinned her destroyed hat and sighed. "How awful."

She didn't have another hat with a mourning veil and doubted she could find another purchase. If she dried the hat, she could attempt to reshape it in the morning. She groaned. This trip had become more than her duty and grief for her father. The journey was two parts horrifying and one portion exciting. Shivering with cold, she worked to remove her wet clothes.

"Second time I have bothered with this," she said, annoyed.

Why am I annoyed? She knew why. Events today, including discovering Elijah's criminal past, served to frazzle her nerves. His weapon secretly tucked away should have given her a clue that not everything with him was as it seemed.

She calmed herself with a deep breath and resolved to dry off. She undid the topknot on the back of her neck and let her hair flow down in wet lengths. It reached nearly to her waist. She had considered trimming it—tired of the great efforts it took to wash. Mary Jane glanced in the large beveled mirror above the dresser. Parted down the middle, her hair didn't boost the usual ringlets and coils about the ears that she normally wore. No...mourning required more restraint. Startled at the high, pink color in her cheeks, she leaned forward and glared at her image. She would manage to wrestle out of her clothing without Elijah's helping hand. When she lived in her little apartment at the college, she had relied on her roommate Sarah for assistance, just as Sarah relied on her.

She remembered Sarah's expression when she'd learned of Mary Jane's disgrace. It still hurt to recall how Sarah had turned away from her, disgusted by what she had learned. Obviously scandalized that Mary Jane and Thaddeus—

No. No more. Do not think on it.

Though determined, it took her some time to wrestle off her clothes and arrange them on a chair near the fire to dry. Water had not reached her undergarments, thank goodness, so she could avoid nakedness altogether. What she would not give for a cabriolet bonnet to weather storms like the one outside instead of a mourning hat.

Her stomach growled, but tiredness beckoned more than the need for food.

She glanced down at the ring on her left hand. With a sound of disgust, she pulled it off her finger and sat it on the dresser. There. She'd give the thing back to him tomorrow and end this charade. She must have lost all sense and propriety agreeing to this scheme, and she refused to be a party to it any longer.

She climbed into the four-poster bed. A nap would do her good after that argument with Elijah. She could dine later. Though anger still pulsed through her blood, calmness started to overtake her. Few moments in her life had ever felt that frantic or fraught with uncertainty. Another comprehension came to Mary Jane. Never in her life had she experienced a disagreement as heated and contentious.

And to her chagrin, she had never felt as excited as she had while fighting with Elijah.

How bizarre. That cannot be normal.

Drat. She did not have her diary once again. Still, her mind mulled over what she would say in her diary, if she only had it.

Dear Diary,

I had the most horrible argument with Elijah today and cannot believe how it made me feel. I must guard against these feelings with everything I have. These kinds of feelings led me down the wrong path with Thaddeus. An awful, awful path. But I digress.

He is a criminal. He was released from Eastern State Penitentiary not long ago. Not only is it scandalous but—

Drat. I do not know how to feel about him and it is making me quite insane. Perhaps I should list his good qualities and his bad.

Good.

He is protective.

Strong.

Clearly does not like to see women harmed.

He speaks plainly, which is not something I experienced with Thaddeus. Thaddeus wove lies like a spinster knits socks. Yes, Thaddeus was a polite, proper liar.

Elijah does not appear to lie. He simply does not tell me everything. He hides his past, and now that I have discovered he was in prison, I can understand why. People would shun him.

I have shunned him.

Still, he deserves it for practically yelling at me in front of the hotel.

To be fair, I poked him in the chest and almost yelled at him.

His bad qualities are many.

He is poor and not likely to ever be rich. I cannot be attracted to a man who is poor. My family would not accept that.

He is Irish and Catholic.

Mother would not like that. A woman should socialize within her class and religious affiliation.

He speaks too plainly.

My mother and sisters would find that awful.

Moreover, he confuses me. He actually seems to like women who are somewhat independent and yet he is determined to play my husband.

Husband. Well, I cannot be too concerned about that since I shall never marry. What is the harm in using the deception to assist me in my quest to reach Pittsburgh unscathed?

Oh, bother.

She reached for the ring she'd taken off just a short time ago and jammed it back on her finger.

Mary Jane clasped her head between her hands and groaned in distress. It was not if she ever wished to marry in the past. But if she was to have the secure life her mother and sisters said she *should* want, she must find a husband somehow, someway, at some point in her life before she became so old no man would have her.

Or, I could remain a spinster.

That was what she really wanted. No man meddling in her life and creating havoc.

She hated confusion, and if there was anything Elijah did to her, it was confuse. She did not want to like him. A man this intriguing could ruin her, just as Thaddeus ruined her with promises he could not keep.

She would do well to remember that a man would always disappoint her in the end. Always.

Damn her infuriating, beautiful hide.

Elijah sat in the hotel bar and stared into the mirror above the bottles of liquor. Drawn and quartered. That's what she'd done to him with her reaction, her scathing assessment of his integrity.

Did he expect anything different?

No.

She'd shown her lily-white, upper crust contempt when she'd judged him.

He grimaced, watching his own frown expand. Damnation, she'd wormed herself into his blood, his mind and thoughts from one moment to the next. He also looked like a condemned man. He'd tried drying his hair in his room, but the thick mat didn't cooperate. Hell, he was just lucky he'd grabbed the last room.

Elijah brooded, glaring into the shot glass he held. He needed time to calm down and keep sober. No need to go mad with drink. He needed a level head in his pursuit of his brother.

Keep your mind on your goal, man. Mind on your goal.

He stayed in the bar until well past dark, nursing a single drink, then decided he required a respite from the smoky bar.

Once outside on the deserted back porch, he peered into the blustery evening. Where could he go from here? Contemplation stalled him from returning inside. He'd discovered through the desk clerk that his room was next to Mary Jane's.

Rain pounded so hard on the roof and porch that it rushed and rolled and sounded like a flood coming to wash them away. Anticipation grew in the air, a strange craving to rush to Mary Jane's room and make her understand.

He wasn't a criminal. He wasn't a bad man.

An ache started in his gut. Maureen had died because he couldn't save her. And his ma rejected him.

What difference did one more female's displeasure and stubbornness matter?

Elijah jammed a hand through his hair and grimaced. *Saints' preserve us. Why do I care that she thinks I'm a good man or even if she believes I'm a criminal.* He settled into a chair against a wall and breathed the cooling night air. Best if he dumped those notions right now.

His only goal remained finding Amos and taking revenge for what the bastard had done. Caring about a woman he'd just met did not figure into his plans, and he'd forgotten that. Tomorrow he'd make sure she arrived at the canal safely. After that, she could take care of herself. She'd taken care of herself for all her life before he'd seen her on the train. She could continue to do so without him.

Bolstered, he rose from his chair and started for the back door.

Out of the long shadows, far to his left, he heard footsteps thudding towards him. A man wearing a hooded mask rushed forward with club raised. Elijah dodged to the side as the runner swung the club. The runner swung again. Elijah met the man head on as he grabbed the man's wrist and club at the same time. They grappled for the weapon. Elijah fell over a chair, his body flying backwards. He met the hard porch with a thud and grunt as pain rippled upward into his head. Stunned, he watched the attacker launch another onslaught. Elijah didn't have time to reach in his pocket for his weapon. The attacker swung and hit Elijah's arm with bruising force. Pain rocketed through Elijah's arm and straight into the socket.

"Hey, what the hell's going on out here?" A shout came from the back door, and seconds later two men ran out onto the back porch.

The attacker ran down the porch steps and into the soggy night.

The men gathered around Elijah.

"Hey, are you all right?" one of the men asked.

Elijah struggled into sitting position, his back and head throbbing. *Damn, damn. Your fighting skills are rusty, boy.* "I've been better." For a second Elijah thought he suffered from double vision, and then he recognized the men. He peered at the two redheads from the station. "You."

The twins nodded. "Us," they said at the same time.

"Looks like you have a whole passel of trouble tonight, friend," one of them said.

"Come on," the man's brother said. "Let's get you inside.

You need a doctor?"

Bemused that they gave a damn, he rose to his feet with their help. He felt a little unstable but shook his head. "I'll be all right."

"Who was that guy?" the tallest twin asked.

Elijah rubbed the back of his neck. "Good question."

He followed the men into the building, and he'd reached the lobby when the world around him started to tilt.

He had about two seconds to react. "Ah, shite."

Then he went face down.

Chapter Seven

A knock on the door awoke Mary Jane from a pleasant, deep sleep. Startled, her heart pounded as she listened. Maybe she imagined the knocking.

Another gentle but persistent knock. "Mrs. McKinnon. It's Robert O'Gannon. We met earlier today in the train station. Your husband's been injured and needs you."

A cold lump filled her stomach and her heart started to skitter and thump. She hastened to light the lamp, hands shaking. "Coming."

Elijah hurt.

Fear added to the mix of emotions bombarding her. She hurried to the door, unlocked it, and threw it open. One of the red-headed men from the train station stood there.

His neutral expression turned to pink embarrassment as he realized she wore only her unmentionables. He averted his gaze. "Uh, ma'am, it's your husband. He's in the room next door." He pointed to his right. "They've sent for a doctor."

"What happened?"

"He was attacked outside on the back porch."

A thousand terrible possibilities scrambled through her thoughts. "I will be right there."

She slammed the door and hurried into her damp clothing. All the while she could think of nothing else but getting to Elijah. She grabbed her reticule and rushed out of the room.

She knocked on the door next to hers. Immediately the door opened and Mr. O'Gannon opened the door.

She pushed past him. "Where is Elijah?"

Elijah lay sprawled on the bed, arm crooked over his eyes. As she barged into the room, Elijah dropped his arm and gave her a disconcerted, almost sheepish look. She dropped to the side of the bed, barely registering that Mr. O'Gannon had closed the door and left them alone.

Mary Jane's gaze danced over him, searching for signs of injury. Other than being a tad pale, he looked none the worse for wear. "Elijah, what happened?"

He eased into sitting position and eased back against the headboard with a groan. He closed his eyes. He sounded all right, and without any outward signs of damage, he looked even better. His hair was tousled over his forehead, and he wore only a white shirt and trousers. Mary Jane's attention landed on the sprinkle of dark hair on his chest. Her gaze dropped down to his bare feet. Big, somehow glorious, bare feet. Heat rushed into all parts of her body. She tried to remember if she had ever encountered a man as unnerving, as impossible.

"By all the saints. I told him not to bother you," he said.

Worry kept her on edge. "Apparently he thought it was enough of a concern to contact me. Now, what happened?"

"Some arse came out of the woodwork and attacked me with a club. Before he could finish the job, O'Gannon and his brother appeared. I had the good grace to faint like a woman." His mouth twisted into a small smile for a couple of seconds, then retreated to his customary frown. "I woke up right away, but they helped me upstairs and insisted on fetching the doctor. O'Gannon's brother is doing that now."

"I am surprised they helped you considering how they acted earlier in the day."

"They told me they were only looking out for you earlier."

"Any sane person would think twice about letting you near—"

"Never mind." He waved one hand. "It doesn't matter. Why don't you go back to your room? After all, I'm a murderer. Who knows what I might do to you?"

His dismissive tone cut to the quick. She wanted to run, to leave him here with his injuries. She stood. "Well, I can see you are quite healthy. Since you are not dying in my arms, I suppose I can leave."

She turned to go, face hot with indignation, her stomach tossing with the sickening belief she was abandoning him.

"Wait."

Half tempted to keep walking, she turned towards him. His gaze assessed her, but this time with invitation simmering in his eyes.

He rubbed the back of his neck. "I apologize. That was...unfair." He paused, and when she didn't respond, he said, "You didn't have to come here. Why did you?"

Flustered, she stayed in place and mumbled her explanation. "I could not very well ignore Mr. O'Gannon's summons. It would have looked strange if a wife did not come running when her husband is injured."

Amusement twisted his lips then exploded in a smile. "I see you left your crinoline in your room, and your gloves. Not exactly proper is it, darlin'?"

His wit barely registered.

That damn smile lit up the room, and she blinked in astonishment. Yes, he'd smiled before. And yes, she'd thought him handsome and charming when he had. Something about this smile...something about it drove every thought from her mind but one.

Oh my, my. With a smile he became unimaginably striking. As his lips curved and amusement brightened his eyes, her heartbeat galloped like a racehorse.

Good humor did something extraordinary to Elijah McKinnon. Life had probably not treated him kindly. Whatever indignities he might have known, her heart hated to think on it.

Despite her resolve to have nothing to do with him, part of her yearned with her heart and that longing threw her into chaos.

As those green-as-Ireland eyes captured hers and held, her breath halted. Her senses spun. Lush, forbidden heat blossomed in her lower stomach. Trying to supply an unflustered answer became impossible.

"I see I have you speechless." He put out his hand. "Come, wife. Sit next to me until O'Gannon brings the doctor. We want to make the proper impression."

He winked.

She almost gasped. *The impudent—*

Her mouth popped open. "I—you are funning with me, sir."

"Yes, I am, darlin'."

Fumbling for words, she said, "I suppose I shall have to abandon asking you not to use that endearment, since you do not seem to listen."

"I rarely do. We'll make an agreement. I'll allow you to continue calling me sir, since you don't seem to listen. And I'll call you darlin' in retaliation."

A smile escaped her, and as it widened her mouth, she almost laughed. "You are the most infuriating man I have ever met."

"In your case, Mary Jane Lawson, I think that might mean something significant." His voice held secrets, lush promises. Exciting possibilities. "I love seeing your eyes wide, your face flushed, your lips parted. Damn me if it isn't the most..."

His voice drifted off, his gaze locking with hers so completely, she wondered if a strange muse had entwined them both. She swallowed hard and shook her head to deny the power he wielded.

As she approached the bed, she did so like a lamb heading for slaughter. "If you are quite healthy, there is no need for me to be here."

"Ah, but I can hope that you were worried about me, can't

I?" He sobered for a moment, his eyes now warm with something that almost resembled affection. "Were you? Worried about me?"

"Of course not. You are...hearty. I only thought..."

"That it wouldn't look proper for you to slam the door in O'Gannon's face and tell him to let me die?"

"Yes."

Mary Jane wondered if she'd lost her common sense. Here she stood with her hands clasped in front of her like a prim school marm, her heart doing an annoying dance.

She returned to his bedside and settled down. When he winced, the apprehension that bombarded her earlier returned. "Are you in pain? Can I get you something for relief? I could have some wine sent up."

She reached out impulsively and brushed the hair back from his forehead. Elijah caught her hand, and with his eyes locked on hers, he drew her hand to his lips. He pressed a heated kiss to her knuckles. "If this is pain, then I'll endure it over and over." His voice went deeper and rough with emotion. "And there is only one thing that would give me relief."

"Wine then?"

"No." His gaze dropped to her bodice and caressed her breasts like a touch.

Once more a mindless yearning flushed through her body. "Elijah..."

"Say my name again, darlin'"

"I..." She could not. Saying it at his command was too intimate.

Bemused and yet excited by his touch, she left her hand in his. He clasped it securely but gently, then released her with an intoxicating slide of flesh against flesh.

"Sir, I am serious."

"So am I."

"You are very rude."

"So you have told me before." His voice went lower. Dangerous and enticing. Coaxing her to forget the world around her and concentrate only on him. "There isn't anything you can tell me about myself I haven't heard before."

"You stare and stare. Did you learn manners in Ireland?"

"None. Wait. Yes, I did. But since seeing you I've lost all reason. I'm capable of nothing more than babbling of your beauty. You've bewitched me beyond saving."

As if caught up in a turbulence he could not escape, he drew her closer, leaning forward until their faces were close. His mouth hovered near hers.

She gasped, but could not speak for a few seconds. "This is madness."

"Yes."

Before she could think of protesting, his mouth took hers.

They touched nowhere else but lips, yet Mary Jane felt his caress as a lightning jolt. He lingered and withdrew, settled and sampled. Hot delight coiled and grew. She pulled back and her hand went to her lips. She kept her fingers there while her mouth tingled. Her gaze locked with his in startled revelation.

That slow, sinful smile tilted his mouth, a devilish and disarming quality she did not resist.

"Mrs. McKinnon, I'm surprised. I'm astonished, as a matter of fact. I thought you didn't like your husband anymore."

She stood, spine straight. "I do not."

He settled back onto the pillows and put his hands behind his head. "That didn't feel like dislike."

"It was." The denial touched her lips but didn't enter her heart. She walked a distance away.

Before she could retreat any farther, he sat up and left the bed. He came to stand near her, his body so stalwart and healthy, she doubted anything could fell him. His chest rose and fell with deep motions, his arms akimbo, his bare feet planted apart. Her gaze snagged on his chest again, mesmerized for a moment on his power and strength. They almost touched chest to chest.

"Why did you come running?" he asked.

Instinct called, and she put a hand out in defense. Solid male muscle connected with her palm. His hand fell over hers, tucking her much smaller fingers to warm, hard flesh. His left pectoral muscle bunched, and his nipple beaded under her fingers.

"Why did you come to my room if you dislike me so much?" he asked again.

"Common decency is expected of all ladies. That should not surprise you."

Slowly he released her hand, and she let it slide along his chest before snatching it away from disturbing sensations. Her body was aflame with unexpected yearning.

"I think you came here because there's part of you that cares about me," he said. "And I'll prove it."

Once more he leaned in and kissed her. Brush by brush, he painted his lips over hers in tender strokes that heated fires everywhere. He fisted his hand in her hair and drew her to his chest, his mouth now working hers with a persistent tasting. She eased away with a moan, but his lips still hovered over hers.

"That wasn't a proper kiss," he said.

"Of course it was."

"How many times have you been kissed?"

She licked her lips, and his gaze caught hold of the sight and burned like a touch. She swallowed hard. "Many times."

He frowned. "Many times? By how many men?"

"By one."

"How old?"

"Forty."

"Ancient."

"To a twenty-year-old woman, it is."

"That's interesting." He kept his voice soft and non-threatening. "So, how old are you now?"

"Twenty-two."

"I'm twenty-six."

"Ancient."

"In five years I've lived a lifetime."

She had no doubt he had, in his own way. "The man was Professor Thaddeus Ricker, a lecturer at the university. He teaches Latin. He was very appealing and handsome, a scholarly man that women respected." She shuddered. "But they should not have. I should not have."

"The old man didn't kiss you properly, and because you didn't find him attractive, you didn't enjoy his kiss."

His brows knitted, and she saw sympathy and understanding there that she did not know if she wanted. Attractive? Oh, yes, she knew how she felt when Elijah stood near, when he looked at her with those hooded, searching-out-every-secret eyes. It was world's above what she had experienced with Thaddeus. Her professor, once so dear in her young heart, seemed a pale imitation of manhood against Elijah's potent personality.

Before she could answer, his touch slid down to her throat and tested the pulse pounding there. "Sure, and there it is. Heat and madness."

"Madness?"

"Your pulse is quick. The way your breath quickens and your heart picks up speed tells me you like our kisses."

"I do not *want* to like it." She blurted the statement with a petulance that surprised and embarrassed her.

"Whether you *want* to like it or not isn't the question. *Did* you like it?"

She knew she hovered on making a step that once taken could not be erased. "Yes. It was...pleasurable."

His eyes turned hungry, their intensity building with her

answer. "How much pleasure?"

"New. Different."

He drew in a deep, shivering breath and trembled on the exhalation. "Do you want an honest kiss, Mary Jane?"

She could not voice it, so she did the one thing that would answer. She slipped her hand through thick, black hair at the back of his neck and eased towards him, brought him nearer inch by inch until...

Their lips met.

And suddenly all the protests within her mind and in her diary faded to insignificance.

Pleasure danced within her body, once more returning the sweet, mysterious longing to her lower stomach and the ache between her legs. His arms enfolded her, drawing her deep into his embrace. Braced along hard sinew and unforgiving muscle, she wrapped her arms around his neck and gave in to the devil. For most certainly that is what mother would call these growing feelings and this dangerous man. His mouth consumed hers without hesitation. Wrapped in this heavenly world, her senses whirled, spellbound with delight. His lips pressed hers open, and his tongue dipped inside to caress hers in one quick touch. She moaned and jerked back.

His arms remained tight around her, his eyes concerned. "What's wrong?"

"What you did just then...it is...is that normal?"

He chuckled, and embarrassment almost caused her to pull away. "Sure, and as certain I am that I was born in Ireland, it's normal. It's passion, darlin'. It's what grows the pleasure." He whispered his next words against her lips. "A man who wants a woman does it, and when she wants him, she participates."

"Oh. The professor never did that."

Still smiling, Elijah said, "Damned fool."

As he kissed her again and his tongue thrust deep, she

gasped into his mouth. The rough, gentle way his tongue brushed over hers sent new furls of sensation twisting inside. Her hands roamed, finding his hair and loving the silken, cool thickness. She arched, wanting to be closer but not certain how to accomplish it. His chest crushed her breasts. His hands wandered her back. She clung to him as she learned the rhythm and twined her tongue with his. He was spice and flavors so heady and luscious she wanted to more and more regardless of consequences. Almost without thought, she kneaded the muscles in his shoulders, tested the power in his biceps. When his hands loosened and came up to cradle her face, she clasped his forearms. Soon one deep kiss translated into two, then three, tastings that translated into more lingering thrusts of his wicked tongue. Though a delicious haze clouded her mind, she sensed this path led to a place she may not wish to wander just yet.

She needed breath and sanity and tore her lips from his. "My goodness."

His chest rose and fell, eyes blazing. "I don't imagine goodness had a thing to do with this, Mary Jane."

Her hands returned to his broad shoulders. She disengaged from him, stunned by what had happened. Yet her body sang a tune that made her wish to dance and sing and exclaim these shameful feelings to the world. She had never imagined sensations and emotions as potent as these existed.

She fumbled for a way to distract him from this path, and to block the madness that threatened to overtake her common sense. "Who attacked you?"

"I don't know, but I wouldn't be surprised if it was either skinny arse or that blond guy on the train."

A shiver coasted over her body. "The men who accosted me the other day?"

"The very ones."

"Why? Because you helped me?"

"Most likely."

Before either one of them could speak, a knock sounded on the door. She turned away to answer it and in walked O'Gannon and an older man in his fifties with graying, slicked back hair. His coat was dripping wet and after he removed it, he put it on a chair. Medical bag in hand, he turned to his patient.

O'Gannon's twin brother arrived—they were dressed differently or she couldn't have told them apart.

The graying man introduced himself as Dr. Franklin Woodriff. "I'll examine the patient now. If you could all leave the room, please."

"I'd like my wife to stay, please."

O'Gannon and his brother left swiftly. As the examination occurred, Mary Jane spent most of her time standing at the window, worried more than she wanted to acknowledge even to herself. She did not like these feelings that demanded her attention, or the helpless need that consumed her when he was near. Since she started this journey, she had experienced so many things that would have shocked and disturbed her friends and family. Yet here she stood, pretending to be a wife...wife to a man who may have committed murder. The idea should have sent her running to the protection of authorities. Yet, when she was with Elijah McKinnon, she felt safe. Protected.

And the forbidden aspect called to that part of her some would call sinful.

Here she was breaking her own rules, the *new* rules of decorum she had vowed to maintain.

Oh, bother.

She sighed and stared into the torrential rain that continued outside. No. She did *not* feel exactly safe. She felt unnerved. Inexplicable feelings that had no name.

"Well, Mr. McKinnon," the doctor said, "you seem to be in good shape. It looks like you've got a bump on the side of your head, but it's very mild. That explains why you fell unconscious. The man with the club got in at least one good knock. You'll be fine."

Relief filled Mary Jane at the man's words, and she turned to smile at both of them. "That's wonderful news."

"That is good news, doc." Elijah swung his legs off the bed. "My wife has been wringing her hands for the last half hour." He winked at the doctor. "She was really upset for me."

Mary Jane wanted to hurl something at Elijah's head and gave him an exasperated look.

The doctor's chuckle confirmed that he believed Elijah's hyperbole. "Well, that's certainly understandable, Mr. McKinnon." The doctor's genuine smile soothed Mary Jane's remaining ragged nerves. "I recommend a good night's sleep and that you keep a watch on your husband this evening."

"Oh, but—" Mary Jane cut herself off. It would sound rather odd if a woman didn't wish to stay with her husband in these circumstances. She nodded. "Of course."

"If there is anything worrisome, you can reach me at this address." Dr. Woodriff pulled out a card with his address and handed it to her.

He returned to the bed and closed his medical bag.

"Thank you, doctor, for coming out in the rain." Elijah shook his hand.

"You are very welcome." The doctor glanced from Elijah to Mary Jane and back. "These are rough parts after dark. I suggest neither of you go out alone. We've had some local trouble with nativists."

Elijah sat up straighter. "What kind of trouble?"

"We have plenty of Irish coming through these parts on their way to Pittsburgh, many of them new immigrants. Last week the sheriff found a man and wife dead behind the saloon. The conductor remembered them as Irish, but everyone else pretended they hadn't seen them in the saloon."

"You're suggesting the person who hit me did so because I'm Irish?" Elijah's question bristled with animosity.

Dr. Woodriff put up a hand. "Now understand I don't have

such sentiments myself. Many a doctor who did would refuse to treat you."

"A hypocrite to the Hippocratic oath?" Mary Jane asked.

The medical man's eyebrows shot up in surprise. "You've heard of the Hippocratic oath?"

She nodded. "I cannot imagine any doctor allowing himself to be influenced away from helping someone in distress."

Dr. Woodriff reached for his coat and hat. "You would be surprised, Mrs. McKinnon, by the strange things even doctors will do given twisted beliefs. I'm telling you this in warning that it's best to keep on guard."

"Thank you." Elijah's mouth turned tight and his eyes troubled.

Mary Jane reached for her reticule to pay the doctor's fee, but Elijah drew the money from his pocket and paid it.

After the doctor left, she locked the door and stood watching her *husband*. "I never thought a train trip could be this dangerous."

Elijah eyes were thoughtful. "Life is dangerous. Now there's even more of a reason for you to stay with me, even if you don't like the thought of rooming with a so-called murderer."

"Everyone on that train and in this hotel thinks I am an Irishman's wife. I daresay I am in more danger now than when I was plain old Mary Jane Lawson or because you were in jail for..." She crossed her arms, angry at the circumstance.

"Come on, you can say the word. Murder. I was found guilty and sentenced. I can understand any woman wanting to run away when she heard that. But I've been proven innocent and released, Mary Jane. I didn't murder anyone."

She drew in a deep breath, daring to meet his eyes. "How long were you in prison?"

"Five years."

A noose squeezed her heart. "You were so young."

"Twenty."

"Not so much older than me."

"I'm surprised you confessed your age earlier. So few women do."

"When a woman confesses her age it often gives men and sometimes women an excuse to treat her differently. That is why I do not mention it."

Curiosity burned in his eyes. "Treat her differently?"

"You are berated for being Irish, even though you are a citizen of the United States. I am berated for simply being a woman."

That statement seemed to hold him speechless for some time. "There's something else you aren't saying, darlin'."

She closed her eyes, weary from the night's events. "At twenty-two, I am quite on the shelf." He laughed, and her eyes popped open. Anger resurged. "What are you laughing at?"

"First, I know the fair sex is maligned by ignorant men. I think men should protect their women. And I won't allow a woman to be mistreated by any man if I know about it. Your age...well, a man would have to be half mad if he didn't see you for more than your age." He walked around her, his gaze assessing. His voice lowered, the husky sound rich with Ireland. "Sure, and a fool wouldn't see your rich, dark hair with those pretty red highlights, or the way your cheeks color when you're furious or..." He stopped in front of her, heat in his eyes. "Or aroused."

Oh. My. Elijah's words played with her senses, engulfing her in a soft but alarming place. "Aroused?"

His voice went even deeper. "I could see it when I kissed you...each time I kissed you. There is a look in your eyes. Hunger. Curiosity. It makes me want to peel your clothes off and find out if that pretty skin goes pink everywhere when I touch you."

Shocked, she wanted to deny the images and feelings his statements produced. The way he looked at her, as if he could kiss her and not stop until this blinding craving swallowed her whole... "No. This is too much."

"You seem like the type of woman who enjoys the truth and recognizes it when she hears it and sees it. From the first moment I saw you, Mary Jane, I knew you were different. You are beautiful, accomplished and intelligent. And you're strong. Yet you keep the real Mary Jane Lawson locked up in stiff corsets and big-arsed crinolines. When you were fighting with me in the rain, well, *that* was the real Mary Jane."

His words spun her around, dazzled her with gratification. Yet the skeptic inside her would have none of it. "It is certainly a pretty speech."

He grunted, his expression returning to granite. "Because no man has had the bravery to say it to your face before, that makes it untrue?"

Oh, she hated how his words threw her into an uncomfortable place. Especially when she couldn't form a word of denial. So she said nothing.

"You really do think I'm a jackass, don't you?" he finally asked.

"This is so complicated. Your mockery earlier leads me to think what you say cannot be trusted."

He shook his head and returned to the bed. He lay back on the bed and folded his hands over his lean stomach. "I apologize if I sounded mocking. It's amazing I can find coherent words at all."

"Oh?"

"Five years in solitary confinement—" He broke off as raw emotion entered his turbulent eyes.

Concern overwhelmed Mary Jane. She walked towards him. "I heard that Eastern State Penitentiary was a model place to reform prisoners."

Darkness entered his eyes, a desire to bury a horror too wretched to imagine. "It is long over."

"Not in your mind." Her voice softened. "Not yet."

He placed the heels of his hands over his eyes, and his words came harshly. "I'll conquer it. I'll drive it out." He lowered his hands and masked the haunted expression. "Everything I've said since you entered this room tonight is the truth. You are beautiful, intelligent, and any man would be lucky and proud to have you by his side. And when you came in the room tonight you were worried about me. I just can't figure why."

Why indeed? Examining those thoughts too closely disturbed her. "I told you. As your wife it makes sense I would be worried."

"Yes, but the point of this is that you *aren't* my wife. You think I'm a rounder."

"A scoundrel at the very least," she said.

His mouth curved in a devilish grin. "There you have it. I'm a man of few scruples."

Elijah's sparkling eyes caught her up in the fun, made her lips turn up even though she did not wish to like either his attitude or him. "How can you make light when someone attacked you because you are Irish?"

"I am used to people wanting to kill me because I'm Irish. For wanting to kill me whether I'm Irish or not."

"That is preposterous. This is the United States of America, not some waterhole in...in..."

"Europe? You don't think there are backwaters here? Places where bad things happen and no one cares?"

She paced, agitation gathering inside her like a beast on a tether. "Not in civilized, polite society. It is unacceptable. Perfectly barbaric." She stopped pacing and turned to him. "Did people try to kill you in prison?"

"No."

"But there are many awful men in prison."

"And women."

"Women?" The thought took her off guard, and then she shook herself.

"They weren't housed with the men."

She almost asked him to explain, then thought better of it. Listening to his sordid experiences could not be healthy for her. Well, her mother would say so, anyway.

"Come and sit down. You're about to wear a hole in the floor, wife."

She halted, not the least surprised by his request. "What difference does it make how many times someone tries to murder you? How indifferent can you be?"

He rose from the bed once more, his stride unruffled as he stood near her once more. She could feel his body heat and smell his pleasant, masculine aroma. "Yeah, I'm mighty worked up over someone trying to do in me in. But I doubt it was the same people who killed the married couple. My guess is the two men are all het up because I spoiled their plans to hurt you in that alley."

Mary Jane's mind whirled with questions. "What I honestly do not understand is why you have gone to such great lengths to protect me. I just told you this evening to stay away from me and that I wanted nothing to do with you. Yet you finagled a room next to mine. Why?"

"I didn't have to finagle a room next to yours. I didn't know it was next to yours until the desk clerk mentioned it. I think he guessed we were fighting and wanted to help us mend the fence."

She sniffed. "Doubtful."

His fingers trailed a warm path from her temple to her chin. He tilted up her face so she must gaze into the searching depth of his eyes. "I'm happy you're with me and that you're safe, Mary Jane. First, any man could see that you're without chaperone and on top of that, in mourning. When those men started watching you like buzzards, I knew what they wanted. They saw a woman without protection. I couldn't live with myself if I let that pass."

"You were staring at me rather rudely."

He shrugged. "I'd apologize, but I'm not sorry. I wondered what had happened...whether you'd lost a husband. I cursed myself because I'd no business thinking you were one of the prettiest women I'd ever seen and there was something about you..."

His gaze turned warmer, smoldering now with a banked heat that drew her a step forward even though it terrified her at the same time. "Something?"

"Yes." Elijah shook his head and broke the spell starting to surround them. He frowned. "Those clothes are still damp."

His abrupt change took her a moment to assimilate. "Yes. Why?"

"Take them off."

"What?"

"We can't have you turning ill. Take them off and lay them on the chair. Climb into bed where it's warm."

Her protest came out without thought. "I have my own bed. You should lie down and rest after your injury."

"You heard the doctor. You're staying here to look after me awhile."

She puffed up. "I will sleep in the chair."

He rolled his eyes. "You can't sleep in the chair."

"Why not? You did the other night when we shared a room."

A muscle jumped in Elijah's jaw line. "I wasn't wearing wet clothes."

She made a mocking sound. "I am not fragile. I can sleep in a chair."

"There is only one blanket on this bed, and you can't sit in a chair all night in your unmentionables. You'll get cold." He turned suddenly cool, detached eyes upon her. "Don't fret, Mary Jane. We can share the bed without me turning into a ravening beast. You can trust me."

She almost refused. Almost stood her ground, determined

to sleep in her clothing. An injured man surely would not touch her inappropriately. Of course, he had already kissed her tonight. Elijah had touched her often since he met her, and yet here she stayed, acting once more as his wife.

What choice did she have? As the rain continued, lightning crackled over the building and reminded her she had no retreat. "Very well. I will gather my other things."

She withdrew to her room, her mind roiling with a confusing mix of distrust and treacherous feelings that would not disappear no matter how hard she tried to banish them.

Chapter Eight

Elijah awoke the next morning wishing that he'd slept in the chair.

As God is my witness, this was not a good idea.

Sunlight streamed under the curtains and sent an arrow over the wood floor and the foot of the bed. Daytime had come, but with it a new challenge.

Mary Jane's sweet bottom nestled against Elijah's erection. He didn't want to wake her by moving, but not moving threatened to kill him. Her delicious body cuddled against him, his left arm encircling her, his palm cradling a lush breast covered by a thin barrier. *Sure, McKinnon, and the fact she hasn't awakened is amazing.*

His fingers contracted over giving, round flesh, and when he brushed over her nipple, it beaded to a hard point. She moaned softly. Satisfaction ate a hole in him. Even in sleep she was aroused. Even if her virginal body had never known a man's thrust, she knew passion when she felt it. God help him, but he wanted her with a raw lust that threatened to erode decency. His body had a life of its own. His cock felt like it would burst. He'd been a damned fool believing he could sleep all night in this bed with this woman and not want her. Wanting and taking were two different animals, though, and he'd never consider stealing something not freely given to him.

You don't have time for this, boy. Mary Jane is a forever kind of woman, and after you hunt down Amos, there isn't a forever for you. Just remember that.

He could abandon the train, get a horse and take off. Leave Mary Jane to her own devices. He'd thought about it more than once. Problem was, he didn't have enough money to buy a horse, and the train would be faster. He didn't know this area well enough to ride over the mountains and arrive in Pittsburgh in one piece and successfully hunt down Amos.

He was stuck with the train and the temptation of Mary Jane.

He wouldn't leave her unprotected, no matter what his goal.

He closed his eyes and committed to memory the soft weight of her breast in his cupped hand. He wanted to lick and kiss and nibble until she writhed, until she begged him to enter her depths and ride her into oblivion. Her slim waist, rounded hips and cushioning ass drove him to this side of insanity.

Damn it, he could blame it on those kisses last night. Thrusting his tongue into her had created a craving so fierce he could taste her even now. Her innocent kisses had grown in skill, but he wanted to tutor Mary Jane until she surrendered everything without hesitation.

Elijah drew a deep breath and marveled at her delicate rose scent. She smelled like comfort and gentleness, home and hearth. Things he couldn't know until he'd killed Amos. Probably not even then. For once he finished off his good-for-nothing murdering brother, he'd be on the run himself. Forever.

A good woman couldn't be saddled with a man like him.

Then again, maybe holding her last night had its benefits. For the first time in a long time, the nightmares had stayed at bay. Or, it could just be his good luck that he hadn't awakened sweating and so frightened he couldn't see straight.

She sighed and wiggled against him, and he stilled like a man on a frozen pond with cracks opening beneath his feet. She shifted enough to allow his cock purchase between her legs. Sure, he wore his breeches, but the heat of her thighs promised more, so much more. Her unmentionables, a camisole and pantalets, tantalized enough to allow his imagination to run wild. He imagined opening his pants, lifting her thigh, and sinking between hot, wet folds and thrusting like a madman. He almost groaned. After more than five years of abstinence it would feel beyond wonderful to sink his body into hers.

And something else niggled in the back of his mind.

Bare brushed against bare as she moved and one of her cold feet pushed between his. He'd never considered feet as erotic until this moment. He allowed his foot to rub over the top of hers. He groaned. *By all that was holy.*

Another sigh left her, as if she dreamed about a happy event. It stirred feelings he'd fought to bury for two days. He didn't want to care for her in any deep way. Knowing if she liked mince pies or peppermint cakes, or if she would scream when he brought her to climax, or just exhale in a breathy moan of pleasure—

God help me.

As if his fingers had a mind of their own, his thumb drifted across her nipple. Heat beneath his fingers renewed desire. Another soft moan. Suddenly she let out a gasp and jerked away from him. Though they were covered almost to their chests, she dragged the coverings higher and sat up.

"What are you doing?" Her eyebrows slammed together in obvious disapproval.

Deciding to keep things serious, he said, "Staying warm. It's not exactly hot in this room."

He let the sheet fall away, and her gaze snapped to his open shirt. Her attention fixated on his chest, then slid down over his stomach. She seemed fascinated with his body, and he admitted to himself her attention felt good. He slipped from bed to escape her nearness. He caught her gaze fixating on the bulge at the front of his pants.

"Something wrong, darlin'?"

She jerked to startled awareness, a pretty pink coloring her cheeks. "What? No. Of course not. But you were... I thought when I woke up that you..."

He guessed what she meant, but he stifled a smile and strode to the window. "I what?"

Her mouth pursed in disapproval. "Your hand was wrapped around my breast."

Elijah crossed his arms. "Yeah. It was."

"Why you—" Her eyebrows knitted with disapproval, her arms crossing as well. "You said you would keep your hands to yourself."

"I woke up that way. Sorry if I can't control my body while I sleep."

Her gaze darted to his cock again and lingered, and the tension it created in his body caused him to grit his teeth. Before he could even walk away and hide his arousal, his erection hardened more. Her eyes widened, then she jerked her gaze away.

She slid out of bed and went to the basin of water where she washed. He couldn't watch her do that either, so he stared out the window. Drawing back the dingy off-white curtain, Elijah took in the weather. Sun had banished most of the clouds, though wading through the waterlogged and muddy streets wouldn't prove pleasant.

He heard the rustling of her clothes as she dressed, and it kept his body unsettled.

"Help me with this corset, please?" Her question sounded tentative.

When she turned her back to Elijah, and he started to work the laces, his fingers almost trembled. His senses noted everything about her. Her floral scent teased his nose, her skin looked smooth and soft. The long, thick length of her hair begged a man to touch it, to bury his face in it.

Jesus, Mary and Joseph.

He gently brushed her hair away and over her shoulder.

116

"Wouldn't want to get this pretty hair caught in the laces." Unable to keep the arousal out of his voice, he continued with, "You have such white skin."

Elijah felt her stiffen, but he didn't stop working the laces.

"I do not spend much time out of doors. My mother always said too much sun is not good for the skin."

He nodded. "She's probably right. No leathery, brown skin for you, darlin'."

God, if I could just have one night to caress her. To feel all that white softness in my hands.

His cock didn't care about propriety or morals. It strained against his trousers. Elijah gritted his teeth as he finished with the corset. "Need help with the buttons on your dress?"

She turned towards him and smiled. "Would you please?"

He didn't think he could take another minute, but he endured as the seconds stretched and he worked on each stubborn button. "Damn, who is the monster that makes these dresses so blamed difficult to manage?"

Amusement painted her voice. "Most of these dresses are designs originally made by a man."

He grunted as he finished the last button. "Dad-blamed fool."

He released a constricted breath and moved back to the window.

Once more, he forced his attention to the road and saw skinny man and blond man stepping across the sodden street. They dodged debris that flooded the way, branches and old boards and piles of high mud caused by swirling water.

What he saw next caused him to curse. "Well, I'll be damned."

"I beg your pardon?"

"Our blond friend and skinny friend are down there talking to that Dr. Woodriff."

Mary Jane arrived at his side. "You are thinking perhaps

Dr. Woodriff is in league with them?"

He looked down at her, all trussed up in her bodice and skirt, and mourned the lost view of lush flesh he experienced earlier. "No. They're probably asking how I am, though. They may have heard rumors that I'm half dead."

"Hmm."

He turned away and washed up. "At the next stop we'll find a tub and have a good soak."

"That would be lovely."

Damned if it wouldn't. His mind wended an inevitable path to her, naked in a tub. With him. His cock jumped to attention again. *Damn it all to hell.* He had to stop this.

She turned away from the window. "The time is getting late. We have to make our way to the station. But first, I have something to say."

She had that school marm attitude again this morning, her hair piled in a severe knot on the back of her head and scraped away from her face. Despite the harshness of the hair arrangement, her face held innocence and beauty.

"Did you hear me, Elijah?"

Sure, and the tone went with the school marm presentation just fine. "I'm listening."

She clasped her hands in front of her. "No matter what sleeping arrangements we come to in the next leg of our trip, you cannot take the liberties you did this morning."

Elijah wasn't sure whether to be amused or annoyed. So he did what worked. He ambled towards her until they stood close together. That way he could enjoy her rose scent, her pretty eyes, and make his point.

"I apologize for the liberties, but I didn't *take* them. You were snuggled right up to me, your sweet little arse tucked into me. You squirmed and moaned. That leads me to think you were enjoying it, even if you were half asleep. And let me tell you, darlin', it was damned hard to keep my hands from roaming more than they did. Do you have any idea how beautiful you are?"

"I—no." She apparently hadn't expected that rejoinder. She closed her eyes. "You are not making this easy."

"I don't intend to. We're caught in this charade to keep you safe." God, he hated saying these next words. He kept his tone firm to convince himself. "If we want to keep you a virgin, we'll have to back off. No more kissing, touching. No more sleeping together."

Mary Jane's lips tightened. "If you recall, you were the one who kissed me first." She patted her hair as if making sure it hadn't loosened, then reached for her mourning hat and veil. Holding it primly in front of her, she gave him another look that screamed condescension. "For my part in this, I apologize. But I will not be lectured by you as if you were my husband." Her mouth trembled slightly. "Not even then."

When she turned towards the mirror, Elijah watched her. Her face was impassive and dismissive. Now he felt like the schoolboy, and he didn't like it one damned bit.

"There may be some flooding up the line, Mr. McKinnon. We're waiting to find out if the canal is safe from here to Duncan's Island and on to Hollidaysburg. If so, we hope to arrive there in fine shape. The next day you'll be on your way across the Allegheny Portage Railroad and straight into Pittsburgh."

The man's pride came through clearly, and Elijah liked the captain's friendliness and efficiency.

Elijah glanced at the wall clock. "At this rate we won't make it to Hollidaysburg today."

"It is getting cloudy again. I surely hope it does not rain again. Things are wet enough as is." Mary Jane's unusually petulant complaint didn't deter the captain.

"Ma'am, I'm sure we'll do our best," the man said.

She nodded and returned a smile, but the soft curve of her

lips didn't seem genuine. "Of course."

"Sure, and are you in a hurry?" a voice said, humor laced in every syllable.

Elijah and Mary Jane glanced over at the entrance and saw one of the O'Gannon brothers there. Elijah couldn't say which.

"You planning on staying another night here?" Elijah asked as O'Gannon walked towards them.

O'Gannon shook his head. "Not if I can help it. How's the head this morning?"

Elijah nodded. "Good." He put his hand out. "I wanted to thank you for getting the doctor and my wife for me last night."

O'Gannon smiled brightly. "That was my brother Seamus who went for the doctor. I'm Robert."

"Thank you to both of you, just the same."

Robert O'Gannon hitched his thumb in the direction of the station open area. "No problem. We don't like to see a fellow Irishman in such bad shape. How long have your people been in the United States, Mr. McKinnon?"

"Ten years."

"And you've been in prison all that time?" Robert asked.

Elijah sensed Mary Jane's unease. Her gaze flickered from here to there, as if searching for escape. "I was in for five years."

"For murder?"

Elijah didn't like the man's curiosity. "I was proven innocent of the charges. That's why I'm out of prison."

Robert put one hand up. "My apologies. That was too personal a question, I can see. Well, both of you take care. Looks like the captain is coming back with news about the rest of the trip."

O'Gannon walked towards his brother Seamus and the captain, his swagger built of obvious confidence. Something about Seamus and Robert made Elijah nervous, and he didn't like it.

The skinny man and blond man arrived at the station.

Tension spread throughout Elijah, but he turned his attention back to Mary Jane.

Before he could comment about the arrival of the miscreants, she said, "You never did explain to me how you were blamed for murder."

"A tale for another time. Let's go."

He slipped her hand through his arm so she accompanied him in an easy stride towards the platform. The look on her face said she wouldn't be placated forever. Telling her more than she already knew about Maureen...no. Deep inside his gut twisted, screaming and aching for a release. He wanted another person to know and accept the agony he once experienced. To banish the demons clinging to him. Yet he couldn't. He just couldn't. Talking about his time in prison would make it real. Make him remember things he wanted desperately to forget.

"Elijah?" Mary Jane's soft voice forced him to stop near the platform while other patrons walked past them. She looked up at him, expression curious and worried. "Are you feeling all right?"

"I'm fine."

Her other hand came up and touched his forearm, a feminine hand so white, the fingers long and the palm small. He visualized those delicate, beautiful fingers palming over his chest once more, trailing down his stomach and lower...much lower.

Saints preserve me.

Good luck, McKinnon. The saints don't want a thing to do with you.

"Your face had such an odd expression," she said. "So sad and lost. So angry at the same time."

Tension locked up his throat, and he took a huge breath and moved along the platform. "I just want to get to Pittsburgh."

Beside him her skirts swished as she released his arm and the captain took her hand to help her into the floating carriage. "We all do, Mr. McKinnon."

121

Duncan's Island to Hollidaysburg and Allegheny Portage Railroad

When rain didn't materialize and the canal trip finished without incident, Mary Jane could not believe their good fortune. They made it to Duncan's Island in record time, and she marveled at the beautiful scenery. Primeval forest and hill met the rivers Susquehanna and Juniata. The canal ran along the southwest side of a mountain, separated from the Susquehanna by a huge wall. They ascended to a timber bridge resplendent with numerous arches and drew the boat across the wide river. They remained on the packet boat that would take them on the Juniata Division Canal. Time passed slowly as they navigated eighty-six locks. She had heard that in the early days of the railroad passengers had changed back and forth from railroad cars to packet boats. Thank goodness these sectional packets made it possible to stay on the same accommodations for the entire trip. They passed Millerstown, Mexico and Mifflin. Soon the towns along the route all seemed to blend one into the other. Waynesburg, Hamiltonville, Huntingdon, Petersburgh, Alexandria and Williamsburg.

At Hollidaysburg they transferred to the Allegheny Portage Railroad tracks. She was glad they did not negotiate the roads, which swam in water until they became nothing more than muddy paths. She heard one man say this stretch of track ran at least thirty-six miles, and that it took most of one day to get from Hollidaysburg to Johnstown. Another man reported that new tracks would soon be laid around the Allegheny Mountains instead of over it. While locomotives made this trip quicker and more efficient than the previous stationary engines and horse drawn railcars, she heard it had all come too late to save this old railroad from approaching economic ruin.

Their passenger train today had a baggage car and two coaches. While the two coaches could haul sixty or so people, today about twenty-five people filled their coach and she had no idea how many filled the one behind them. With slow progression they headed up the eastern slope of the Allegheny Mountains. One by one they traversed ten incline planes, hoisted by a locomotive. Plains and valleys were left below as they traversed bold and rugged terrain as dangerous as anything she could imagine.

Alas, the rain caught up with them once more, and she watched with trepidation as the storm pummeled them without mercy. The windows fogged, and seeing much became almost impossible. Elijah had fallen asleep on the seat across the aisle from her. She remembered this part of the trip on the way to Philadelphia and at that time it had seemed long, too. She peered out of the window, trying to gather her bearings. The Allegheny Mountains ran from northeast to southwest, a five hundred mile stretch. She tried to imagine herself roaming among them and the idea sent fear dancing inside her. She'd never seen a place so vast and intimidating. Yet she'd survived this trip intact so far. Mary Jane smiled to herself because if she'd heard one of her friends relate such a trip, she wouldn't have believed it.

While she watched the Alleghenies slide by, she went deep into thought and reflection. She wished she had time to write in her diary all the words she had imagined putting to paper in the days before. So she closed her eyes and thought about what else she would tell her journal when she reached Pittsburgh.

Dear Diary,

Since taking this trip to bring father home, I have experienced events I believed only happened to other people. Other women kiss men wantonly, allow them to stroke and touch and plunder. Other women defy an outrageous and handsome man while standing on the threshold of a hotel. How many women can say they spent the night with a man accused of murder, nursed him after a beating, been rescued from ruffians by the same man and, well...

Dear diary, it is too much to take in, to know how to react from moment to moment.

No, telling mother or my sisters about this amazing adventure would not do. I certainly cannot speak of it to my mother and sisters.

I confess I am concerned. I have taken dangerous steps towards an unknown end. Unknown ends always frighten me. Always. I have not acknowledged that fact until now. Have not explored what it meant. Discovery always means peril, and that means foolish notions and possibilities. Elijah McKinnon attracts me, and although it is not at all wise, I find myself drawn to him with the fiercest of emotions. His life is downtrodden, his past uncertain. He is dangerous, and yet I know in my heart he must be different than other men...Thaddeus in particular. Especially Thaddeus. There is substance and fortitude, and reliability within Elijah that I can sense. Most would say I am gambling with my emotions like I did with Thaddeus.

To my absolute shock, I am excited.

Exalted in the most bizarre fashion, by those same possibilities I should find frightening. Such folly brought me into moral peril with Thaddeus. Am I truly so weak? Am I destined to make the same mistakes over and over?

Perhaps I should stay on guard, and I have told him that intimacies are not permitted.

Yet...

She opened her eyes, losing her ability to imagine the words. Putting her feelings into words had never been difficult before with her diary open in front of her. Why did she find it so impossible to describe exactly what she felt and what was happening to her? Why she would abandon her resolve that she would no longer involve herself with men of dubious connection?

The steam locomotive chugged and strained up one laborious incline to another. Drop offs and rugged edges came on every front. Trees hugged the ridges, their profusion of hemlock and other greenery reminding her of Elijah's mysterious eyes. This land proved vigorous, a challenge to all who dared cross it. To her, these mountains and this excursion became more than an event to survive. It became about the learning, the total understanding. Contentment came out of nowhere, and she embraced it, not knowing how long it would last. She only knew it felt wonderful and real. Delicious and uplifting. Her father's death brought sorrow, but maybe she had learned about herself along the way. She noted the others in the car, including the haughty woman and her husband Fritz, remained silent. Perhaps they felt this magic, too.

Elijah awakened abruptly, a gasp on his lips. Another nightmare?

She almost reached out to him, but he blinked and rubbed his eyes. "Where are we?"

"Incline six I believe. Almost to the Summit Mansion Hotel."

"Did you stay there on the way to Philadelphia?"

"No. We managed this trip far quicker coming from Pittsburgh."

The train came to a laborious stop into the station. Before long a conductor entered the car behind them. Rain chased people towards stagecoaches awaiting passengers.

Mary Jane sighed with disappointment. "Oh, no. Don't tell me this all we are going today?"

Before Elijah could comment, the conductor came on and announced the bad news. "Sorry, folks, but the weather down the Western Slope is too rough to proceed for the rest of the day. You'll find accommodation at Lemon House or Summit Mansion Hotel."

Mary Jane stood in front of the Summit Mansion Hotel and decided they would stay here—it looked more elegant than Lemon House. Built next to the turnpike, Summit Mansion Hotel was a white, three-story, wood frame building.

"Humph." Elijah's male grunt said it all as they stood

125

outside the hotel on the dirt road and took stock. "Looks high on the horse."

She smiled. "If we enter and you object to the folderol, we can try the Lemon House. Agreed?"

He looked down on her, a brooding quality in his eyes. "Agreed."

They entered and found a well-designed and distinct world. The interior at first glance showed moderation with furnishings, nothing too ostentatious and nothing too rustic. Mary Jane scanned the lobby, front desk, and what looked like a parlor and dining room. Several people lingered in the lobby, most of them men. Their rough work clothing spoke of coal miners, rail workers and other laborers. Only the train passengers looked none the worse for wear.

After Elijah and Mary Jane waited in line to check in, the dark-haired, rugged man at the front desk smiled brightly at both of them. Mary Jane could not help but notice the man behind the desk paid particular attention to her.

"Pleased to meet you, Mr. and Mrs. McKinnon. I'm Douglas Campbell, son of the owner. I think you'll find our hotel most comfortable. We opened for business in December, 1833, and our hotel is the best around," the desk clerk said.

"Oh?" Mary Jane gave him a genuine smile. "Right around the time the railroad started."

Campbell leaned on the desk and continued to spread on the charm, apparently just for her. "You know about the area, Mrs. McKinnon?"

"Only a little I have picked up here and there."

"Well, once you've stayed here, you'll come back again."

Elijah did not appear convinced. "How many hotels are around here besides this one," he gazed around, "and the Lemon House?"

Campbell's warm brown eyes danced with zeal for his subject. "Well, Summitville has grown to over four hundred people just this year. There are four hotels in Summitville." He scratched his chin. "Another four outside of town too. There are even five boarding houses nearby. Lemon House is a lovely establishment, but it's a bit farther away."

"Humph." Elijah grunted his enthusiasm, and Mary Ann wanted to smack him with her reticule.

Campbell rushed on, apparently determined to impress. "We've got eight-foot ceilings, long hallways, and forty-two rooms. Each room has a bed, dresser and washstand. Our kitchen has indoor water piped from a spring. Though with all the rain we've been having, we've had enough water for a lifetime." Campbell's chuckle sounded false to Mary Jane, but she took the polite approach and smiled. He continued with, "We have a room on the second floor just for you."

Mary Jane glanced over at Elijah. "What do you think?"

Elijah waited so long to answer, she wondered if he heard her. He pulled out his money. "We'll take a room. Can you have my wife's trunk sent up?"

"Would be my pleasure." Campbell held his hand out to shake. When he took Mary Jane's hand, though, he held on longer than necessary and smiled into her eyes.

Elijah pointedly took her hand from the other man, picked up the key and turned to the staircase.

As Mary Jane and Elijah headed upstairs, Mary Jane pulled her hand from his grip. "Is there something wrong, Elijah? You were a little impolite back there."

"I saw the way he was looking at you." They reached their room number, and Elijah unlocked the door. They stepped inside and after Elijah relocked the door, he tossed the key on the washstand.

He sounded almost petulant, almost...jealous. "And?"

"The man's a wife stealer."

Mary Jane worked on removing her hat. "You think he will steal a wife you do not even have?"

"Yeah."

She placed her reticule and hat at the foot of the bed and took a chance on this temper. "That is ridiculous, Elijah. I have no interest in him. Besides, I have no interest whatsoever in attracting any man's attention."

"Sure, and why don't I believe that?"

Half amused, she took another gamble. "I know this could not possibly be true, but you sound jealous."

Sure enough, he turned away from the washbasin and stalked her way, all prowling masculinity and hard edges. His eyes flashed. He leaned in close, his fresh male scent teasing her senses. "All right, I'll confess." Elijah continued his predatory walk, circling her like a man reviewing property at an auction. "I will get this off my chest and then say no more about it." He stopped in front of her, his gaze hot and hungry. "When he touched you, when any man gets near you, I go a little mad."

Startled and aroused by his possessiveness, she managed one question. "Why?"

"Because I'm keeping you safe. I made that vow, remember?" He leaned in closer, so much closer her breath caught. He smelled wonderful and male, and she longed to reach out and stroke his face. "Against my better judgment, I might add."

His eyes still burned, but he turned away and sat on the bed to remove his shoes. Disappointment settled inside her. Had she wanted more? And if she had, *what* exactly? To hear a declaration of affection? Of undying love?

Preposterous.

When Elijah drew off his waistcoat, cravat, and unbuttoned his shirt to the waist, she received an eyeful before averting her gaze. She closed her eyes but could not vanquish the vision from her brain of sculpted chest, broad shoulders, and muscled stomach sprinkled with dark hair. She felt too hot, too confined. Staying caged in this room with pure male animal made her fidget.

She reached for her hat once more, regretting the need to

place it on her head again. "I say we should have an early meal before everyone else has the same idea. We can talk."

He tilted his head to one side and managed a lopsided smile. "What else do we have to talk about?"

"Anything. Everything. The real reason why you are traveling to Pittsburgh since you have never said."

His mouth tightened, all humor lost. He lay back on the bed and crossed his hands over his stomach. "I do *not* have to tell you that."

She walked towards him and caught the faraway look in his eyes. "You constantly confound me, sir. I do not understand you."

He sat up and scooted to the edge of the bed. His thighs spread wide, and she realized with a start that she stood between those encompassing limbs. What troubled her most was her inability to move away. "Maybe it is best if we kept it that way. I don't know you and you don't know me."

She dared to make a bolder move, tired of playing games that required dancing and dodging to arrive at a coherent answer. "Perhaps five years in a prison made you afraid." Defiance grew in his eyes, and Mary Jane knew she hit on a truth. Yet she understood fear too well...this entire journey had her teetering on a pinhead. "I will make you a wager, sir."

"I like the sound of that." His voice dropped into a husky, sensual tone that brushed like a touch along her skin. "But I have a price."

Chapter Nine

"A price?" *Oh, Mary Jane, what are you doing?*

The arrogant Irishman leaned back on his hands. "I'll tell you a little of what you want to know, then you pay."

A warning jumped into her thoughts. *You're taking this too far. Retreat. Retreat.* "With what?"

"After each answer, you have to kiss me."

Her mouth popped open. "That is outlandish."

His eyes said he didn't lie about what he wanted. "Maybe. But it's the price you'll pay if you want answers."

She tried self-defense and moved away to stand in front of the mirror over the washbasin. She placed her hat on the washstand and stared at her wide-eyed expression in the mirror. *Oh my.* She looked as startled as a small child. "You are playing the rascal."

He made a sound low in his throat, somewhere between a contented sigh and the purr of a languid cat. "That sounds about right."

Mary Jane's throat tightened, but that imp inside refused retreat. He thought he could challenge her to a battle of wits. Well, she would show him. She worked open the throat of her dress, knowing it would distract him to catch a glimpse of female flesh. Perhaps if she attempted charm...

She undid her hair pin by pin. It fell about her shoulders and dropped to just above her waist. It needed a good brushing, but the chignon had given her hair some wave. She could not see him from this angle but sensed his piercing attention.

She should not do this.

Yet she could not stop.

She turned towards him and saw the ploy worked. Elijah's eyes turned molten as his gaze fastened on her throat and breasts. Perhaps this adventure had loosened her inhibitions more than they should. She trembled on the edge, almost ready to back away from the silly venture.

He patted the bed beside him. "Sit next to me and get comfortable."

Comfortable? Oh, she could *not* feel comfortable sitting anywhere near him. "What about our meal?"

"Are you hungry?"

She shook her head.

He patted the bed again.

She sat and turned slightly towards Elijah, keeping at least a foot between them.

Weighty silence gathered and accumulated before she forced a question passed her lips. "I hardly know where to start."

He returned the favor and angled his body towards her, his knee hitched up on the bed, his forearms leaning on his thighs. "What are you burning to know, darlin'?"

"Did Maureen break your betrothal because you were accused of a crime and imprisoned?" His mouth twitched, and she saw the denial welling. She put her hand up. "I know you said never to ask you about her. But whoever she is, she is important enough to give you a nightmare."

His eyes clouded, but he nodded his agreement. "That she was." He sighed. "All right. You asked for the truth. I was convicted of murdering Maureen."

Mary Jane's hand went to her throat as goose bumps prickled along her arms. She could not believe it. Did not want to believe it.

"That is not the half of it," he said. "The man who really killed her was my own brother. Amos."

Mary Jane did not react for a few seconds, stunned.

"Does this make you want to run from me?" he asked.

"I suppose it should."

"So your mother would say."

"Most definitely."

"I don't see you running."

"I admit that I am horrified. But not of you. For you."

She had not expected the pure gratitude she saw in his eyes. "Thank you, darlin'." He leaned closer. "I gave you an answer." His voice went low and soft. "Kiss me."

Elijah's plea touched a new place within Mary Jane. She wanted that experience, to relight the flame. The conservative angel on her shoulder went silent.

Mary Jane leaned forward, taking initiative. He waited for her at first, then met in the middle. A slow, tentative kiss brushed over her lips, and a tiny flame flickered in her belly. He drew back, surprising her.

When he sat back, his forearms once more resting on his thighs, mischief danced in his eyes. "That wasn't half bad."

"Half bad?" Her indignation came to the forefront.

"You need to really kiss me, Mary Jane. Or beg me to teach you more."

Her cheeks flooded with heat. "Me? Beg you to teach me...well, I do not think so."

He laughed and the seductive sound coiled and caressed her like the brush of fingertips all along her body. "Ask me another question."

She huffed. "Very well. Why were you accused of murder rather than your brother?"

His face became reflective, eyes deep with emotions that flickered from anger to resignation. "Because the evidence pointed in my direction. Because my brother had friends who swore he was with them the night she was killed."

An ache started for him, and she feared how far she could press without bringing him more pain. "This sounds like a long story."

"It is."

"Start from the beginning. How did you meet Maureen?"

"You didn't kiss me after the other question."

Again she expelled a sigh. "Come here, then."

He smiled at her demanding tone. He met her halfway, scooting closer. When their lips touched this time, delicious sweetness coiled in her belly as his lips stroked and warmed. This kiss went longer, but no deeper.

She drew back, breathless. "There. Now answer my other question."

He scrubbed one hand over his jaw. "It started a long time even before I met her. My mother left Ireland with me, Amos and my other brother, Zeke. Zeke is six years older than me. Amos is five years older than me. My Da used to beat us all when he didn't like something we did or said. Or even if he'd just had a bad day. Amos took after our Da, and he terrorized Ma sometimes and me. I started off as a puny thing and that made it easier for Amos to hurt me."

"You? I do not believe you could ever be puny. How tall are you now?"

"That's another question. Two as a matter of fact. You owe me two kisses first."

"Elijah Jonas McKinnon, you are quite the...the..."

"Blackguard."

"Indeed." She leaned forward and settled a lukewarm peck on his lips. Quick. Efficient.

He touched his fingers to his lips. "I barely felt that one. Try again."

"Oooh." She wanted to smack him. He dipped his head, and

their lips met. Brushed, released, brushed and released.

She backed off. "Tell me more."

He continued. "I'm six foot and three and a half inches. How tall are you?"

"Five feet and five inches."

"Hmm."

One of her eyebrows quirked. "Continue your story, sir."

"We had a piece of land in Galway and farmed it well. Still, we were always in poverty. I never knew anything but scraping by moment by moment, day by day. Amos hated poverty, but not the way the rest of us did. He hated it like it was a person. He fought with us all the time and took sides with Da. Said we all needed beating. Da finally kicked the stuffin' out of him one day and that put an end to Amos's loyalty. Amos didn't stop taunting or hitting me, though."

She stared at the drab dark blue quilt on the bed as tears of anger for what he once endured threatened her eyes. "That is horrible."

"I fought back and sometimes Zeke managed to keep Amos away. Not always, though. Zeke couldn't be there every moment of the day. I've got scars from our scraps. But everyone I knew in Galway lived this life...the poverty and sometimes the abuse of man to wife or child, so I was used to it. When I was fifteen, Da decided he'd rather kill us than take care of us. He tried setting fire to the house with us in it."

Mary Jane recoiled. "That is despicable."

"Ma managed to stop him and a neighbor restrained him. Authorities came and took my Da away. They planned to put him on trial for attempted murder, but Ma didn't wait for the trial. She realized that if he wasn't proven guilty, he'd come back and finish the deed. She didn't want to take that chance. She packed up what she could carry and booked passage on the next ship bound for America. She'd saved some money that Da didn't know about. We escaped and arrived in Philadelphia on January 4, 1840."

"Coming to a new country must have frightened you."

He nodded. "No more than the thought of my own Da killing me." His solemn expression didn't alter when he said, "Kiss me."

Though she was curious to hear about his venture to the United States, she wanted to explore his kiss just as much. She complied. His mouth barely moved under hers, so she coaxed him deeper. She tasted, lingered over his top lip and then the bottom, allowing her feelings, her need to heal him come to the fore.

That stopped her cold.

She wanted to banish his pain. Understand him on every level. The knowledge shook her.

Oh, Mary Jane, you have indeed gone way too far once again.

He drew back, eyes betraying his amazement that she had taken such initiative on the kiss.

She managed to ask the next question. "What happened after you immigrated here?"

He shifted and drew himself around so both feet planted on the floor. He leaned back on the palms of his hands. "It was hard going. We heard about an Irish organization in Philadelphia, so we traveled there. Luckily for us they helped Ma find a job in a sweatshop." He shrugged. "Working in a sweatshop is hard, dirty, unpleasant work, but Ma wouldn't let us starve. We did what we had to. We lived in a tenement in Kensington in the Irish Third Ward and shared rooms with another Irish family. It was crowded. One parlor, one kitchen, two bedrooms. My Ma and us boys slept in one room, but we each had a bed. The other couple and their two small boys slept in the other."

Mary Jane winced. "To think I have never shared a room with my sisters. We...our house would qualify as a small mansion of sorts. Twenty rooms in all."

"Small?" He snickered. "That's all right, darlin'. You

shouldn't have to apologize for your wealth." He looked into the distance for a few moments, as if he envied her cushioned life but would never complain about it. "During that time we roughed it, but we were happier than we were in Ireland."

"What happened after your mother worked in the sweatshop? Did you and your brothers work?"

"Zeke was a blacksmith, Amos a gunsmith. They took to the trades easily. I hawked papers on street corners to start, then learned blacksmithing from Zeke."

"When did you meet Maureen?"

He turned only his head towards her at first. "That's two questions and two kisses. I'll let you give them to me one after the other."

Finding that she had no desire to complain, she met him in another kiss. Warmth flowed over her body and removed all sense of cold or damp. She eagerly joined her lips to his. Time seemed to slow and stop until all she noted was a flowing sensuality that grew and grew. Elijah kept his hands to himself and left each movement to her discretion.

Instead of pulling back for a second kiss, she kept the first one alive. Her fingers tangled in the hair at the back of his neck and enjoyed the silky, cool texture. He moaned and it snapped her into reality. She pushed away, breath uneven and heart ticking an unsteady beat. Staring into those verdant eyes, she saw his need build. His lips parted as he licked them. His chest rose and fell with quicker breaths.

"That was one kiss." He moved in, turning full towards her and obviously intent on another.

She put her hand to his chest, and he stopped. "Elijah, I..."

His eyes narrowed. "What is it? You promised a kiss for each question."

"I know. I just..."

His fingers came up and traced a delicate line over her chin and down to the pulse in her throat. "Your pulse is fast, and the way you kissed me..." He paused. "I know you like it. If you didn't you would give me a short peck and dance away." When she looked down at her lap, he titled her chin up. "Are you afraid of me?"

"Yes."

His brow furrowed. "By all the saints, darlin'. You know I'd never harm you. I'm here to protect you."

She shifted, and he allowed his hand to drop. "I do know that, but..."

Her uncertainty, she knew, warred with her curiosity. Curiosity about him as a man. Curiosity about these powerful physical sensations, the yearning pulsing raw and almost unrestrained within her body. Her time with Thaddeus paled in comparison. She reached behind his head to take another kiss, but it turned into a half-hearted peck.

He crossed his arms. "Go on, then. I know you have more questions."

Eagerness pushed her to ask again, "When did you meet Maureen?"

His hands dropped to his thighs. "At the sweatshop where Ma worked. I went there one day to walk Ma home because there were threats against Irish women by this madman lingering in the area around the sweatshop. Ma introduced me to Maureen, and we all left the shop together. I escorted Maureen home first and then went home with Ma. Our relationship grew from there." He took a long shuddering breath. "During the nativist riots in Kensington in 1844, I was caught in the commotion trying to get home from work. Maureen had left the shop early to gather some food for her family. I saw a man trying to accost her and saved her from his attentions."

"A nativist attacked her?"

"No. An Irish Catholic."

"And you...once more the savior. Do you make a habit of saving women from evil men?"

He turned his gaze on her. "The only women I've needed to

save were my Ma, Maureen and you. Women I care about. And when it came down to it, I couldn't save Maureen."

Women I care about.

One sentence and her longing for him increased. A primal desire to touch, to show him surcease from the trials he'd faced in life. "You care about me?"

"That's another question."

She kissed him, and he twisted his mouth over hers for an intimate fit. Not just one kiss, but another and another in a fiery, passionate response. Both hands speared into her hair and drew her closer. He groaned against her mouth. Her nipples tightened and rubbed against her chemise and corset with an irritating prickle that needed attention. Restlessness grew inside her that she wanted desperately to assuage and yet did not know how.

He drew back, his breaths rasping in his throat. "No more. We need to stop. We must stop."

Her breath came as harsh as his, and she understood the wisdom of his words. "You are right, of course. But I have more questions."

"How many are there?"

"At least ten. Do you think you can survive that many?"

"I could count that question among them and lower the count to nine."

"That is hardly fair, sir."

"Who said I am fair?

"Perhaps I should start charging you for each of *your* questions."

A wicked gleam entered his eyes. "And how would you charge me?"

Her mind scrambled for a reasonable idea. "Perhaps more kisses?"

"Let us stick with what you owe me and on another night we will talk about what I owe you."

"But we may not have another night, Elijah."

He tapped the tip of her nose gently with his index finger. "Ask your next question, minx."

This new endearment started a far larger blaze inside her. Excitement crackled like the lightning that had speared the heavens. While she acknowledged the danger inherent in continuing this folly, she also wanted it with a sinful ache.

She swallowed hard and asked her next question. "When were you betrothed to Maureen?"

"We found our passion...fervent. We wanted to marry before we sinned." His mouth twitched at one corner. "Though we sinned some anyway."

Her cheeks heated. "Oh my."

"We'd known each other a month, if that, before Ma gave me the ring you're wearing now, and I planned to give it to Maureen. One day I fell at the blacksmith's shop and cracked a rib. Zeke encouraged me to go home. I planned to meet Maureen at the sweatshop. When I got there, Ma said Amos was walking her home. When I reached her home, though, her Ma and Da said they hadn't seen her. She came walking up a few minutes later with Amos. Amos had this strange smile on his face." Elijah's eyes darkened. He lay back on the bed, his legs hanging off the side. His hands clasped over his stomach.

She waited, her breath almost suspended as she waited for him to resume. Tension drew her muscles into knots.

"Maureen seemed in a strange melancholy and wouldn't talk to me. I asked Amos what was wrong." He gave a humorless laugh. "The bastard told me Maureen was considering switching her affections from me to him."

Mary Jane couldn't miss the hurt in his eyes or his voice.

"It turned worse from there. She avoided me for days. I didn't know what I'd done wrong. I was furious at Amos, and we almost came to blows a couple of times. Ma and Zeke separated us." He jackknifed into sitting position, then stood and started pacing, hands in his pockets.

As his agitation increased, so did hers. She dreaded and longed for the end of his tale. She must know what happened.

He stopped and stared into nothingness. "One Sunday while her parents left for church, she begged off and said she was ill. I left church and went to check on her. I was worried and I thought maybe if I got her alone, she'd talk with me. She answered the door."

"Then you talked with her."

"Yes." He closed his eyes and his mouth twisted. A shuddering breath left his lungs. "We talked. She confessed she was afraid I would break our betrothal. Terrified, in fact. She said she loved me, but that she'd disgraced herself. When Amos had walked her home, he pulled her into an abandoned house and forced himself on her."

A dull, painful ache thudded inside Mary Jane's chest. "Oh my heavens."

"He raped her." His voice was thick, raspy. His eyes turned tormented as he stalked the floor like a jungle animal. "He forced himself upon her and then said I'd disown her...that her whole family would disown her if she told them."

"Surely, they would not have."

How could she say this when her own family had almost disowned her?

Raw pain filled his gaze as he stopped pacing and stared at her. "Her father was a bastard who taught her to think she wasn't worth a half-penny. Her mother was a tiny, timid thing that couldn't defend her daughter or herself." Elijah shivered as if he suffered a fever and then righted his expression. Cold, hard fury replaced the pain. "Amos had told her she was a whore and a bitch and deserved what she got. That if she didn't break her betrothal with me, he'd tell everyone that she'd led him into the abandoned house and begged him to dishonor her."

Mary Jane swallowed hard, her mouth so dry but her eyes prickling with tears. "That poor girl. She must have been in such terrible agony not knowing what you thought. You believed her?"

He leaned back against the washstand, his dark head bowed as he crossed his arms. "I believed her because she was a wonderful woman and Amos is a bastard beyond measure."

She did not yet ask another question. Not because she feared another kiss. Because sorrow washing over his strong form slumped his shoulders and lowered that proud head. She hated seeing him saddened and could not imagine him any more broken than at this moment. Maybe if she allowed herself to think on it, it would break her, too.

He finally lifted his head, and his eyes held remnants of pain. "I told her it didn't matter what Amos said. My anger was all for him. My hate was all for him. I'd never wanted to kill anyone before. She begged me not to go after him, as it would only hurt me in the end." He drew in a deep breath and let it out. "Maureen told me she was pregnant with his child." He tipped his head back and gazed at the ceiling. "She begged me not to abandon her, and I vowed I never would. The child was innocent and Maureen was innocent. We planned to run away together the next day."

She swallowed hard. "But you didn't?"

Elijah's gaze, direct and sad, gave her the answer. "The next day I felt like damnation, but I packed my meager belongings, left my mother a note and headed to the meeting place we'd agreed on—the church not far from where she lived. When I got there she was nowhere to be found. I somehow knew something was wrong. I searched the neighborhood and eventually found her in a back alley nearby. She was stabbed through the heart. A knife was left nearby."

Mary Jane's throat ached with unshed tears. "How awful. I can only imagine what you must have felt."

He nodded and tore his gaze from hers. "I loved her more than anyone. Before I could run for the authorities, a man and woman saw me with Maureen's body. I'd picked her up in my arms, and her blood was all over me. She couldn't have been dead too long. When the police came, I was still there. I wasn't going to run—I wanted to find the killer as much as they did."

She wiped her eyes as tears fell. "Oh, no, Elijah. It must have gone all wrong."

He made a half-strangled laugh. "Very wrong. The police blamed me of course. I told them when Maureen told me about Amos, but when they found Amos he was at a home a block away where his friends claimed he'd been all night sleeping off a drunk." Gazing down at the floor or his boots, he sighed. "Zeke and Ma vouched for me, of course. They all testified that I'd been at home that morning when Maureen was killed. They believed me. At least Zeke did."

"Your mother didn't?"

"She had doubts, I could tell. Eventually she blurted out that maybe I'd done it after I left the house. The police decided all the evidence pointed towards me. My note to Ma saying I was running away with Maureen, for example. They interrogated me and said that I must have gone into a rage when she refused to leave with me."

"Why was she out of the house so early?"

He rubbed the back of his neck. "We planned to meet at the church yard, but maybe she wanted to leave early to make sure her Ma and Da didn't try to stop her."

Tears continued to rain down her face. Elijah's own eyes shimmered.

"Then they convicted you?" she asked.

"There was no proof against Amos, and I was the one they'd found in the alley with her."

"But..." She shook her head. "You must have had witnesses to your good character. To the kind of man you are."

He shook his head. "Didn't matter. I looked guiltier than anyone else. Even her Ma and Da went from loving me to thinking I was the scourge of the earth. When they declared me guilty and sentenced me to twenty-one years of solitary confinement, I decided there and then I'd pray each day to say sane. To make certain I'd survive twenty-one years so I could kill Amos."

She shivered at the coldness in his declaration. "Yet they released you in five."

The bleakness in his eyes did not retreat. "Because Zeke refused to let it go. After I was thrown into Eastern State, Zeke knew Amos had done it but he couldn't prove it at first. Ma and Zeke disowned Amos, though I heard from Zeke before I came on this trip that Ma relented and let Amos back into her life. Zeke kept working for my release. It took him some time, but he convinced two men who'd been friends with Amos to tell the whole truth. Amos had killed her and come back to the house to tell them all about it."

"Five years. I cannot imagine what you must have endured."

He shook his head. "You can't know. You must *not*."

She stood and as he walked towards her, wanting so much to ease his pain. "I am not a woman of delicate sensibilities."

"No?" He reached up to brush away the last of her tears. "You are strong, but you're crying for me."

She drew in a deep breath and acknowledged the truth. "Any woman with an ounce of feeling would cry."

"Not every woman would believe a word I've said."

"I doubted you in the beginning."

The darkness in his gaze lifted somewhat. "Maybe you still should."

She frowned, disturbed. "Why?"

He traced a path down her back, feathering over the long length of her hair. Her heartbeat picked up, her pulse seeming to race with a new and furious pace. He slipped under her hair and cupped the back of her neck. "I'm not a nice man, darlin'. When I find Amos, I plan to kill him."

She gasped but didn't pull back. "You are planning to

murder him? For revenge?"

"Yes. That's why you shouldn't think too highly of me." He leaned in until his lips hovered within a breath of her ear. "And when I'm near you I want things I shouldn't. I need things I shouldn't. My body craves yours."

He was right. She was frightened. That he would murder anyone in truth seemed impossible, but his harsh words tangled with a feral attraction she felt helpless to avoid.

She was driven. Driven to the edge by sensations so delicious and forbidden they must translate to sin. To a path she had trod before and would take again at her peril.

Elijah's mouth angled, then tasted hers, but this time without the slow buildup. His tongue surged into her mouth. She moaned as his hands plunged into her hair and held steady. Repeatedly his tongue seduced, thrusting with a primitive rhythm that aroused. Rushes of sensation assaulted virgin territory. Desires meshed and blended as her breasts ached and filled with heat. She clutched his shoulders as they eased down onto the bed. Her heart pounded as his gentle caresses moved over her face, hair, and down to her shoulders. Hunger ignited as she groaned and shifted against Elijah's insistent searching touch. He released her only long enough to shift until he lay half over her. Once more he kissed her, and his tongue rubbing over hers urged her into a firestorm of response.

Fascinated with his strength and drawn to the power she knew resided inside him, she ached to experience more. Her heart pounded with a furious beat. Breathless and astonished at her own response, she did not wish to stop this headlong flight.

He drew back and stared into her eyes. Turbulent emotions played over his features. When he sat up, he turned away from her and buried his face in his hands. Torn between mortification and blind desire, she sat up.

Trembling, she could not speak at first. Elijah had said

more than once that she shouldn't fear him, and now he seemed determined to scare her into not caring for him. She found her voice a few moments later. "Elijah, I am sorry I did not trust you before when I first heard you were convicted of murder."

The green in his eyes shimmered, a sea that flowed from sand to ocean depths. She could become lost in them and drown in delicious sensations.

"Any woman would believe as you did. And now that I've told you I plan to kill Amos, you should be wary of me."

"No. You are not a murderer. You wouldn't have come to my aid."

"I would if I wanted to manipulate you."

"Yes, but you have not."

His smile was weak, but she thought she saw relief in his eyes. "Many women would slap my face for what just happened."

He stood, his expression wry and self-deprecating. Her gaze snagged on the front of his breeches, and she stared as his manhood pressed hard and thick against his trousers. Power surged through her at the thought she had done this to him. She created a desire within him this strong, and that astounded her beyond anything else. Thaddeus had become aroused, but the feelings she shared with Elijah overpowered anything she had felt for the professor. For a man who had given her nothing. No protection. No dignity.

"I could have continued," he said. "But I won't take what you'd regret giving me later. But I'll be wishing all night I had. Five years of living in an eight by twelve cell, never seeing anyone but my jailer...it does things to a man, Mary Jane. Things dark and strange that he can't rid himself of no matter how he tries. My need for revenge is deep, and I won't be swayed from it."

"You aren't a dark soul, Elijah McKinnon, no matter how much you claim it."

One corner of his mouth tilted. "You don't know me at all, Mary Jane. Not at all. And maybe you shouldn't."

That stung. Stony coldness swamped his features. "Let us go downstairs and eat before the dining room closes."

Chapter Ten

Alleghany Portage Railroad

I am closer to home.

As the train plugged along through a new thunderstorm, Mary Jane rejoiced. They were on the final stretch westward down the mountains. Conversation stayed muted on the train, as if no one possessed energy or will to speak. The steady clacking noise of wheels against rails continued with monotony.

The previous night returned to her thoughts again and again. After they had eaten dinner and gone back to their room, the evening had passed as if Elijah never revealed his tragic past and his desire for revenge against Amos. As if everything had drained clean out of him, he went silent and retreated to the chair to sleep. This surprised her. She thought for certain he would want to share the bed again.

You should be happy you did not share the bed with him again.

He might not be a murderer yet...but he soon could be.

No.

She did not believe he had it in him.

The idea of waking up with his body so near hers, with his hand caressing her, started a panic and a yearning. She spent a restless evening waking every two hours, her mind spinning nightmares of hiding in a dark alley with a faceless murderer stalking her every move. Only the realization that Elijah slept in the chair nearby kept her from lighting the lamp. She sighed. It was just as well he had not shared the bed. Soon her journey would finish. She could leave Elijah and his troubled life behind. They shared nothing in common other than the strange situation they had found necessary to create. Yes, she would feel relief when they parted ways.

Somehow that did not feel as satisfying as it should.

The train had just lowered onto a long plain with a gradual down slope when things changed.

A huge rumble jerked her from musings. The train shook.

Impressions flew at her too fast to process. She heard another explosion, and her heart lurched.

Elijah sat to her left and he tensed, one hand gripping the back of the seat in front of him. "That's an explosion."

"Are you blinkin' daft?" an English accent said somewhere in front of them. "That's not—"

A high-pitched shriek of metal and brakes laboring came from somewhere near the front of the train. The whistle blew. Murmurs started all around her. As the train swayed, she wondered if the earth convulsed as it sometimes did when the land was angry and split and shuddered. More metal screamed, the whistle blew again, and fear rose up like a beast to grab her throat.

As the train slid to an unceremonious halt, a shout came from somewhere in the carriage. "Everyone, hands up."

Haughty woman ejected a blood-curdling scream. Mary Jane jerked around to face the threat. Blond man and skinny man both stood at the door of the train car.

Skinny man held a weapon in his hand, and it pointed straight at Elijah. "Don't anyone move or we'll put a hole in you bigger than Virginia."

Blond man sniggered. "Yeah, we'll put a hole in ya."

Time seemed to slow. The O'Gannon brothers were in front of her and too far away to disarm the skinny man. Elijah could not do anything without being shot. The men closest to skinny man and blond had to be in their seventies at least. She doubted they could help.

Fritz grunted. "What do you men want? Money? Is this a train robbery?"

"Oh, it's a train robbery all right," the skinny cretin said. "But it's a whole lot more. By the way, my name is Herbert Jackson Claypool. You need to remember my name. I want it in all the papers."

Blond man threw a dagger-filled look at his gun-toting friend. "And I'm Stanton Archer. Hoop is what my friends call me. But you ain't my friends, so you can call me Stanton to show respect. And if you don't show respect, well—," he chuckled,

"—then you are just gonna be dead."

Mary Jane glanced at Elijah. He sat with his right arm on the back of his seat, the other hanging almost casually at his side. His waistcoat was buttoned, but she remembered the weapon hidden there. Her mind whirled. Would he use it? How could he unbutton his waistcoat *and* get to the gun quickly enough? He would be killed. Her heart, racing in time to the frantic throbbing of her pulse, stopped at the thought of these men hurting Elijah.

One of the O'Gannons made a movement.

A loud report split the room and the haughty woman screamed. Mary Jane pressed one gloved hand over her own mouth to stifle a cry. O'Gannon's hand went to his shoulder as blood spilled from a hole in his waistcoat. His eyes rolled up, and he fell as his brother, wide-eyed and with denial on his lips, lunged to catch him.

"Son-of-bitch. You goddamned son-of-a bitch," Elijah said just under a growl, his accent thick with reproof.

She was unable to look away from the rage in Elijah's face. In the short time she had known him, she had seen his anger and witnessed his disdain. This...this was something darker, more feral. His mouth turned to a hard line, eyes bleak and determined. Recklessness and valor etched in every line of his handsome features. She feared deep in her heart he would try something that would get him killed.

"Now see here," one of the elderly men said. "We will give you our money. Please do not shoot anyone else."

Hoop smiled smugly. "Yeah, you'll give us yer money. Now. One by one, empty yer pockets and give us them purses."

Gladly. She'd gladly give him her money to make them leave. One by one the crooks tromped down the aisle as men removed pocket watches, rings, and their money. Elijah kept his attention on the two criminals. She felt his tense awareness as if it belonged to her. He reminded her of a coiled snake ready to strike.

They reached her, and she started to slide the reticule off her wrist, when Hoop grabbed her arm. She gasped in surprise and pain.

Elijah jerked, his body starting to come out of the seat, his mouth curled with anger, eyes blistering with contempt. "Get your black-bellied, whore lovin' hands off her."

Claypool cocked his weapon. "Uh-uh-uh." He moved his gun back and forth in a shame-shame motion. "Don't move. We'd kill you right now, but there's someone that has a bone to pick with you, murderer."

Mary Jane stiffened, her mind reeling as Hoop's fingers tightened to the bruising point. "Please, I will give you my money. Just let me go."

"I don't think so." Hoop's grip tightened. "We have plans for you."

Horror rose up inside her, but she fought it. The haughty woman sobbed.

Hoop swung on the frightened woman. "Stop yer howlin', bitch."

The woman pressed a handkerchief over her mouth, eyes wide with terror. Conscious of her own almost paralyzing fear, Mary Jane made a pact with herself. She would not lose control.

She would take some of that grit and vinegar her mother had insisted was her downfall and use it to good advantage.

"I will go with you," she said to the criminals, her voice as low and calm as she could manage. "Just don't hurt anyone else."

As she said it, she caught Elijah's gaze for a split second. He shook his head enough for her to see the movement. She chose to ignore his admonishment. She feared he would place his life on the line for her...for anyone on this train.

"Get up." Hoop pulled Mary Jane into standing position. "Walk in front of me down the aisle."

As Claypool continued collecting money and valuables and stuffing them in a bag, Hoop kept his hand fastened to her arm. They reached the O'Gannon brothers, and the unwounded O'Gannon held his unconscious brother in his arms, pressing a hand to his wound. The uninjured brother hurried to empty his pockets and his brother's.

Once finished there, the criminals came back at a methodical pace. They moved past Elijah as if he didn't exist.

How odd.

Hoops prodded her to walk in front of him. They passed the haughty woman and her husband, who looked more frightened than anyone else. All the bravado the woman had displayed in previous days had vanished. Her husband did not try to console the woman.

Claypool stepped into an empty seat, and Hoop squeezed passed Mary Jane. Hoop manhandled the back door until it opened.

He turned back to Mary Jane and snagged her arm. "Come on."

"What? No—"

Hoops pushed her inexorably towards the door connecting their car and a baggage car. "Come on. Get down there."

She took each step carefully, trying not to trip over her

crinoline and holding her skirts up. Fear breathed down her neck. As she took that last jump to the ground she wavered on her boots and almost fell on one rail. She heard the locomotive belching and hissing. Up ahead, at the front of the train, smoke rose.

Hoops jumped down behind her and clamped his beefy hand around her forearm. "Come on, sweetie, let's go." He started towards the thick forest ahead. "Hurry up."

She tripped as he dragged her ruthlessly forward. "Unhand me—"

She struggled, and he smacked her across the face. Flesh stung as her head snapped back, a cry escaping her throat. Tears of anger, fear and pain rose in her eyes.

Claypool stood at the opening, his weapon trained on those inside the car. "Don't anyone try and follow or we'll kill her."

She placed one hand over her stinging cheek as Hoop yanked her forward with a painful grip. "Get a move on."

Rocks threatened to trip her at every turn and as they entered a thick stand of trees, she twisted her foot and fell to her hands and knees with a yelp.

Hoop's fierce snarl lashed her ears. "Damn it, wench. Can't ya walk?" Once more he gripped her arm and pulled upward with brute force. "Walk or we kill ya. That's all there is to it." He leered into her face, his crooked teeth giving him a monstrous appearance. His foul breath gusted over her face and she flinched away. "Maybe I'll take my pleasure on ya before my friends join up with us, eh?"

Something hard and determined surged inside her. She would be damned if she would allow him to put one more hand on her flesh.

"Please," she said, "I think I twisted my ankle."

More angry and frightened than she'd ever been, she leaned over as if to inspect her ankle under her crinoline. She reached for a sizeable rock and came up with a rapid swing.

And connected with his temple.

Hoop's eyes opened wide as he groaned, then his eyes closed, and he fell like the stone that clobbered him. His eyes stayed wide open, unblinking, his lips slightly parted over that ugly mouth.

It took several moments to register what she had done to the odious man.

She had killed him.

Nausea boiled up inside her, and she clutched at her stomach. *I've killed a man.*

Shaking and aware that Claypool would not be far behind, she dropped the bloodied rock. She lifted her skirts and ran. Heart hammering, she splashed through a puddle and raced to find somewhere to hide. Thunder crashed overhead. She flinched and scrambled over larger rocks, hampered by heavy, damp skirts. A sharp report from the direction of the train dared her to look back, but she did not see the train or anyone behind her.

Rain poured in huge sheets, and she shivered as the coldness soaked her. Her breath rasped in her throat, her side aching, her body protesting rough treatment. Another loud report echoed in the air.

Shooting. At me. Must get away. Where to go?

Dark clouds lowered into the valley as terrain became steeper, more unforgiving. Shoving aside thoughts of how she would survive out here, she hurried forward. If Claypool caught her...

Now is not the time to think about that. Hurry. Hurry.

Mary Jane ran forever. She dropped down behind some thick scrub brush. Her heart pounded so hard she panicked and gasped for breath that would not come. She put her hand over her mouth and tried not to groan.

Calm. Must calm down or they will hear.

As she kneeled in the dirt, rain pounding her unmercifully, her mind whirled. What happened to Elijah? Had they hurt or killed him? Anguish gripped her already raw throat.

153

Rain reduced to a steady but less forceful deluge. She did not know whether to feel grateful or dismayed. The rain would slow Claypool and other accomplices if they meant to chase her. She did not dare think what they would do if they caught her. Escape was her only option. She stayed crouched behind the bushes, shivering and quaking. Senses heightened, she peered through the sheltering brush. Time crawled onward. She looked at the timepiece on the chain around her neck. Thirty minutes had elapsed.

Cold, so cold.

The shivering turned into a desperate need for heat. She disregarded her desire for warmth and concentrated on not moving. Then she saw Claypool coming from around a tree about a hundred yards away.

"Hey, little girl, I'm going to find you and you're going to pay. You killed my friend, you bitch. You heartless bitch!"

Tears surged into her eyes as Claypool, weapon in hand, advanced on her. She swallowed the whimper clogged in her throat.

"Where are you, bitch? Huh? Come out and I'll make it easy on you."

Oh God. Please.

She heard another shot and saw Claypool jerk, mouth opening in a silent gasp, eyes wide in surprise. He tumbled forward and lay still.

What on earth?

Mary Jane clamped both hands over her mouth, trembling, anticipating anything. She looked around for a stick, any weapon she might use. A figure came out from behind a stand of trees, not far from where Claypool fell. The man was tall and familiar. He held his revolver at the ready.

Elijah.

The dearest sight she had ever seen.

He scanned the woods, looking frantically in every

direction, his chest rising and falling as if he had run for miles. She shifted and a twig snapped.

Elijah's attention pinpointed in her direction, and he walked towards her. Relief made her legs weak, her knees practically knocking together as she came to her feet slowly.

"Elijah?" Her whisper was low and tentative.

"Mary Jane?"

"I am here."

"Shhh...keep your voice low. They're coming."

She stumbled from the bushes, and relief filled Elijah's face in a rush. He walked towards her, and she dashed forward.

He crushed her to him. His face buried in her hair, lips close to her ear. "By all the saints, darlin'." His voice sounded broken, deep with unguarded emotion. He pulled back, cupped her face in one hand. "Are you hurt? Did that feckin' bastard—"

"I killed that man. I killed him." Horror mixed with disbelief.

Her fingers twisted in his shirt, and she was more relieved than she could say, shaking with reaction and residual fear.

"We've got to go. More are coming to kill us."

"What—how—" She could not force the questions passed her lips.

Rain poured down his face as he urged her deeper into the woods. "We must keep moving." His eyes blazed down into hers, anger and something so manic within his face that she feared what he might do. "There are two more men on our trail and they've got horses. One was my overseer at the penitentiary. The other is my brother Amos."

They crashed through underbrush and swerved around trees. It was hard not to make noise. Elijah's firm grip on her hand didn't let up. Her side burned, her breath coming hard, her legs ached.

She could not continue.

She must.

Elijah darted between two large boulders. Giving a burst of power, she hurried to follow.

Her skirt caught and jerked her to a halt. "Wait."

He stopped as she tried to yank her skirts through the rocks. She pulled and the dress ripped.

"Damn it," Elijah hissed his words.

He reached down and grabbed her skirts and the material caught. It tore in his hand. "Hold this." He stuffed the material into her hand. "Come on."

"Why am I holding this?" She gasped the question as he snatched her hand and they ran.

"We can't leave anything behind for my brother to track us."

She did not have the breath to ask more questions and knew he would explain...maybe, when and if they had time later.

If.

Renewed fright gripped her and she corralled it with effort. Memories of how this adventure started crowded through her headlong flight for survival. Grief had tangled her emotions when she left Pittsburgh, but she never suspected that less then two weeks later she would find herself most of the way home and halfway to her death.

No.

She refused to give in that easily. She barely kept up with Elijah's endless plunge through brush and stands of hemlock. Without remorse he pushed onward, his grip on her hand ruthless. Her legs became leaden but she forced them forward. Until the toe of her boot caught under a rock. Her toes stung, and she fell forward, straight into his back. He stumbled, lost his hold on her hand. She went straight down on her left side. Pain ripped up through her ribcage. She gasped and closed her eyes, rolling through a painful wave. Angry tears shot to the surface but she squeezed her eyes shut to ride it out.

"Darlin'?" Elijah crouched over her, his hand slipping under neck. "Open your eyes." His voice grew urgent and low. "Mary Jane, open your eyes."

Her eyes snapped open as tears rolled down her face. Her throat ached. "I am fine."

Worry etched his features, but he took her word for it and helped her to her feet. He cupped her face again. "Just a little farther."

A little farther? To what?

She stumbled along in his wake, no energy to ask why they pushed onward into the woods where no one from the train could help them. Thinking that far ahead caused more trepidation, so she concentrated on planting one shoe in front of the other. After what seemed an endless time, a rocky outcropping and massive hill rose in front of them.

"Thank the saints." He tugged her forward. "Here." He released her hand long enough to shove aside shrubbery and reveal a tall opening. She saw his throat work as he swallowed hard. "Damnation. I don't want to go in here, but we must. I'll go first, you follow."

His voice snapped like a general, and she flinched. His eyes went hard, unyielding.

The darkness beyond the crevice appeared to be a wide mouth without teeth. What horrors lay inside? Unreasoning fear stilled her courage. She sucked in a quick breath. If Elijah could conquer his apprehension, so could she.

He crawled in, headfirst. When he disappeared into the maw, all went quiet. Even the wind didn't stir, and the rain stopped. Her entire body quaked. Nightmares of deep, unknown places from childhood tormented her from the edges. They beckoned, dared her to stay brave and to remain sane.

Elijah's hand came out and then his head. "It's larger than I thought. It's a deep rock shelter."

She clasped his hand and leaned down. He released her once she started inside. She crawled on hands and knees and

157

discovered enough headroom to stand and several feet on both sides. Light penetrated from a large crack in the ceiling.

He inched around in front of her and made certain the hole stayed thoroughly covered by the foliage. Turning back, he stopped. He put one finger to his lips in a gesture of silence. He pulled his weapon from the inner waistcoat pocket and held it, prepared for use. They stayed that way for several minutes. Time stretched in front of her, an eternity of waiting, of anxiety ridden breaths and heart pounding apprehension. Safety still felt far removed. Now that they had stopped running, she heard her own breath rasping, her heart pounding in her ears as her body slowed. Reaction came without remorse. Tears flowed and fell to her cheeks. She regulated her breath by slow turns, and yet her body remained tense. After what seemed an eternity, he made his way past her and sat against one wall. He gestured for her to come closer.

She eased towards him on her hands and knees, her crinoline bunching up in the way. Frustrated, she frowned. She never hated fashion more than this moment.

"Take off the crinoline. We're leaving it and the corset behind," he said.

She hesitated and then realized the wisdom in his request. Mary Jane rose to her feet. "Help me. I have to remove the dress first."

He nodded, his face etched with a harsh determination. She turned away from him. Methodically he unbuttoned the back of the dress while she pulled the hatpins out of her hat and hair. As his fingers moved, a fleeting thought raced by. Even in these desperate moments of flight, his fingers brushing with heat through dress, corset and chemise somehow made her incredibly aware of him as a man. Then the thought fled.

She tossed the pins in a corner and flung the hat aside. She was surprised the thing had not fallen off before now. Her dress stuck to her, sodden with rain and made the buttons more difficult to undo. She would have to dress in it again once she removed the corset and crinoline, but what choice did she have? Before she knew it the shoulders and the tight sleeves eased away from her skin. Eager, she pulled the garment off her arms until she peeled it all the way down and it fell around her waist. She wriggled to shove it off her hips. She stepped out of the dress and worked on the ties that held the crinoline in place. As they remained quiet, a sense of urgency filled the air. They must hurry in case his brother found them and they must fight. She shoved the horsehair padding downward, and he came around to the front and knelt in front of her.

"Here," he whispered. "Lift your legs one at a time, and I'll pull it off."

She complied, and quicker than she expected, Elijah crumpled the nuisance and shoved it into a corner. Without speaking he returned to stand behind her and made short work of the corset laces. When it loosened around her ribs, she sucked in a breath. That felt so much better. Though she never worn her corset particularly tight, removing the garment was liberating. She took one deep breath after another. When he loosened it completely, he pulled it over her head. It, too, went into the corner.

Now that she stood in nothing but chemise, pantalets, stockings and boots, she trembled with cold. His hands rested on her shoulders for a second, and then he turned her around.

His eyes had lost their harshness, but they held no awareness of her as a woman. He had shut down for the fight, all efficiency in the face of danger. "I know the dress is cold and wet, but you have to put it back on. If they find us here..."

She put her fingers over his lips. For a few unguarded seconds, his eyes flared. She'd never imagined green eyes could burn this bright and hot with emotion. Quickly he shut it off, like a flame doused under a rush of water. He helped her back into the dress, which went much faster.

Once done, he sat, propped his back against the wall and stared at her. He drew up one leg and propped his forearm on his knee. With his disheveled hair, sweat beading on his forehead, and a harsh look in his eyes, he looked every inch the dastardly criminal. Part of her wanted to run from him too. After all, she was in this predicament because his brother had a vendetta with Elijah. His rumpled waistcoat hung open, dirt and something red smeared over one side. Worry speared her.

She sank to her knees in the damp earth in front of him. She grabbed the lapels of his waistcoat and parted them. "You are bleeding."

"No. I'm not. That's the blood of the man I killed."

Her lips parted but nothing came out at first. She struggled with her words. "We both... I hit that man with a rock, Elijah. I killed him."

"I know, darlin'." His voice softened, the rough understanding lowering his husky voice. "I know."

More tears came, and as they rained down, her face crumpled.

"Shhh..." He reached for her and pulled her into his lap.

He cuddled her close, his powerful arms providing shelter she desperately craved. She wept quietly, holding back the screaming fear. She shuddered and quaked. She saw a misery in his gaze, a genuine sorrow. She touched his face and felt the bristle of beard growing there. In those quiet moments, Mary Jane heard nothing more than gentle breaths, felt nothing more than his heat beneath her, cradling and comforting.

Understanding, like that she had witnessed before, warmed his eyes and softened his visage. His lips parted. She stared at that handsome mouth and wanted it on hers with undeniable desperation.

Closer, closer still, he tilted towards her until...his mouth touched hers with exquisite gentleness. When her lips parted under pressure, his tongue pushed inside. Retreated. Caressed. Owned her mouth with sweet, deep thrusts. She arched into that kiss, breath puffing into him, mouth moving in response, tongue tangling in carnal dance.

Elijah broke away with a gasp, eyes still blazing.

He leaned closer until he whispered in her ear. "If we were anywhere else and completely safe, you would be beneath me. Naked."

Blunt as his words were, they excited Mary Jane and made her forget their harrowing flight.

"But we can't." His burning gaze lingered on her mouth, then recaptured her eyes. "I would put you in danger, and that's the last thing I want. Promise me something."

"Anything." The word, so definitive and complete, left her throat without a pause.

"If they find us here and anything happens to me, you fight with everything in you. You fight to live. You understand?"

"No—I— you are not going to die." Her voice broke. "That will not happen."

"If there's one thing I learned incarcerated in Eastern State, it was that bad things happen and you cannot always stop them. If that bad thing happens, and I cannot keep you safe...you do what you need in order to live." His gaze was fierce and demanding. "You understand me?"

"Yes." The excruciating thought twisted a hot knife in her breast. "Yes."

He kissed her forehead and then her nose. "Pray it won't come to that, darlin'. I'll do everything I can to keep us alive."

"Why? Why would you sacrifice so much for me?"

He went silent, those thickly lashed eyes now devoid of passion but hard with truth. "I failed to keep one woman safe. That won't happen again."

"Maureen."

He nodded and closed his eyes.

"Tell me more about her." She lifted her left hand. "She must have been special if you honored her with this ring."

His eyes clouded with pain beyond bearing, then dissolved into resolute anger. He clasped her left hand and held it for inspection. "I would have left it on her hand because she was my betrothed, but my mother and Zeke told me to keep it as a memento."

As the truth penetrated, he gently shifted her off his lap. He had told her more about his life in one moment of vulnerability.

Elijah spread his legs open and bent his knees. "Lean back against me."

Still processing his revelation about his betrothed and his brother, she turned until her back pressed against his chest and his arms wrapped around her. At least this way she could escape his encompassing gaze. Since the first day she'd met him, which seemed such a long time ago, he'd laid siege to her thoughts, her world with an extraordinary power. Two warring feelings battled within her. Trepidation and acceptance. If they did die here... If Amos found them, she would have known an extraordinary time with Elijah. One she could not have found in any other time or place.

Like a big, protective animal, he surrounded her in security. For the first time in what felt like hours, she could loosen the tightness in her muscles.

He leaned down until his lips touched her left ear. She twitched in reaction.

"Easy." His breath puffed hot in her ear. "We're stuck like this until I'm sure they didn't see us come in here."

She shuddered against him, and when his lips touched her ear this time, it was with a gentle kiss. This time Mary Jane's quiver felt different. As it had when they shared a kiss in the hotel, as when he touched her body so intimately, this felt like caring...like affection. She eased her head back until it rested along his right cheek. His breath puffed gently against her left ear with each exhalation.

Mary Jane relaxed point-by-point, minute-by-minute. Elijah's grip around her waist loosened until his palms slid outward and cupped her ribcage. His strong thighs pressed along her hips, and now that she no longer had the barrier of corset and crinoline, her senses absorbed so much more. Her nipples beaded against the fabric from the cold, and they almost ached. Warmth spilled low in her belly, arching out from the point where his hands held her. As she calmed, an uneasy silence invaded.

"When do we leave here?" she asked.

"In the morning."

Elijah heard Mary Jane sigh, and he held her tighter. Soon, she fell asleep. As the storm blanketed the forest, he was certain his brother had stopped searching for now. If he'd been alone and the moon had shown high and full this evening, he would have stolen into the night. With the precious cargo in his arms, he couldn't risk it.

Precious. Damn her, she had become too important. As she sighed again and her breath deepened, he didn't have the heart to rustle her awake.

Besides, if she slept maybe he could ignore the way she felt against him, nestled with such trust. He drew in a deep breath and caught her scent—pure woman and a hint of the escape they had endured. Damn, but she'd proved brave. More courageous than many men he'd known. His admiration increased.

Yeah, keep telling yourself that's all this is. Admiration.

No. It was something else he couldn't think too much about. His thoughts bounced from recognizing stomach-clenching danger to pounding lust. He closed his eyes and allowed a moment's luxury in letting go. Her body curved into Elijah's, warmth pressed against his erection. Her head nestled back against his right shoulder. When he watched her undress, he'd almost lost it. Almost gave into the soul-stealing lust that had slammed into him without warning. He'd heard other men speak of how danger heightened the senses, and when said peril vanished, desire replaced battle-lust. They claimed a man often required proof of life in sex. Slipping into a warm woman's body could satisfy his urges and bring release from the blood churning emotions still coursing inside him. Yet the thought of just any woman under him, accepting his thrusts...no, he didn't want it. Only one woman could satiate him.

His hands slid up her ribs and paused just under her breasts. Sweet Jesus, he longed to cup her, to squeeze and plump those round breasts. Without the enhancement of a corset, her breasts still would fill his hands. He licked his lips imagining his mouth encircling a delicious nipple and sucking. He bit back a groan as his cock throbbed.

He took long, slow breaths and strived to push away his lust. All that mattered was staying alive and finding a way out of their predicament. With that sobering thought, he opened his eyes and stared into their darkening, small shelter and waited for dawn.

How many hours passed, he couldn't say for certain. He drifted in and out of sleep, nerves still primed for action and danger. When night closed in, he found the darkness both comforting and disquieting. Sometime during that quiet, she shifted in his arms and moaned. Her head lolled to one side, and he realized she dreamed. Her movements became more pronounced. She started to writhe in his grip.

"No, please. I did not mean to kill you." Her voice whimpered, not loud but filled with horrific self-reprisal and fear. "It was— I had to escape from you." Her voice became louder. "No. Please no."

Aware that she could alert Amos to their presence, he gently shook her awake. "Darlin'. Darlin', wake up. It's only a dream."

Immediately she jerked to alertness. "Elijah?"

He smoothed his hands up and down her arms and kissed her ear. "You're safe. It was only a nightmare. I'm here."

She sighed. "I never imagined killing anyone...in my dream he was in my face again." Her body shuddered. "He was going to..."

"I know." He kissed the side of her neck. "He can never harm you again, Mary Jane. He can never harm anyone again."

Sobs shook her, and the agony spiking through Elijah took him off guard. He thought the pain might banish when he'd found her unharmed in the woods, but this grief pierced him like a sword. He rubbed her arms, soothed her with his touch and body heat.

"Softly, darlin'. We must stay quiet."

But as he admonished her to remain as silent as possible, he held her into the night.

Chapter Eleven

Elijah felt the cold bunk under his back once more.

Fear choked his breath as he pushed back the blanket. He bolted upright, a cry on his lips. Back in prison. He was back in prison with this feckin' smelly blanket and the cold moonlight streaming in the skylight above. As he left the bunk and ran for the door that prevented escape from this living hell, Elijah realized he couldn't take another minute, another day of silence, a day where his throat ached to speak, to utter a solitary word.

Before he reached the door, he yelled. "Let me out of here, you bastards. Let me out."

He stopped dead as his hands hit the metal and wood that made up his door. Then the door rattled, and he heard Amos talking.

"You in there, Elijah? 'Cause if you are, I'm making sure that Varney keeps you in there forever. No one is coming to get you out, you hear? You're going to rot forever in there little brother. Rot!"

"Elijah?"

He jerked, startled by Mary Jane's feminine tones. "What? Where—"

She eased around to look at him, breaking his grip on her arms. Light spilled between the foliage at the rock shelter entrance and filtered the dawn. Dust floated in the light. "You were having a nightmare again."

"Damn it." His mouth felt pasty, his heart banging against

his ribs.

"I was afraid you would cry out and alert our pursuers."

He took a ragged breath and shook off the dream. "I'm sorry."

Her eyes held sympathy and understanding. "It is all right. Someday you will have to tell me about the dreams in more detail."

That made him uncomfortable. "No."

"Why?"

"Because..."

He trailed off. The small cave pressed down around him, his breath threatening to strangle in his throat.

"Elijah?"

He gasped. "I'm all right."

"Is it the cave? Does it remind you of your cell?"

He closed his eyes and took two deep breaths. "When we first crawled in here, I didn't even think about it. Now..."

"It is all right. We are going to be fine."

He didn't have to force a smile. Somehow his heartbeat began to return to normal with Mary Jane's sweet, comforting voice wrapping around him.

Morning came, and with it, fresh challenges. Tough, damn near insurmountable challenges with a woman at his side. On the other hand, she was far tougher than he believed when he first met her. His confessions to her, though perhaps ill advised, had taken him by surprise. He'd spoken of things he had never told another person, not even his Ma. The last thing he expected was to feel relief he'd confessed so much. The anvil he carried around his neck remained, but now it felt lighter.

They had frittered away precious time sleeping. The earth waited for no one. Birds chirped outside. The scent of rain and earth permeated their hiding place. Wishing for fog cover seemed a futile venture with sun rays drawing bright bands along the rock and dirt shelter floor.

With reluctance, he removed his arms from around her. "We need to leave, darlin'."

Aching with the cold, he shifted her away. Mary Jane groaned softly. "Do you think they are looking for us? Why were they looking for us? None of this makes sense."

He kept his voice low as he expressed his suspicions. "They must have staged the hold up as a two-pronged attack. My brother placed Claypool and Hoop to follow us on the train."

"Then your brother somehow knew what train you would be on when you left Philadelphia? How?"

Elijah shook his head. "He probably didn't. Someone must have told him I was getting out of the penitentiary. He knew I'd come after him and that the law would be all-fired to catch him as well. He ran but left instructions for his friends to watch me. They had to follow me everywhere—that's the only way they could have known which train I was on. My brother and the buzzard with him must have camped on the incline."

"Even so, they would have to know which train you were on."

He scratched the beard growing on is chin. "They played their odds. If they didn't get the right train they could still rob it. If they got the right train, Claypool and Hoop would rob everyone and then deliver us to my brother. Simple. Claypool and Hoop probably paid off the engineer so he'd stop the train if he saw anyone ahead getting ready to blow the track." He tapped the side of his head with an index finger. "Amos used black powder or something to blow part of the tracks. The only way the iron horse would have stopped in time without derailing would be if the engineer already knew when and where to stop. Someone paid him. Times are hard on the Allegheny Portage Railroad. It is getting old and worn. There's probably more than one engineer who needs the money."

She stood and shivered, her eyes wide and face pale. "That is quite a conspiracy, sir, but I think you must be correct."

He stretched into a stand, his muscles cramped, his body

weary from trying to stay warm at night. "That means my scallywag brother has taken significant steps to kill me."

"Just as you have formed plans to kill him?"

Anger edged upward. He hadn't said a thing about killing Amos, so she had to be guessing. "I wouldn't put innocent lives in danger to kill Amos."

"Of course not." She sighed. "I am sorry."

He almost growled back, but her softened words stopped him cold. He had put her in danger, a complete innocent in his sordid situation.

"I apologize, Mary Jane. I drew you into this trouble." He laughed, but the sound was filled with self-loathing.

Freed of her corset and crinoline, Mary Jane appeared more vulnerable and less stoic. A freedom flowed around her like the loose trappings of her skirt. Thank the heavens her long hair was tied up to her head instead of loose around her shoulders. Not only would it tangle in their headlong flight for survival, he wouldn't have resisted touching it. Despite her admirable courage, how could she survive this wilderness?

Bleakness darkened her expression. Irritation raised its head. Irritation because he placed her into this position through no fault of her own.

"You're right, Mary Jane. Every guiltless soul on that train is in danger because of me. I tried to protect you and brought you peril instead."

She shook her head. "No, I am sorry, Elijah. You have done an admirable job of protecting me. You could not have known your brother would try and harm you."

"Fate has a way of placing obstacles in our path, doesn't it?"

"That is for certain. Now, I am a murderer. What will the law make of what I did?" She put her arms around herself, drawing in tight as if she could disappear into the rocks. "I killed that man, Elijah. I saw a glimpse of his open eyes. I took his life from him."

"You defended yourself against his attack. That is not murder. But it's never easy to kill."

Her gaze flashed to his. "Who did you kill?"

"Only Claypool. I shot back at him after he shot at me first. When they dragged you off the train, it scared me, Mary Jane. Scared me so bad I could feel it tightening around my throat like a noose on the gallows." Harsh memories gripped him. "As soon as Hoop took you into the woods, I pulled out my weapon and told Claypool to give up his. He turned and fired. I moved just in time and took my own shot. I missed. He ran into the woods and that's when I went after him and you. He turned on me and fired again. I shot him in the chest."

He didn't like reliving those moments when he crashed into the woods. "I feared the worst. Instead I found Hoop with his skull dented in and you nowhere to be found. I was relieved because he was dead, but worried. All I knew was that I had to find you."

Her expression slid from harsh recollection to stoic resignation. "I...thank you, Elijah. I would not have survived without you."

He brushed the end of her nose and removed some dirt. "Don't thank me too soon, darlin'. We're somewhere between Cassandra and Portage. There is plenty of wilderness left to survive, and we don't have supplies."

She sighed. "We are caught out here in the middle of wilderness with no defense from monsters, and I do not mean of the animal kind."

"There are those too."

She waved one hand. "Do not remind me."

Elijah walked towards her and clasped her shoulders. When he spoke, he meant every word. "I vow I'll get you out of here. I won't let anything or anyone harm you."

"I know." Her voice sounded soft and convinced, and her eyes reflected new hope.

"We survived last night with nothing more than the clothes

on our backs. There may be hunter's cabins this far down the mountain. If we continue southwest we will either run into one at some point or run into the town of Portage. In the meantime, there are other ways to survive."

Her eyes warmed, and some of the worry disappeared. "If I had to find myself trapped in the woods, there is no one I would rather be trapped with, sir."

Overwhelming affection struck him between the ribs and demanded action. He slipped his arms around her waist and brought her into his body. As she sighed deeply, his body relaxed. He'd lost Maureen because he couldn't protect her against Amos.

I'll be damned if it happens to Mary Jane too.

He kissed her forehead and tucked her head against his shoulder. She felt far better and more comforting in his arms than the weapon tucked in his waistcoat pocket. Drawing strength from her life, her beauty, the extraordinary emotion she'd already shared, he held her close.

"Do you trust me?" he asked.

She leaned back far enough to see into his eyes. "I do."

He nodded and released her. "Good. Then we need to leave quickly and walk as far as we can before the end of the day so we can find shelter. If we're lucky we'll stumble upon those hunter's cabins or maybe a farm or other abode. I have a few shots left in my weapon, so we're good there. Stay close to me at all times. We'll find water first."

They left her corset, crinoline and crumpled hat in the rock shelter and headed into a cool morning. A mist settled along the ground like the smoky trail of a mythical dragon. He didn't know whether to hope it wouldn't rain or to wish it would. Rain would slow down Amos's search, but it would impede their progress, too.

Elijah's breath sluiced in and out as he measured what to do first. Damn good thing he had a sense of direction. Mary Jane walked alongside him. Though she kept her gaze mostly on the ground and held her skirts up so she could see where she walked, the determination in her face gratified him. She was strong and healthy, and he wouldn't fail her.

"Thanks be to St. Patrick," he said.

She glanced at him with a bewildered expression. "Pardon me?"

"I'm thanking St. Patrick that you're a clever, strong woman."

She clambered over some large rocks in her path. "Am I?"

"I'd bet my life on it."

"Please do not, Elijah. You cannot imagine..."

"What?"

"When I was running from that man I was sure they had already killed you, and I was on my own. I was terrified. I was not strong. And the thought of you dead..."

"Yes?"

"I could not... I could not imagine it."

He sensed she held something back in her confession. Could she have some deeper feeling for him? He thought maybe she did, and though he shouldn't want it and an alliance between them would never work...by all the saints, he yearned for a woman's affection. For one woman to trust him and care for him.

"You fled for your life," he said.

"Like any person would. It is natural, not brave."

He didn't look at her, but the anxiety in her voice had stifled what he planned to say next. *If anything happens to me, you continue on. Don't give up.* He'd told her last night, but it might need saying once more.

Elijah kept moving, though he almost stopped and gathered her into his arms. "You put enough power into that rock to kill the man who would have...who knows what he would've done. You did what you must to survive, and most women wouldn't think of that so quickly."

Elijah reached for her forearm and held secure as they forded more rocks and a mud patch.

They remained quiet as he led her towards water. Traversing through thick, enormous stands of hemlock, rocky terrain and tall grass presented a beautiful and demanding landscape. He wished Amos planned this so-called robbery closer to a town. Yet he knew Amos's mind well. Of course he would pick an isolated spot. Blowing rails in the twisting, treacherous areas of the railroad would prove too daunting, but out on the long incline it had not hampered the outlaw. Amos was a bastard, but a clever one.

Elijah followed what he'd learned in Ireland about wilderness survival. His Da, scum that he was, had taught them at least that much. Da had taken Elijah and brothers to a God-forsaken mountain near Galway that promised hellfire land and unforgiving weather. Land in Pennsylvania outmatched Ireland for animal hazards, and that worried him.

Thirty minutes later, he spotted a stream trickling over and between rocks. Mary Jane looked relieved beyond measure, her face pale.

He crouched beside a mini waterfall where a heavy cascade fell about three feet over a large bolder. "Here. This water looks clean." He put his fingers into it, smelled it, tasted one finger. "Smells and tastes fresh. Drink your fill. We'll follow this stream."

She stepped nearer the water and almost slipped. She righted herself before he could reach for her. Kneeling streamside, she cupped clear water in her hands and brought it up to drink. She consumed several handfuls, then splashed her face a couple of times. She wiped her face on her long sleeve.

As he watched, she opened the neck on her dress almost to her breasts.

When she caught him gazing at her creamy flesh, she smiled shyly. "Are you staring, Elijah?"

"Yes, ma'am." He tossed a grin her way. "But I'll look away

to preserve my sanity."

They continued, their silence at odds with the forest, which came alive around them with chirps, wind rustling the treetops, and the cracking of twigs beneath their feet. He wished they could make quieter tracks, but with brush underfoot, it proved near impossible. He quickened their pace until they reached a hill that sloped upward into the blue sky. Clouds started to settle low. Perhaps more rain would come.

"Darlin', we're going up this." He pointed at the hill. "I am, anyway. Stay down here for the moment while I see what is on the other side."

She shook her head. "I will not stay down here by myself."

They worked their way through the brush that pulled at their clothes and scratched exposed skin. Upward, upward until he heard her breath rasping. Her face flushed, dewed with the beginnings of sweat. They halted at the crest.

She sighed and shaded her eyes with her right hand. "More trees."

More hemlock and other trees he couldn't identify sprawled across in endless wonder, but he saw the railroad tracks from here through a tall stand. Deeper into the woods, and not quite within sight of the tracks, stood a small cabin. Smoke curled lazily from its stack.

Riding alongside the tracks two figures on horses made their way.

"Is that—," she started.

"Shhh." He caught her hand and pulled her down so they crouched and barely could see over the ridge. "If that's Amos and his accomplice, we don't want to go anywhere near that cabin."

Within a few moments the two figures headed towards the structure. One figure left his horse and went to the abode. Elijah waited, his hand still clasped in Mary Jane's. Suddenly the man who had walked towards the cabin stumbled back. A woman left the cabin and stepped onto the porch, rifle pointed at both men.

Elijah strained to hear conversation. He couldn't hear a thing except a bird twittering and squawking above his head. With a defiant shake of her long gun, the woman gestured for the interlopers to fall back. Rather than fight her, the man climbed onto his horse and his partner kicked his own horse into flight. Both riders urged their animals into the woods and farther west.

"What was all that about?" Mary Jane whispered her question.

He stood and brought her with him. "A brave woman living alone, or her man isn't home."

"Is it safe to approach her?"

Elijah shook his head. "Let us take one challenge at a time. If we make it down this hill alive, I'd say we'll have time then to consider whether she's safe or not."

"Good thinking, Elijah."

"No, darlin'. It's pure fear."

When she tossed him an irreverent grin, he realized she didn't think he'd meant it. He kept her hand secure within his and started the journey.

Mary Jane tightened her grip on Elijah's large palm as they made their way down the crumbling hillside with cautious steps. Her boots had little gripping power and rocks under her feet shifted. Elijah's Hessian boots performed much better—he did not slip once. The water she consumed earlier helped her feel stronger. She had felt faint before they discovered the healthy stream. Her breath rasped in her throat, her heart pounding from exertion and apprehension. She gathered her voluminous skirts in one hand. Her small reticule, which she managed to keep in her headlong flight from the train, banged against her wrist. She had kept her gloves and that helped every time her hands met bare earth.

"I wish I had trousers to wear right now," she said in a low

175

whisper of frustration.

He did not look back. "Mrs. McKinnon, I'd give about anything right now to see you in those trousers."

A small giggle escaped her throat. "Sir, you are quite incorrigible."

He glanced back once and paused on the hill to throw her a teasing smile. Not long ago she couldn't have expected more than a grim expression. His smile, when it came, warmed her heart clear through. With a man like this, a woman could not rely on a cozy and conflict-free life.

She had never scaled or descended a hill this steep before and turned her attention to reaching the bottom safely. She gripped his hand like a lifeline.

"Any tighter, darlin', and my hand will fall off."

She loosened her hold but did not say a word—trying not to stumble took priority. As Elijah edged down the slope with careful precision, she could not ignore an odd reaction to him gathering inside her. His body flowed like a wild creature, each step certain. Strength, potent and feral radiated from Elijah. His hand, so large and capable, held hers firmly but gently. Despite everything she knew already, this man possessed secrets she longed to understand. Stranded in this wilderness, she did not know if she would ever have opportunity to discover his hidden depths. Striving for survival must remain her only thought. They reached a clearing and took stock.

"I'd suggest that I approach the cabin alone, but that might make the woman suspicious. So we should go together," Elijah said.

They walked slowly towards the structure, and her apprehension rose moment by moment. What if the woman came out firing? It did not bear thinking about, so Mary Jane banished the fear to one corner of her mind. They approached the cabin from the east side.

As their feet echoed across the small porch, the door swung open and the woman stepped out, rifle pointed at them.

Chapter Twelve

Time seemed to slow as Mary Jane and Elijah confronted the older woman. Silvery gray hair piled atop the woman's head and her sack-like, dark gray dress showed her heavy black boots up to the ankle. Though the generous size of the dress obscured her figure, the lady appeared thin and considerably shorter than Mary Jane. Her craggy face, lined with furrows and heavily wrinkled about the eyes, proclaimed great age. Yet she looked sturdy and invincible, like a goddess who had lived in these mountains and had no plans to ever leave.

The woman brought her rifle up a little higher. "What in tarnation do you want?"

Elijah held up his hands. "We mean no harm, ma'am. There was a train robbery up the incline, and we escaped."

The old woman nodded. "You see those men who came by the cabin? Those the robbers?"

"We believe so," Mary Jane said. "At least from the hill we thought it might be them."

"They are part of a gang." Elijah said. "Two of the robbers are dead. The men that stopped by your cabin...one of them is my brother."

The woman's rifle had sagged in her arms, but she brought it up to full bear on her visitors. "Your brother?" The woman's aqua eyes flashed. "You're not a part of his gang?"

Elijah shook his head. "No, ma'am. As sure as God is my witness."

The old woman shifted on her feet. "That don't make no sense."

"It is a long story." Mary Jane put out one hand. "I am Mary Jane...McKinnon and this is my husband, Elijah McKinnon."

The lie slipped from Mary Jane's lips, and she chastised herself for telling it. On the other hand, it made sense to keep the woman in the dark as far as their marital status.

"I don't see no ring on your hand." The woman looked at Mary Jane's gloved hands. "Is it under them gloves or did the robbers take it?"

"No, ma'am." Elijah shook his head. "It's in my pocket." He gave the old woman a gentle smile. "You see, Mary Jane and I had a bit of a disagreement, and she threw her ring at me. It's in a box in my pocket along with my weapon."

"Weapon?" The woman lifted her rifle higher and pointed it directly at Elijah.

Mary Jane gasped. "Please, do not hurt him. He is telling the truth. In fact, I would like my ring back. Would it be all right if he reaches in his pocket to get it?"

After the woman's gaze darted back and forth between them for some time, she nodded. "Iffin' he was my man, I'd make him earn the ring."

A soft laugh escaped Mary Jane, and she stole a glance at Elijah. His respectful expression had not changed. "Well, he saved me from one of the robbers. I would say that is enough."

The grizzled woman stepped nearer but kept her rifle aimed. Her expression lightened and a smile passed over her face so quickly Mary Jane could not say if she honestly witnessed it. "That's all right then. A man who protects his woman, that's a mighty nice gesture. 'Course a woman like me learnt a long time ago to rely on herself. Best you learn that, too, young lady."

"Indeed." Mary Jane took a slow step towards Elijah and removed her gloves. "Now can I claim my ring?"

The woman gestured with her rifle. "You there, Irishman. Take your weapon out nice and slow."

His face remained a hard mask. "I've no designs to hurt you, ma'am. I'll need my gun to protect my wife."

Once more the woman's alert and intelligent gaze darted from Mary Jane to Elijah. "Your man good as his word?"

Mary Jane nodded. "Absolutely. He would never harm a female."

"Good then. Take out the ring and put it on your woman's hand and speak your vows so I know you're a might serious." The woman's gun made a motion. "I mean every word, young man. This rifle is my honor."

"Of course," Elijah said as he drew the ring box from an inside pocket.

Mary Jane did not know whether to find the woman's request ludicrous or funny. Elijah opened the small box and reached for Mary Jane's cold fingers. As his warmth enveloped her flesh, Mary Jane shivered in delight. Even in a flight for life, she found his touch arousing and comforting.

As he slipped the ring onto her left hand, he stood close and looked into her eyes. His powerful gaze held a wealth of emotions, many she could not identify. All of them blended together and started a firestorm, a yearning that declined to wait for privacy or safer circumstance.

"With this ring, I thee wed." Elijah's voice was deep and strong, sincerity in each syllable until she could almost believe them. "I promise to love and honor and cherish you until death do us part."

When Mary Jane could do nothing more than sink into the warmth of his eyes, the woman prompted her. "Go on then, Mrs. McKinnon. Say your vows to him."

Mary Jane swallowed hard. "I promise to love, honor and..."

Elijah's eyes twinkled. "Obey?"

The old woman cackled, but Mary Jane ignored her.

"Cherish. I promise to cherish you."

Elijah drew her left hand to his lips and kissed her fingers. "That will do very well, darlin'."

Tears filled Mary Jane's eyes at his tender declaration. Their quick vows could not have meant more to her than if they had stood in a church. The revelation stunned her.

"Looks like your woman has a fine, loving heart Irishman. You best treat her right." The old woman lowered her weapon and winked at Mary Jane. "I never did obey my husband either, girly. Come into the cabin, and I'll scrape up some food. I have some fine fixins."

Mary Jane bit into the hot cornbread and sighed in ecstasy. Not even the hard bench beneath her or the gnarly wood table in front of her could put her off the buttery taste. With a fire burning in the huge fireplace and stew simmering in a pot over the flames, she realized how cold she had been. Welcome heat sank into her bones and gave her almost as much pleasure as the sustenance. She inhaled and caught scents of beef, wood smoke and dried herbs. Though the cabin appeared tiny from the outside, it boasted a living area with a horsehair stuffed settee, a wingback chair and a long wood table with bench-like seat on either side. A small kitchen and hearth graced one area, plus there was a mudroom and two rather large bedrooms. Not only was the place clean, the old woman kept tidy in every other respect. Calmed by the heat and comfort food, Mary Jane could almost forget the mind-numbing trauma of the last two days. She sipped from a goblet and sighed in pleasure as water bathed her throat.

Mary Jane saw the approval in Elijah's expression as he sat across from her, his plate full. He, too, drank an entire tankard of water in one gulp.

The old woman, who called herself Mrs. Peg Connor, stirred stew in a huge, black pot over a healthy fire.

"This is delicious, Mrs. Connor," Mary Jane said. "I have

not had cornbread in...well, I have only had it once."

Mrs. Connor's eyes widened, and a quizzical expression crossed her face. "Only once, child? What was wrong with your mama?"

Mary Jane laughed, and Elijah's serious expression eased as he joined their amusement. "My mama, as you call her, has not cooked a day in her life. I come from a wealthy family, and we have kitchen staff. I also have never cooked much myself, though I would like to learn. Cook gave me some lessons until my mother caught her and demanded I stop."

The woman's face grew more puzzled, and then Mary Jane realized her mistake. "You ain't cooked for your husband?"

"Oh...well, um...he does most of the cooking. It is an unconventional marriage."

Elijah's eyes darkened with caution. "I learned cooking from my Ma, Mrs. Connor. She is a fine baker."

"Uh-huh. I see. I always say whatever works for a couple works for a couple. There's no special rhyme or reason to it, whatever people might say."

"I doubt you ever listen to those people," Mary Jane said.

Mrs. Connor's laugh turned into a cackle again. "That's a mighty true, young lady. Now you eat that all down. This stew is almost done."

Elijah dug into his cornbread, then ate the other food on his plate with equal gusto. Mary Jane noticed that Elijah always ate as if someone might steal his food at any minute.

"This is most generous of you, ma'am. What is this white food? It's very good," Elijah said.

"That be hominy, Irishman. My husband, God rest his soul, brought the recipe from down south. He was from Missouri, and had particular likes and dislikes with food. Can't say I miss that part about him."

Mary Jane laughed, and the old woman joined her. "This is too much food, ma'am. Surely you will have some."

181

"Never you mind. I'll have some later. You need something in your belly afore you trek into the forest again. I won't send you off without it." Mrs. Connor turned back to them. "Now I know you're heading to Portage, but you won't get that far without the right supplies. I'd give you my horse, but she's the only ride I got. I have a pack you can carry, Irishman. We'll stuff it full of food enough to carry you to town."

Elijah swallowed. He'd thrown the food down his throat like he hadn't eaten in twenty days. "We'll pay you."

Mrs. Connor planted her hands on her hips. "That ain't my way. You two need help, and I can see that. I ain't going to make things worse on you by taking your money. It's my Christian duty and besides that, I want to."

Mary Jane liked the warmth she witnessed in the woman's eyes. When Mrs. Connor first came at them with the rifle, Mary Jane thought the eccentric old lady meant to shoot.

"Is there water where I might freshen up when I finish eating?" Mary Jane asked, feeling so grimy she wished she could soak in a tub.

As if she read Mary Jane's mind, the old woman said, "There is at that. I got a tub in the extra room. We can heat water for you. I got soap I made from plants that works every bit as good as that stuff you buy in the stores. Clean you right up...both of you."

"Thank you." Mary Jane could not believe their good fortune. "This is so wonderful. I cannot tell you—"

"Then don't, Mrs. McKinnon. You're a mite tired, I can see. You'll both want to rest here tonight."

Elijah chewed before adding his thoughts. "We need to get to Portage as quickly as possible before dark and alert authorities about the train."

"My guess is, and my guesses are almost always right," Mrs. Connor tapped the side of her forehead with an index finger, "that someone already knows about the train. They probably all think you're both dead. But if you leave now you won't make it to Portage afore dark. There's a marauding mountain lion about these parts that's causing havoc. You don't want to encounter that creature at night. Best to set out fresh first thing in the morning."

Elijah did not argue, and the half amusement in his eyes showed he appreciated the woman's candor. "You have room for us tonight?"

Mrs. Connor sat on the bench next to Mary Jane. "That I do, Irishman, that I do."

"We thank you, then." Elijah smiled.

"I'd purdy much do anything for a fellow Irish."

"Connor is an Irish name," Elijah said. "Was it O'Connor at one time?"

"That it was. Was O'Connor many moons ago when my husband's family first came over in the sixteen hundreds. Now my side was a mishmash of German and French and maybe a tad dratted English. My husband's father changed it to Connor 'cause people had a prejudice, you know. Dropping the O was the only way to make most of the high and mighty ignorant of his heritage."

The woman's expression filled with enjoyment as she related several tales of her ancestor's adventures. Whether any of them could be true, Mary Jane could only wonder.

Elijah's initial appetite slowed, and he pinned Mrs. Connor with an intense look. "Why are you out here in this defenseless place?"

Mrs. Connor nodded towards her rifle propped up near the hearth. "I ain't defenseless. I've been widowed near twenty years."

Mrs. Connor stood and went to a cupboard where she grabbed two wooden bowls and filled them each with stew. She placed a bowl each in front of Elijah and Mary Jane and provided worn but clean spoons.

"How did your husband die, Mrs. Connor, if you do not mind my asking?" Mary Jane asked after chewing one bite of delicious meat and potato.

Mrs. Connor's eyes went cloudy with distant but painful memories. "An old mountain lion done ate him."

Mary Jane's mouth popped open—the revelation left her shocked.

"I'm sorry," Elijah said. "That must have been horrible."

The woman nodded, but then smiled. "He was a mite older than me...my husband that is. Twenty years older in fact. He said his time would come sooner rather than later, and he taught me how to live off the land." She settled onto the bench, beside Elijah this time. "Leastwise, he taught me what I hadn't learnt already from my folks afore they died."

"That is wonderful." Mary Jane meant it. "Your husband sounds like a fine man."

As her eyes seemed to turn a brighter shade of aqua, Mrs. Connor sipped water from her own tankard. "These here pewter tankards were a wedding gift from some friends. We were young couples together. They're gone now." Her eyes grew misty and took on a far away glaze. "They was killed during a train wreck on that there damned Allegheny Portage Railroad near ten years ago. I don't take that damned steam contraption to get over the mountain. You shouldn't either."

"We're going to Pittsburgh, Mrs. Connor." Elijah explained their circumstance and how Mary Jane's father's father had passed away.

"Horror of horrors, young lady." Mrs. Connor reached across the table and patted Mary Jane's hand with gentle concern. Her veined, callused hand felt comforting. "Bless you. I'm sorry to hear about your loss."

"Thank you. I am ashamed to say it, but the wreck has wiped him from my mind." Mary Jane's gaze met Elijah's. "I cannot believe I could forget poor Father's body."

The old lady drew her hand back. "Don't you fret none. That ain't your daddy in that body. Your daddy moved on to heaven."

Somehow this woman, with her deceptive hard outer shell, made Mary Jane's guilt evaporate like dew under intense sunshine. "You are right. He is at peace."

"Now, on to more practical matters. I have a map that'll get you to Portage faster than if you was navigating on your own. Now, you're such a nice couple I might let you borrow my horse anyway."

"We couldn't let you do that." Elijah shifted and stood to his full height. "You've already done enough for us. How would you know if we'd bring the horse back to you?"

"Nonsense, boy. It was wrong of me to suggest you hoof it to Portage on your own weary feet. It's a goodly ways from here. You're honest and I can tell. You'll get Matilda back to me."

"Matilda?" Mary Jane asked.

Mrs. Connor's broad smile teased. "My horse, young lady. My horse." Mrs. Connor filled them with wild tales of hunting in the mountains for deer and bagging the occasional bear. "Not too many mind you. I figure the animals got as much right to live here as I do. They was here first. I figure those train robbers are not honorable. The animals, you know, they kill only to live. Train robbers, well, they kill for greed and hate and revenge. Revenge is a sick motivation if you was to ask me."

Mary Jane's tankard stopped halfway to her lips as she threw a startled glance towards Elijah. If he'd drawn personal offense from the woman's statement about revenge, he didn't show it.

Instead he sipped the last of his water and placed it down on the table. "Right you are, ma'am. A wise woman."

Did that mean he would abandon his quest for revenge?

The sun started to go down before they considered retiring for the night.

"Now, how would you like a bath?" Mrs. Connor asked them.

Once they heated water and poured it in the large tub in the second bedroom, Elijah told Mary Jane he would wait out in the living area while she bathed.

The old lady would have none of it. "Mr. McKinnon, now you get in there and help your Mrs. bathe. Better yet, the two of you can bathe together. Makes it quicker and you look a might tuckered out the both of you. You should go straight to bed right after."

Elijah started to protest, but the insistent lady poked him in the ribs with her fingers. "Go on now. I'm about to find some sleep myself. I'll be out like a candle in a wee moment."

With that the petite woman stomped into her room and closed the door. A lock *snicked* shut.

Warmth blossomed in Mary Jane's belly and her heart pounded a new beat that spelled anticipation and maybe a smidgen of fear. She headed into their designated bedroom and Elijah followed. He closed the door and took Mrs. Connor's idea by sliding the small bolt to lock.

That lock and the predatory gleam in his gaze caused Mary Jane to take two steps back. And another.

Elijah caught up with her and slipped one arm around her waist. He whispered, and his hot breath in her ear made her shiver in delight. "Keep your voice low so she can't hear. Go ahead and take your bath. I'll stay turned away."

"But we cannot. I...you...we are not truly married."

"No. But I have self-control and so do you. There's no help for it."

He released her and walked to the single small window where light hardly reached as night came early in this mountainous area. Quivering with a combination of delayed excitement and disappointment, she undid her clothes. She accomplished this before in his presence. She could do it again.

"I need assistance with these buttons."

He complied, working swiftly to undo the small buttons on the back of the mourning dress. When the dress gaped in the back and the bodice slipped forward, she caught the material before it could fall to her waist. He swiftly turned back to the window.

After easing from the dress, she hurried to shuck her chemise and pantalets. The cool air nipped her skin, even though a fireplace snapped and crackled on the other side of the room. She tossed them onto a primitive wooden chair and made her way to the tub. She stepped in and found the hot water a soothing balm to banish the cold. She slipped and landed in the tub with a squeak and splash. Water lapped over her face. Strong hands gripped her shoulders and drew her upward. She sputtered and choked.

Elijah stared down at her with worry. "By the saints, darlin', are you hurt?"

She laughed, embarrassed. "Goodness, how clumsy of me."

Easing her down into the water, Elijah gentled his grip. His gaze turned sharp and hungry when it landed irrevocably on her breasts. While she could have protested his presumptuous stare, she did not.

She wanted this. Feared this.

Elijah leaned his forearms on the tub. "You are more beautiful than I dreamed."

"You dreamed of me?"

"More than you know." He allowed his fingertips to slice through the water, stirring a response that ached between her legs. "You're a goddess."

"Surely not, sir."

Caressing her with a devouring look, Elijah's murmured, "I'll help you wash."

His attention slipped to her waist, to the curled hair of her mons and down her legs. She should feel outrage. Modesty. Instead all she could imagine was allowing him every liberty. Of learning what it would feel like to discover physical delights with Elijah Jonas McKinnon.

But no. There could be no delights beyond this. Her experience with Thaddeus had proved...unsatisfactory. Could making love be any different with a man like Elijah?

As she glanced down at Elijah's breeches, his manhood pressed solid against the strained material. Clearly he wanted her in the most carnal way. Fists clenched as his sides, his eyes also betrayed him. Did her face mirror all the emotions tumbling chaotically inside?

"Darlin', talk to me. Tell me how this trip has changed you. Are you going back to Pittsburgh the same woman who left there?"

Elijah's surprising question gave her significant pause. How did she answer truthfully if at all? Images tumbled through her mind. First, meeting him on the train, his brooding countenance intense and purposeful. Second, the way he kissed her as if he had loved her all his life. Despite everything she could not understand, she did know this one thing...she trusted him deep in her soul. Even if he did plan revenge against his brother, she did not think he could actually kill Amos. The man she came to know, no matter how damaged and raw, would only kill to defend.

"I am not the same person, Elijah. I do not think I ever will be again."

"What would your family think? Will they accept and like the changes?"

She shrugged, then reached up to undo her hair. She reached for the soap on the table next to the tub. "I can only imagine, but I doubt it."

"You'll tell them you took a bath with me?"

Her eyes widened. "Are you serious?"

"Yes. "

She watched as he straightened and shrugged off his waistcoat, and that was when she noticed the sleeves were wet. He tossed the garment on the bed and unbuttoned his shirt.

"What...what are you doing?" She knew the answer, but wished to voice a maidenly protest.

"Doing as our hostess bid us. Taking a bath with you, wife."

Chapter Thirteen

Wife.

The word was gruff, not with anger but a sultry, glorious sound in Elijah's compelling voice. Mary Jane could not take her gaze off him as he pushed his fingers through his hair, and the sight of rippling muscles parted her lips in astonishment. Yes, she had seen him like this before...yet not. As he lifted his arms, his biceps bunched and flexed. Shoulders a mile wide and a delineated, glorious chest added to his powerful appeal. Hair sprinkled across his pectorals and lined down over that flat, muscled stomach. Imagining a man more fabulous, more godlike in his physique than Elijah seemed impossible.

She had never seen Thaddeus's naked chest, but she could not imagine in a million years it could look anywhere as wonderful as this.

"Elijah?"

"Yes?"

Without taking his gaze off hers, he sat on the edge of the bed and did away with his boots.

"How did you stay in such fine form while in prison?" She licked her lips, nervous. "You are physically...imposing."

He smiled. He slid off his socks and as he stood again, unfastened his trousers. "There was an exercise yard. Each inmate had a small one outside their cell that was open to the elements. We were allowed twenty minutes outside. I exercised."

"I see. You had enough to eat?"

He paused, his features stone hard. "They didn't starve us, darlin'."

She sighed. "That is good."

As he slid his trousers down his legs, female fear kept her gaze away from his most private area. Even when he stood naked, it took a few seconds for Mary Jane to dare look down.

What she saw delighted and excited her more than she could have guessed.

His manhood stood erect. Thick, long and hard. Below this masculine evidence, his balls hung between his thighs.

She stared. She could not help it. After all, she had never seen a man's arousal exposed. She had not actually seen Thaddeus's manhood even though he had...

She swallowed hard remembering the pain of Thaddeus thrusting against her, his length rasping. Hurting.

Her gaze snapped to Elijah's, and heat curled hot and alive in every centimeter of her body as she recognized the awareness in his eyes. She had seen one of her father's history books and within it, a carving of naked Adonis had shocked her. Yet Elijah was so very much more. His body was a study in extraordinary masculine strength and potency. Her pulse skittered and farther down, lower than her stomach, a hollow need begged for completion.

He strode towards her and stood at the side of the tub, his eyes turned bright with lust, with obvious hunger.

Before she could speak, he stepped into the tub and slid down into the water with her. "Get your hair wet, and I'll wash it."

A mingling of relief and continued anticipation drew her to comply. The day drew much from her, and yet being with him in this intimate moment returned some of her flagging energy. She danced between exquisite possibilities and feral needs. She scooted down in the tub enough to dip her hair, then returned to sitting position.

He grabbed the soap from the stand next to the tub and

created lather between his hands. "Turn around until your back faces me. Then scoot closer."

A wild thrill coursed through her body as she complied. Getting closer to Elijah's naked muscle made her shake with anticipation and virginal fear. Sweet torment, all of it. She closed her eyes and felt him shift close to her back. His long, heavily muscled thighs and calves pressed along the outside of hers. She kept her eyes closed and savored the sensations. Hot, male muscle against feminine softness delighted and challenged her. The hair on his thighs sent soft tingles along her skin. Warm water lapped, as soft as a lover's tentative touch and a delicious discovery. Her nipples beaded and tightened, and gooseflesh prickled along her skin.

As his fingers massaged soap into her hair, she sighed in pleasure. The soap smelled good, and she wondered what Mrs. Connor used to make it. She gave into the rhythmic movement of fingers over her scalp. He knew how to touch without hurting, and the motion soon eased into a languorous caress.

She barely registered how long he washed her hair before he spoke. "Now we need to rinse."

He left the tub long enough to pick up an additional bucket full of water. As she tilted her head back and closed her eyes, he poured the water over her soapy hair until it came squeaky clean. He stepped back into the water and returned to his place behind her.

Husky with an emotion she couldn't define, he uttered his next request. "Lean back against me, darlin."

Apprehension returned. "I do not know if I should."

"Should? Maybe not. What do you *want* to do?"

Ah, well *wanting* was another matter. She shifted backwards until her back pressed his chest. She felt his chest, his rippled stomach, and most of all, the undeniable evidence he still wanted her.

"Relax, Mary Jane. Relax against me."

Those hard thighs bracketed hers once more with a

dominating presence that sheltered but didn't command. Then, without giving forethought, she palmed the top of his thighs. He sucked in a breath, and that hardness pulsed against her back. She moved, wriggling to get nearer, and with a rough sound of delight, he kissed the side of her neck.

Tingles danced over her skin. "Oh, Elijah."

"Mmm?"

"What are we doing here? We are not married."

"No." His denial did not stop his touches, or the tender kisses trailing over her left shoulder and then her right. His fingers splayed out over her hips as he groaned softly. "No. By the saints, darlin' you are a fire in my blood. But if you deny me...if you don't want my touch, you have only to tell me at any time, and I'll stop."

As his hands drifted over her shoulders, smoothing the soap with sensual strokes from her wrists to her elbows, she could not refuse him. Up. Down. Up. Down. All this felt too good, too fragile to illuminate with light and vision so she kept her eyes closed. She licked her lips and matched his exploration by stroking along his thighs. She savored hair over hard muscle, the strength inherent in his body.

"This is dangerous, darlin." His voice went guttural. "Very dangerous."

"Oh?"

Rather than answer her verbally, he gripped her waistline and then smoothed downward. He feathered over her thighs, and she jerked in surprise.

"Easy, Mary Jane. I won't do anything you don't wish."

Once more his hands glided upward and brushed past the side of her breasts. She moaned. Her breath came faster, the excitement pounding in her veins. She relaxed. Flowed with his touches until they started to blend together in a beautiful collection of sighs, whispers and surging desire.

Hot lips feathered over her ear and his tongue flicked inside. She gasped and wriggled. His breath puffed warm and seductive, setting off shivers of delight. She moaned and shifted in his hold, determined at once to renew and escape the feelings, wanting them and hating them because they drew her nearer a precipice. Around and around he palmed and circled her belly, setting new fires before another lay extinguished.

Her back arched as he plucked one nipple. "Oh."

"Your breasts are so beautiful, Mary Jane. So beautiful."

His tongue flicked her earlobe, then he settled into torment as he lightly strummed her nipples with his thumbs. She arched into his cupping palms, into each ruthless brush over her nipples.

He pleasured with exquisite slowness, finding and touching and caressing until Mary Jane writhed within an exquisite madness.

Oh, she should not do this... She should not but...

She wanted it. Ached like she'd never ached for anything else.

Resisting ecstasy seemed futile in the face of what they experienced together. They had scaled heights of fear, of danger, of tramping through a wilderness that promised more perils as yet unexplored. How did one describe tumbling towards an abyss and not caring how far or how long one fell?

She abandoned last restrictions and threw away thoughts of resistance to whatever came next.

His fingers flirted with the underside of her breasts, then drew around and around the fullness as they filled his palms. His hips moved as he pressed a granite length of male flesh along her back. Much more and she would succumb to everything he wanted, a woman captured by his spell and denying him nothing. Oh, but did she care? Did she honestly wish to escape his charm, his affection and fierce devotion to her safety?

As she leaned fully into him, his hand played with her left nipple. Elijah trailed a tantalizing path down, down until his fingers brushed lightly between her legs. She gasped, her head back against his shoulder, his mouth caressing the side of her neck.

One touch caressed the lips of her most private area. Astonished, she jerked. He tried again, teasing along sensitive folds, discovering secrets as he stroked. She smoldered inside, reaching for a feeling she could not escape. His fingers twisting and tormenting her nipple, his touch stroking between her legs—it was all too much. Too amazing.

She clasped his hand between her legs. "Please—I—"

"It's all right." He went still under her grip, his voice gentle. "Do you want me to stop?"

Ecstasy and pleasure danced just out of reach. Did she want to banish them forever? "No."

"Then feel it, my darlin'. Let yourself fly."

He eased two fingers straight into her core. She gasped.

"Am I hurting you?"

"No." She twisted, eager and loving the fullness. "More."

He complied and the growl that purred from his throat drew her arousal higher. Back and forth, his stroke moved within her, drawing her slick heat outward. She writhed in his grip, a sob of excitement and torment tightening within her, ready to explode.

"That's it." His voice was hoarse against her ear. "Feel it."

His touch whispered over her nipple and he slid his fingers deep into the heat and wetness between her legs. His thumb came up and flicked over her hottest need until she couldn't contain low whimpers issuing from her throat. He panted against her ear.

A tingling quiver threatened to erupt, along with sweet pleasure arching through her every time his thumb moved and his fingers caressed.

Thaddeus had never touched her like this. Had never given her such amazing pleasure. Out of control, quaking, she drove towards an indefinable finish line. She could not stand a moment more. A knot tightened, threatened to burst. She shivered and moaned as white-hot pleasure erupted. Shudders jolted Mary Jane from head to toe as a bliss she had never imagined existed engulfed her. The ecstasy jolted her to the core, bringing soft gasps to her throat she could not contain. She quivered as the sweetness slowly ebbed.

Time drifted for an eternity until she realized his arms were wrapped around her waist and his lips teased her shoulder.

"Elijah?"

"Mmm? Did you like that?"

Heat filled her face she kept her eyes firmly closed. "It was wanton. Incredible. Do decent women even feel this way?"

He chuckled, muffling the laugh against her skin. "You're a decent woman, Mary Jane. You're beautiful and strong. Any man would be lucky to have you on his arm."

His praise and reassurance gave her more confidence, and she opened her eyes. "Thank you." The water had not quite cooled, and his arousal still pressed against her back. She turned in his arms so she could see him. "What about you? Do you want to...uh..."

A wicked smile matched the carnality in his eyes. "I do, but I won't. You're a virgin, and I won't take that away from you. That honor is for you to give when you do marry."

Disappointment and surprise filled Mary Jane with an uncomfortable sadness that erased her joy. She wanted to tell him the truth. If he turned away from her, if he thought her a fallen woman he wanted nothing more to do with, so be it. The idea twisted inside her, hurting more than she thought possible. But she owed him honesty and would give it.

"I am not a virgin."

His arms loosened around her. "What?"

"You recall when I told you that my mother and father and sisters disapproved of me."

"You said something about it. Yes."

She sighed. "My mother and father despaired of my inability to follow strict decorum so they gave in to an idea I had to attend the university."

"Women do not go to university."

There was no disapproval in his voice, only statement of fact, so she continued. "I did not attend lectures. I worked for a small stipend for a professor and shared an apartment with another girl who did the same. We both worked for Professor Thaddeus Ricker."

"The man who does not know how to kiss a woman."

She could not help but smile. "Apparently not. But I spent considerable time with him, assisting with his notes, his administrative duties. I loved it. He was so intelligent, so kind, so understanding and not the least condescending to me. Soon, I thought I loved him." When he said nothing, she rushed to finish the story, more afraid now of what Elijah would think when he knew the entire tale. She tensed. "I was very devoted to him and imagined a life with him as his wife. I took a risk and confessed to him that I loved him. He kissed me, then said he loved me. I was so happy. He locked the door to his office, closed the shades..."

Her throat tightened.

"Jesus." Elijah's voice deepened, rough with building anger. "What did he do? Tell me, darlin'. What did he do?"

She cleared her throat and managed to force the words. "He started to kiss me again, to caress me, to touch me in ways I never imagined a man could touch a woman. It did arouse me...a little. But then he asked me to turn around and put my hands on the desk. I could not imagine what for. Then he lifted my skirts, tore my undergarments. He shoved my feet apart and before I knew it, he thrust. It hurt Elijah and I did not like it. But I thought I loved him and I thought that is what happened when a woman loved a man. That she submitted to him in this one way. In many ways."

She could not continue as humiliation washed over her.

Elijah would want nothing to do with her now. Nothing.

Elijah's arms tightened around her. His voice rasped against her ear, "My God, darlin'. The bastard. That fucking bastard."

"If I had not been improper none of it would have happened—"

"No. That is not true. He used you for lust after you confessed your love." He rubbed her arms with soothing strokes. "It was not your fault. You were innocent and didn't understand what was happening. If he really loved you he would've..."

She looked into the water, her mind spinning with questions and a breathless anticipation. "He would have what?"

He rubbed her shoulders. "He never would have hurt you."

Relief doused a portion of her fear. Perhaps Elijah did not think poorly of her after all. She owed him a full confession. "When he finished I was disgusted and thought I never wanted a man to touch me again. I was confused and wondered how I could also feel so repulsed by a man I loved. Less than two days after that, he was accused of stealing important papers from the university. I confronted him because I had seen the papers among his work. He asked me to lie and I refused."

His hands coasted over her arms. "That was very brave and admirable."

She shook her head. "It came to me what a stupid woman I had been. I went to the university authorities and told them about the papers." She took a deep breath. "It created a huge scandal. Even though the authorities found the papers and realized what a bounder Thaddeus was, and even though they relieved him of his position..."

"What happened, darlin'?"

She made a small helpless gesture with her hands as tears filled her eyes. "I was also relieved of my position, and though I kept quiet to everyone about my relationship with Thaddeus, the word got out."

"The bastard told people he took your virginity?" Elijah's voice was harsh.

"Yes. He did. Most people I knew at the university, the very people I thought were my friends...they shunned me. I had no choice but to return home a fallen woman in the eyes of everyone."

"Damn. How long ago did this happen?"

"Two months ago. For the last two months I have tried to be proper. To act the way I should have acted all along—"

"No. Don't say it. You are fine just the way you are, Mary Jane Lawson. You are the bravest, most giving, strongest woman I've ever known."

His strident praise surprised her, and as gladness filled her heart, she turned slightly in the tub to see his face. His eyes had darkened to storm clouds, his mouth a tight line, the fierceness of his belief in her amazing. She smiled. "Thank you, Elijah. But if I had not—"

"Don't." He shook his head. "Don't ever think on it again. You were wronged by a man who ranks no higher than a buzzard. And that's saying too much for the man. You deserve a man who cares how you feel, who makes love to you, not takes from you."

Then he closed his eyes for a moment, the harsh lines of anger still creasing his face.

In the silence, her heart expanded, her feelings for Elijah deepening. "Like you care for me, Elijah?"

His eyes popped open, and he shook his head. In his eyes she saw emotions flicker, but she could not define any single one.

"Let's finish our bath," he said. "Wash my shoulders?"

She frowned, puzzled at his change. "Of course."

Despite the heaviness of their conversation and situation, she could not ignore the physical and mental feelings he stirred within her. Confessing to him had done something she had not

199

expected.

She felt free.

Truly free in a way she had never experienced before.

Oh my.

All the wantonness she had locked up and thrown away roared back to the forefront. She wanted to defy all the conventions, to throw away the binds that had restricted her for two months.

She wanted to touch him with abandon.

They changed places, and as he turned around, the incredible view of his back and buttocks caused her to sigh. His buttocks were firm and muscled, and for a wild second she imagined cupping each cheek in her hand. Warmth pulsed and tingled in renewed desire, and when he sat in the water with his back to her, erotic feelings reemerged. As her legs sprawled along his long thighs, she started washing his back. Soap slid over shoulders carved with muscle. Though his skin was pale from the long confinement of five years, there was nothing weakling about him.

He moaned softly, and she smiled. She worked soap over his biceps and closed her eyes as she savored the power within his forearms. She should make conversation.

"Tell me more about your life in prison."

"I'm not sure I should."

Determined, she pressed him. "Please. Tell me. I want to understand what you went through. I have learned so much about you already, but I feel there is a little piece I have not reached. You exercised and what else? What could you do?"

As she dropped the soap and laced a teasing path over each ridge of muscle in his stomach, he sucked in a breath. "I couldn't do much." He took a deep breath. "You want to know right from the beginning what my prison experience was like?"

"Yes."

"Very well, darlin', but don't say I didn't warn you."

"I am not a delicate flower, Elijah. You cannot say anything at this point that will shock me."

"Really?" Doubt tinged his voice.

"Really."

As Mary Jane continued her slow caresses over his body she wondered if he felt the same way she had when his hands had drifted over her.

"So be it. Where do I start?"

"What does the prison look like?"

"It's a fortress, like a picture you might see of a castle in Ireland. A torture chamber that started as a good idea and became a nightmare. It opened in 1829, founded on principles of penitence through solitude and labor. Several famous people like Benjamin Franklin thought prisons were horrible places that needed reformation, and they worked to build that place. They thought it would work, but little did they know..." He shook his head.

She continued her soothing touch, hoping it would provide solace as he confessed what he knew. He dunked his head in the water so she could start washing his hair.

"Governments around the world copied Eastern State Pen," he said. "I heard Charles Dickens visited it in eighteen forty two and called it cruel and wrong."

"Is it cruel and wrong for the guilty?"

"A good question. I can't answer for anyone else but myself." She slowed washing his hair, and he continued his tale. "The place has a double gateway with a portcullis flanked by two towers. After your belongings and clothes are taken from you, you're washed down with cold water. You're given a pair of wool trousers and a long-sleeved top. They put a mask over your head so you can't see where they're taking you."

"You are talking about yourself in the second person."

He stopped. "Damned if I'm not. I guess it's to forget what happened. The fear was...when I was riding the carriage to prison, I wasn't afraid. When they put that hood over my head, though, that was it. I was damned terrified. As if they were walking me to the gallows right then."

She tried to imagine this powerful man afraid of anything. Yet his words whispered of fear and pain and genuine remembrance from within his soul. Her eyes filled with tears at what he must have suffered.

"I forgot to mention a prisoner is given a number and photographed when they come into the pen. From that point on a man is his number and nothing else. I was eight, eight, eight. For the longest time my jailer called me eight man, but he knew my real name and would sometimes call me that."

"Your jailer?"

"An overseer named Gulliver O'Toole. People called him Mouse. I couldn't call him anything."

"Why?"

"Solitude, remember? I was there for twenty-one years of solitude. That was my sentence."

She swallowed hard. "I cannot imagine five years of solitude much less twenty-one."

"Don't try, darlin'. Don't try." He cleared his throat. "Mouse put my food tray through the slot in the iron door and let me into my exercise area. For a long time I had a garden, if you can believe that. Not exactly manly, as Mouse said over and over, but I didn't give a gobshite. Pardon my language."

She shrugged. "I have heard cursing before, although yours is…different from most I've heard. Continue."

"I grew flowers in my garden my Ma would be proud of, if she'd ever seen them."

Loneliness echoed in his words, and she wondered how anyone could bear such a place. "What did they feed you?"

"As I said, we ate well. Beef and pork, a pound of bread each day and as many feckin' potatoes as I liked. You know, it may not be Irish of me, but I ate so many damned potatoes in the pen I don't want to ever see another."

She laughed softly. "Anything else?"

"We got coffee and tea and sometimes cocoa."

"It sounds better than what some poor eat on a daily basis."

"It is. The intention wasn't to punish by starving. The solitude was to give us time to establish a relationship with our creator. Since I wasn't guilty, I thought about everything *but* penitence. Four years along I wondered if maybe God had decided this was the best way to punish me for some unknown slight." Those broad shoulders shrugged. "I heard many souls there asked to see a chaplain, but I didn't want to see him. I finally knew what my worst sin was. I didn't protect Maureen."

"Oh, Elijah. How could you have saved Maureen?"

"I asked myself that day after day and never came to reasonable conclusion."

She wished she could remove his guilt as easily as taking the next breath. Whatever happened in the next few days or years, only Elijah could make total peace with himself.

As she allowed her touch to linger on his lower back, he shivered.

"Did your mother and Zeke send you letters?" she asked.

"Not until I was almost out. They allowed me to send my Ma a letter right before I was released." He explained his Ma's desire that he not come and see her.

Filled with an uneasy dislike for his mother, she said, "That must have hurt."

"More than you know."

Her hands settled on his trim waist. "Were you allowed any visitors?"

"None."

"You talked about your cell but not what was in it."

"Not much. Indoor water closet, if you can believe that. My door was made of solid wood and metal. There was a good-for-nothing air vent below the sill of my garden yard door and one in the skylight above. Didn't get much air through that. I was there a year when I got a fever. I ignored it at first until..."

She tightened her grip on him. "Until?"

"I started coughing and couldn't stop. My ribs ached, and I was weaker than I'd ever been. I passed out one day in the garden, and Mouse took pity on me, and with the help of another jailer they carried me over to the infirmary. Doctor Given was kind, and that surprised me. I had pneumonia."

"Oh, Elijah, that is awful. Did they put you back in the cell?"

"I thought they would, but they kept me chained to a bed in the infirmary. It took me three weeks to recover. Sickest I've been in my sorry life. "

"You could have died in there." Her eyes filled with tears, and she let them to drift down her cheeks, allowed what he once suffered to remind her of the privileged life she enjoyed.

"I'm too tough for that." The amusement in his voice lifted her spirits.

"I believe you are right, Elijah McKinnon."

Once more she caressed his stomach, but this time her touch drifted lower. She stopped right before the thatch of hair encircling his manhood.

His breath sucked in sharply. "Mary Jane—"

"Were there women there?"

"Prisoners? Not many, but they were kept near the administration offices mostly in block seven. The authorities probably thought they were even less use than the men. We were disposable people, Mary Jane. We were sinners or possessed."

"And you never spoke a word while in prison?"

"Most of the time, no. I wasn't allowed to speak to Mouse, but he talked to me. I talked with the doctor because he insisted on it, but that was it. Men who tried to break silence were normally punished."

"Simply for talking?"

"Yes. There was this device..." His breath hitched.

The suspense of not knowing forced her to say, "Tell me."

"It was called the iron tongue. They used it more in the early years of the prison, but they still used it from time to time while I was there. When a man talked or tried to communicate with other prisoners, the jailers could strap him in a chair." His shoulders started to heave as he took one deep breath and another. "Then they put this...they put this damned thing in a man's mouth that grabbed onto his tongue. If he tried to move his tongue it ripped into flesh." His entire body wracked with a shiver, as if the device had once torn his flesh. "There was this man in a cell next to me who wept every day. I could hear him. One day they took him away. Mouse told me they put him in the tongue, and he choked on his own blood."

Her arms twined around his waist, and she placed her cheek against his back, hoping she could comfort him in some small way. "That is barbaric."

His shoulders heaved again. "There was more. Do you want to hear it?"

No, I do not. "Yes."

"Other men they tortured by hanging them outside in the winter by their wrists. They poured water over their heads. Some were tied to a chair and left for days until their limbs turned black."

She stifled an exclamation of horror, her imagination lending a clear picture. "Did you...Elijah, did any of those things happen to you? Did they punish you?"

His laugh was a bark of derision. "I was lucky I had Mouse for a jailer. He could have punished me at least once or twice, or just made up that I was talking when I wasn't so he could punish me. He never did. Even after I..."

"What?"

"One cell next to mine had this man in it... Mouse said he was near fifty. The man had killed his wife and two kids and had been there seventeen years already. Anyway, I heard this horrible choking noise and pretty soon I realized that something bad was happening. On instinct I cried out for help. Jailers came running. The man died. He choked on his own meal."

"They did not punish you for talking?" she asked in amazement.

"Mouse argued against it. I heard him telling the other jailers that I was only doing the decent, Christian thing trying to get the man help. Mouse was a piece of shite in a lot of ways, but he wasn't all bad. Not all bad."

She rubbed his shoulders and sat up straight, her tears still a slow trickle. "How did you manage to survive thinking you would be there twenty-one years?"

"Why didn't I rot? I thanked God every day I wasn't dead, that I had a chance to kill Amos when I got out." In an achingly raw voice, he said, "Rinse my hair, please."

She climbed from the tub and used the bucket. A dark lock fell over his forehead, curling in the middle with roguish impudence. She almost reached out to touch it, to explore the masculine lips that evoked sensual promises with a kiss. Feeling a bliss that perhaps had no merit in the situation, she climbed back into the water and proceeded to lather the soap over his chest. What she couldn't see, she could feel. Oh, how she could feel. Every ridge, every slab of hard muscle teased her. When her fingers lingered over his nipples, he gasped, and the flesh peaked just as her nipples did. Ah, another feature of his wonderful body she loved exploring.

"That place was like a castle," he said suddenly.

"What place?"

"Eastern State."

Elijah's voice retained a husky flavor that teased her senses. Right now, in her frazzled state, it didn't matter what he said, but how he said it. Somewhere in untouched recesses within her heart, she hungered for the passion that rumbled in his tone and betrayed the condition of his soul.

"You never should have been in there." What words could she use that wouldn't sound unequal to the enormity of his experience? "Never."

"It was as awful as I let it be."

His words rang with conviction, as if the stone walls of Eastern State had imbedded into the fabric of his skin, his mind, his heart. The strange, rough sound in his voice, overlaid by his accent, sent swift and soft reaction over her skin.

"How can such an experience ever be escaped?"

"Can't. And I don't plan to forget it, darlin'. It's one of the reasons why I'm alive right now. Maybe, if they hadn't thrown me in that devil's hole, I'd be dead."

The thought of him dead ate away at her like a disease. "Why?"

"Because when I found Maureen, I was damned tempted to jump off a bridge."

She wanted to offer the comfort a mother offers a child who has fallen. At the same time, her body yearned for another connection she did not dare identify. "What truly kept you alive in there?"

"Like I said before. Revenge. Amos murdered my woman. He didn't spend five years in that prison. He didn't rot every day he couldn't speak. He didn't live with the fear of wondering if he might go mad every day with nothing more than his garden to keep him from thinking too much. He didn't have to wonder what it might feel like to taste a woman again, to sink deep and find release inside her. Even the most pious man imagines that once or twice."

Her pulse raced, her heartbeat quickening in a race to overtake her breath. Heat warmed her face at his audacious statement. "Did you wonder about it once or twice, Mr. McKinnon?"

"Oh, I imagined it more than twice. And I'm imagining it

now."

Mary Jane wondered, with painful clarity, how it would feel to learn someone precious had been torn from her arms. What would it feel to be loved as fiercely as this man had cherished his Irish Maureen?

He chuckled, and his throaty laugh echoed with deliciousness in her belly and lower. Rasped over her senses like a warm blanket on the coldest night. Inside her the wanting started again, a thrilling, aching call to sin.

She longed with her heart to know a man's love this profoundly. "I'm so sorry."

"Don't be sorry. It happened and it can't be taken back."

Despite the horror of what he told her, she wanted more than ever to give him solace, to mend yet a meager portion of what the prison experience had done to him. She curled her body closer around his, until her femininity pressed into him, her breasts touching his back. She reached down and clasped the base of his manhood.

He jerked in surprise and curled his hand over hers, holding her fingers over his smooth heat. His breath sluiced in and out. She closed her eyes and felt his power pulse beneath her fingers. "Elijah, tell me what to do to help you forget."

Elijah's fingers tightened around hers. Wordlessly, he gave Mary Jane an answer.

His hand moved hers up and down in a slow rhythm. Up. Down. Up. Slowly down. After he released her, she continued the movement, soap lathered in her hand aiding the motion. His thickness swelled beneath her ministrations, the power and mystery of his pleasure revealed to her one exhilarating minute at a time. Emboldened by her desire to wipe bad memories from his mind, she increased the pace.

Elijah's breath hissed through his teeth, and his head went back as he shook in her grip. Her other hand braced on his chest, and she felt his breathing come faster as she increased the pumping motion. She sensed there was more she could do to bring him additional pleasure, but he did not demand more. Caught in his obvious pleasure, she kissed his back and caressed his stomach. White-knuckled, he gripped the tub and a moan left his throat. His hips moved with her motions.

"Mary Jane," he managed to gasp.

How long she pleasured him, she couldn't say, but his body told her how much he loved what she did. His head went back again as he stiffened all over and groans strangled in his throat. His manhood throbbed in her hand as his hips jerked and twitched. Something hot and wet spurted over her hand again and again.

He trembled and shook, each panting breath declaring his pleasure. "Oh God, darlin'."

Chapter Fourteen

Amos stared at the snapping, dancing campfire and a curse burst from his throat. "Damn it. Where is that flea bitten, no-account brother of mine?"

Varney took a huge bite out of his jerky and chewed. "Keep your voice down. It's enough to wake snakes."

Amos sneered, his petulance well earned. He glared at Varney and his habit of smacking his food. Amos suspected Varney did it to spite him. Varney's cold eyes never wavered as Amos settled firmly onto the blanket that would serve as his bed tonight, and the saddle nearby his pillow.

Rather than argue the tone of his voice, Amos chewed his own jerky and wished he'd never agreed to pay Varney to track down Elijah. The man was a damned nuisance.

Behind Amos a horse snorted. Wind danced in the trees as fog drifted nearby the warming circle created by fire. Last thing he wanted was to admit to this idiot in front of him that Elijah had bested him. Elijah never had the upper hand once in his life, and by damned, Amos wouldn't let him start now.

"I never should've let you do it this way." Amos took a swig of the most disgusting coffee he'd every tasted.

"You?" Varney threw another sneer Amos's way. "You think you got power over me?"

"Your good-for-nothing men didn't do the job!" Amos's temper flared. "They got themselves killed!"

"Land sakes, McKinnon. What bug flew up your ass?"

Varney laughed softly, but the rusty sound edged with cruelty. "You paid me and I'll earn the rest of my money one way or the other. Hoops and Claypool didn't mean nothin' to me. So your brother and his bitch killed 'em. So be it. Elijah is somewhere in these here hills, and we'll find 'em."

Firelight played over Varney's angular, devilish features. He pulled a flask out of his pack and unscrewed the top.

Amos cleared his throat. "Don't get all corned."

Varney took a swig. "I ain't been corned in a coon's age, McKinnon. Don't you worry none." After a long time, Varney continued. "It ain't time to hang up one's fiddle, McKinnon. We'll find your brother. And when we do, we'll kill him and the bitch."

"I'll do the killing. And the woman is also mine. I'll decide what to do with her."

Varney snorted. "Yeah, I'll just bet. What you gonna do? Carve her up? Rape her?" Varney laughed, clearly enjoying the thought. "Amos, you're as savage as a meat axe."

Somewhere in the night, a coyote or maybe a wolf howled. Unfamiliar with all the creatures in the mountains, Amos felt a strange exhilaration increase his bravado. Living in the city had softened him, but now he yearned for wildness. He'd make this situation work one way or the other. He wouldn't stop until Elijah's eyes were stone cold dead.

Varney spit and it flew to the left. "Well, your brother ain't no dummy that I can see. After five years of having his brain marinated in the penitentiary, I would've thought he couldn't think his way outta a sack."

Amos pitched the remainder of the coffee and put the cup by the fire. "I reckon he learned something Quaker on the Sabbath. Maybe he has more religion than I gave him credit for."

"That should make you hate him more, don't it? Bein' more Catholic and all. Tell me there, McKinnon. What made you hate papists when you was born one?"

Varney's question threw Amos. "I told you that already. Besides, Fenwick is my boss, and he pays me to hate them. That's all it is."

Sarcasm in Amos's tone wasn't apparently lost on Varney. "Pay for hate. I like it."

Amos didn't like how long it was taking to find Elijah. After all, the fog might stay for a long time, as he'd heard it sometimes did in these parts. Not long after Varney had helped him blow the tracks, they'd discovered the passengers on the train were plain scared. They didn't resist further robbery. One man on the train was bleeding like a stuck pig—shot by either Hoop or Claypool. Didn't look like he'd make it. Amos had almost taken the one old battle axe on one carriage and had some fun with her. That would have been tasty, but he decided it would take too much time from his main goal—finding his brother.

Amos and Varney figured they'd find Hoops and Claypool easily. What he didn't expect was to locate their bodies and no sign of their quarry.

"Sakes alive, McKinnon, I told you I could do this with Hoop and Claypool."

"Yeah, well, you didn't, did you? Hoop was a sorry puke and Claypool an idiot." His anger made his accent thicken. "Sure, and they got themselves killed, didn't they? That woman must have cracked Hoop in the head with that rock. He sure as hell didn't fall on it by accident."

Varney chewed the rest of his jerky, tossed back the rancid coffee as if it tasted like fine champagne, and then spit into the fire. "What the tarnation are you worked up about? We'll find him."

"If we don't, you'll be as poor as Job's turkey."

Varney frowned and leaned back on his hands. "That so?"

"That's so."

Varney's eyes glittered in the campfire. As bad eggs went, Varney was the worst, and he'd hired him for evil. Yet Amos couldn't trust anyone, least of all a man like this.

Varney sighed. "Well, you're the biggest toad in the puddle."

Amos took a deep breath. "You know that ole bitch in the cabin?"

"Yeah?"

"Well, come morning we'll visit her again. I got a feeling she'd hide those two," Amos said.

"We're miles from there."

Amos snickered. "Not that far. Yeah, we'll visit her again."

Elijah stilled, his hands gripping the sides of the tub, his body still quaking from the spine-melting orgasm. His senses seemed heightened. He could see and hear all around him with painful clarity. Wind rattled the single window, and an owl hooted in the darkness. The fire crackled. His breath rasped in his throat.

He opened his eyes and hung his head. His body started to soften, muscles releasing tension. And Mary Jane's lovely, small hand still gripped his penis, his essence covering her thumb and index finger. An almost animal instinct demanded he snatch her up and sit her down on his hard manhood. He wanted to come again, spurt his seed into her womb with a primitive drive almost frightening in its intensity. He gritted his teeth and forced that idea right out of his head. It wouldn't do. He couldn't, no matter how much he wanted to sink inside her, take her after what she'd told him.

But not because she was no longer a virgin.

No, he wanted to tear apart that Thaddeus what's-his-face for taking a treasure that should have been reserved for a better man. A man she could honestly love. Her husband.

Tears dried on his cheeks, for even as she'd caressed him and arousal had fogged his brain, he'd cried under her sweet attention. A woman had never given him so much. Maureen's love had been innocent, a gift. Mary Jane's affection twisted his insides as she forced him to reckon with his past. He didn't know how he felt, other than drained and aching with awareness. He wanted nothing more than to lift Mary Jane from this tub, dry off, and lay her on the coverlet. He would lick remaining droplets off her pretty skin and devour the beautiful body she hid during the day under layers of mourning.

"Darlin', that was..." He trembled, emotion catching in his throat.

She released him. When she spoke, her breathless voice, full of awe, comforted his soul. "It was amazing, Elijah. Such power. Such amazing power in your body."

He stood and water sluiced off his skin. He turned to face her, and Mary Jane's eyes reflected uncertainty, and to his surprise, fear.

Her gaze flicked to his penis, then she blushed. "You are still...um..."

"It's like that sometimes after a man spends his seed."

Stepping out of the tub, he grabbed a towel from the stand and secured it around his waist.

"How long does it stay like that?"

Her innocent question made him smile. "For a bit."

"Oh. Thaddeus was...well, he was nothing like you."

Oh, indeed. Any more questions of the same ilk, and he'd have to explain more than he wanted. No, couldn't explain it. He'd want to *show* her.

He held out his hand. "Come. It's time we got some shut eye."

Trepidation retreated from her eyes, and calmness replaced it. She placed her hand in his. Once she stepped out, she dried vigorously, shivering with cold. Knowing she feared more intimacy, he dried himself and returned the towel to his waist. He sat on the bed. On occasion she'd look up at Elijah and catch him staring. He couldn't help it. Nothing would please him more than to touch her round, full breasts again, her nipped-in waist and rounded hips. She wasn't a skinny woman, but neither did she hold excessive weight. Her delicate bone structure reminded Elijah of a fragile and sacred pagan goddess. A mystery from Ireland's past, when gods and goddesses ruled the earth. When she'd wrapped her fingers around him and stroked, offering mind-bending release, it had taken everything he had not to love her.

Swift panic rose inside him. Love her with his body, that is.

He couldn't afford a deeper emotion beyond affection. Beyond delivering her to Pittsburgh and safety. Anything more he refused to permit.

Elijah stood, resolve renewed. "We need to dress in those clothes Mrs. Connor gave us."

She used the towel to blot water from her hair. "Why?"

"Because we have to be ready to leave at a moment's notice."

She nodded and sighed with obvious regret. She reached for the chemise and pantelettes. "It feels wonderful to put on clean clothes."

Gratified that she didn't quiz him about what happened between them, he started to dress. The pants fit too loose at the waist—Mr. Connor had obviously weighed more in this area. Elijah tightened them with a belt and stuffed his feet into clean socks, then shoved on his boots.

He was buttoning the shirt when she said, "That shirt is almost too small for you. It strains across the shoulders."

"It'll do. Might be too big around the middle, but there's no help for it."

He wrinkled his nose as he looked at his waistcoat drying over a chair. It smelled, but there was no helping that, either.

She slipped into the threadbare gray dress. "Bother. This is too snug across the bosom."

Elijah's lips twitched, but he stifled a laugh. "I like it. I won't complain."

Her gaze flicked to his, and clear understanding lit her eyes. "Why, sir, I think you enjoy seeing my breasts unbound."

"I like them bound or unbound."

She made a *tsking* sound. "Well, the dress is barely long enough." Mary Jane walked across the room with her hands on her waist. "Men shall see my ankles." She shrugged. "I suppose with my boots on it will not be so awful."

Truth be told, he didn't like the idea other men would see her nipples pressing against that bodice or her ankles revealed. Watching Mary Jane finish dressing made his stomach clench and his body hardened again. He breathed deep and remembered they shouldn't feel too safe.

When she required buttoning, he assisted. "Come, let's sleep. We're off early in the morning."

He extinguished the lamp. They lay on top of the quilt, and his body curled around hers like a spoon.

With one of her whispery, erotic sighs, she said, "Elijah, you are poking me."

Several seconds passed before he understood her meaning. "Sorry, darlin'. Holding you does that to me."

"Tonight was wonderful." Her voice held sleepy sensuality. She clasped his arms and held tight. "I will never forget it. I regret one thing, though."

"What's that?"

"I made you sad. That is the last thing I ever want to do."

Awash with confusion, he answered her the only way he could. "I'm not sad."

"You were when we discussed the prison. I felt it in your body. In your voice. The pain is still inside you."

She was right, damn her sweet hide. "I'll allow that. I'm fine now. Go to sleep." After a short time, he realized he had a question. "Darlin', did your family blame you for what happened with that professor?"

Her voice held infinite sadness when she said, "Yes.

216

Especially father. He...he said that I would likely never marry because I was wicked and sinful, and my mother said she was ashamed. You see, they think I disgraced the entire family."

"That's shite."

"Is it?"

"Absolutely. If you were any more...what did you call it? Deported, you would have a stiffer corset than you already do."

She did laugh, then...a giggle of pure delight. "Deportment. Deported is not the right word, sir. But no matter. I cannot undo what happened."

"No, you can't. But get it right out of your pretty head that you're sinful and wicked. You're..." His throat felt tight, the ache building inside him as he spoke the truth. "You're a beautiful woman that deserves a man to love her. Any man with a lick of sense would see that."

She squeezed his forearm. "Thank you, Elijah. That is very sweet."

He snorted. "It isn't sweet. It's the truth."

She laughed softly. "Then thank you again. You arc an extraordinary man."

Elijah's gut tightened as her revealing words filled him. She'd told him an important piece of information. One he wasn't sure he wanted to know. Mary Jane must trust him, and that she thought him extraordinary...no one had ever called him that.

She'd allowed him to take a bath with her, to touch her intimately. To stroke his cock until pleasure had sent white-hot streams of ecstasy from his body.

Satisfaction and something close to deep affection coiled around him like the warmest blanket.

No.

He couldn't allow her feelings to deepen, or his. It simply wouldn't work.

Elijah had the important business of revenge to complete.

Her breathing deepened. She'd fallen asleep, apparently feeling safe even when she shouldn't. For she wasn't safe from his brother and accomplices, and she wasn't safe from him. From this moment on, he would make sure no further lovemaking passed between them. A man like him, with a dubious past, could never have a woman like her. She'd play his wife for the rest of this trip, but that's where it ended.

Resolved that he'd done the right thing in not taking their lovemaking to the next level, he fell into a restless sleep.

"I'm afeared your husband is right bothered." Mrs. Connor placed another biscuit on Mary Jane's plate and assessed her with worried eyes. "If I had my druthers, I'd say you two had a fight last night."

Mary Jane slathered jam on the biscuit and bit into it with relish. Her hunger seemed unusually healthy this morning. "Oh, believe me, Mrs. Connor, we did not argue."

Mrs. Connor's face split into a big grin. "While I can't say it's fittin' to admit, I did hear somethin' and wasn't sure I heard what I did."

Heat blossomed in Mary Jane's face and inflamed her body. She finished chewing. "I am so sorry, Mrs. Connor."

What could she say?

"Don't worry none, girl. You'll get no wrath from me. After all, you're married."

Mary Jane dipped her head in agreement, but the lie burned in her gut like poison. She did not care for the charade, but what choice did she have? Lying to the woman felt somehow unclean, after all Mrs. Connor had done for them.

"Mrs. Connor?" Mary Jane stood and walked towards the older woman. "Thank you for everything you've done for us. I cannot thank you enough."

Then, totally on impulse, Mary Jane hugged the woman.

At first the smaller lady remained stiff in Mary Jane's arms, and Mary Jane wondered if she'd crossed a line. Then the woman wrapped her arms about Mary Jane and patted her back. "There, there now, girl. Don't get all blamed sentimental or you'll give me a powerful need to tear up, and I don't cotton to that."

Mary Jane laughed and restrained tears. She heaved a deep breath and moved out of the woman's embrace. Before she could speak, the door opened and Elijah entered.

His gaze took them in. "Time to go."

His voice sounded clipped and sharp, and Mary Jane acknowledged Mrs. Connor had detected his cool mood. When Mary Jane awakened this morning, he seemed less affectionate and more detached. Immediately she'd recalled her mother and father's admonishments. Besides fornication being ordained only under marriage, this was why a woman kept her physical affections and virginity until she married. A man never wanted a woman if he already possessed her virginity...what mattered. And other men did not want used goods.

No matter that Elijah had been kinder to her than any man she had known, he had one thing on his mind, and she knew he would not be deterred.

Revenge against Amos.

She should be repulsed by the thought of Elijah wanting to kill anyone. She did not know what she thought of it anymore.

Mary Jane did not wish to test his mood, so she gathered her paltry belongings from the bedroom. She returned with her reticule and an old, rather floppy hat on her head.

Mrs. Connor handed her a wrapped package of jerky and biscuits. "You take this now. You'll be needin' it."

"Thank you for your generosity." Mary Jane smiled. "How can we ever repay you?"

"No need to repay me, young lady."

Mary Jane hugged her again.

Elijah kissed the lady's hand like a gallant. "Thank you for use of your mare, Mrs. Connor. We'll have her returned to you in good condition."

"Matilda is an old lady like me, but she'll get you there." Mrs. Connor waved one hand. "Now get out of here. Daylight is breaking higher. Wait. There's an extra rifle in the small shed out back. I'll get it for you."

The old woman left by the back door.

A short time later, a loud report outside split the air.

Mary Jane's pulse quickened. "What was that?"

"Gunfire. Sounded like it came from the shed." Elijah retrieved the pistol from inside his waistcoat. "Wait here."

His command kept her stock still, heart racing as he left by the back door.

Before she could move, the front door burst open and a man as tall, dark-haired and handsome as Elijah forced his way into the room. A short cry of fear and surprise left her throat. A long, deadly looking rifle pointed right at her. Fear sent icy tentacles marching up and down her back and paralyzed her throat. She wanted to scream for Elijah, but a new fear interrupted that thought. What if Elijah returned to the cabin? He would die in seconds.

She could not bear it.

Whatever happened to her, she could not allow Elijah to be harmed.

"Hello there, girl." The man's voice held a hint of Ireland, and she knew in a flash his identity. "Scream and I'll kill you right here."

Amos McKinnon.

His icy green eyes, so much like Elijah's, taunted her. Yet there was something vital missing from this man's gaze. His grin held satisfaction, as if he had consumed a bellyful of the most gratifying meal. His hair was clipped shorter than Elijah's and neater, his nose a little bigger and jaw a tad wider. His clothes were certainly finer. Yet the coldness in his eyes belied any hope that Amos possessed the capacity for morality and caring like his brother.

Before she could react, he grabbed her around the waist and dragged her towards the door. She twisted in his grip. "Let me go. Let me go."

She stomped on his foot but caught the edge of his boot. He grunted but did not release her.

"Bitch!" He cracked her across the face with his hand. "I'll teach you to disobey me."

Pain lashed through her skin and reverberated in her skull. Pinpoints of light danced before her eyes. He pulled her relentlessly through the door and down the steps. Four horses stood beside Mrs. Connor's old mare Matilda. Head still reeling, she stumbled and almost fell.

She heard another sharp report, then another and another from behind the cabin and near the barn. *Oh God. God, please protect Elijah. Please.* Tears filled her eyes. She shook them off. She couldn't afford to be weak. Not now.

The man dragged her towards one horse. "Get on."

She stalled, glaring at him. "Damn you! Damn it all, let me go. How could you do this? How could you?"

He released her long enough to stick the business end of the rifle against her stomach. "Get on or I pull the trigger."

White-hot fear replaced defiance. Her breath came in spurts, chest heaving as she tried to calm. She did as he commanded, swinging into the saddle with ease.

"Well, aren't you a little horsewoman? I wouldn't have figured Elijah's whore to know how to ride a horse."

Hate surged inside her, a harrowing emotion she had never experienced before. With difficulty, she held back a retort.

Another man ran around the side of the house, his left side bloodied. He stumbled and almost fell. He motioned with one hand, the other clutching his rifle. "Go, go!"

Amos glared at the other man. "What the hell—"

"I done killed them both! Leastwise I'm pretty damned sure." The wounded man swung onto his horse, a grimace marring his already ugly countenance. He snatched one packhorse's reins. "Heyahhhhh!" He used the long reins and his spurs to urge his horse into flight.

"Feckin' hell," her captor snarled the words as he swung up behind her and urged their horse into movement. He wrapped one arm around Mary Jane, practically bruising her ribcage. "Get up, you feckin' horse!"

He grabbed the reins of the other packhorse.

As the animals carried her and the two men into the woods with reckless swiftness, she dared speak. "You are Amos."

He laughed, and the wicked sound sent chills over her. "That I am." He directed his question to the man on the other horse. "You stupid bastard, I told you not to kill anyone until I gave the word."

The wounded man tossed them a wild-eyed glance, as if he'd lived in the woods for a century. He threw a big grin her way, eyes twinkling with a hideous amusement she could only guess at. "That old bitch was too good a shooter. Had to defend myself."

Grief and horror gripped Mary Jane, twisting in her stomach until sweat broke out on her skin and choked her with its strength. Nausea boiled in her stomach, and she pressed one hand to her mouth.

Elijah. God, not Elijah.

Oh, Elijah.

"You goddamned arse." Amos's words fired at the other man. "I told you to hold them for me, not kill them. My brother was for me to kill."

Tears poured down her face. The hurt inside stabbed like a crippling lance, as hot as a poker thrust into her heart.

She vowed she would kill these men herself. She did not care what happened to her after that.

With her heart shattering into a thousand pieces, she finally understood Elijah's need for vengeance.

Chapter Fifteen

Elijah awakened to a throbbing on the right side of his head that stung like all Billy Hell. He touched his forehead and groaned. Disoriented, he opened his eyes and blinked into the bright sun. That hurt worse, and he covered his eyes with his hand. His fingers came away bloody. Slowly and painfully, he rolled to his left side and tried to remember what had happened. Was he drunk? No. He'd only been drunk one time in his life and vowed never to do it again.

He lay still and breathed deeply, riding through the ache in his skull and inability to recall a bloody thing beyond his own name. Wind rustled trees and birds sang happy songs. Too bad he couldn't feel as jolly about the situation. He registered that a small shed lay not far away to his north and a watering trough south at his feet.

Watering trough. He'd flipped backwards over it when—

Seconds later he cursed as memories slammed into him. "Damned son-of-a-bitch, feckarse!"

Swiftly he sat up and moaned as his head protested the movement. He squinted against the pain and took several deep breaths. *Amos and Varney. Damned Varney was in on this.* Like lightning the memories flashed in his head. He'd made it out the back door and found Mrs. Connor lying on the ground, blood spreading out over her left side. Before he could get off more than one shot at Varney, the prison jailer had shot him. He'd fallen straight over the trough because he'd been standing in front of it before Varney fired. The bullet must have grazed the right side of his skull. He reached for his weapon, which lay not far from his left side.

Struggling to his feet, he staggered around the trough and saw Mrs. Connor where he'd left her. "Mrs. Connor?"

He fell to his knees next to her, checked her pulse and found her breathing. Thank God. Through his scrambled thoughts, he remembered Mary Jane and terror gripped Elijah with cruel jaws.

Oh, Jesus, Mary and Joseph.

Mary Jane.

He pushed past the pain and ran towards the back of the cabin, pistol set to fire. Half suspecting he'd encounter Amos and Varney in the house, he didn't yell her name. He looked in the back windows. No sign of them in the bedrooms. He crept around the left side of the cabin. Step by step he checked the windows at the front, then came to the open front door. Elijah stepped in with his gun raised but saw no sign of Mary Jane or the culprits. Fear wrapped icy fingers around his throat, and he ran out the back door to tend Mrs. Connor. By this time, she'd come to her senses.

When he ran towards Mrs. Connor, she sat up, clasped her left side and cursed louder than he had. "That cussed, flea-bitten, son-of-a-cur. He shot me."

He dropped onto his knees beside her. "Got me in the head."

Grimacing with pain, the old woman kept pressure on her wound. "You're bleeding like a stuck pig, boy. We gotta get that taken care."

"No time. They have Mary Jane." Nausea curled in his stomach. "I don't know how long we've been out. They could be miles away."

Without asking for permission, he lifted the woman in his arms and headed for the back door.

She wriggled. "Land sakes, boy, put me down. I can walk."

He ignored her. Once inside the cabin, he placed her on a couch and rushed to round up clean bandages. She fussed that his head was still bleeding, but it slowed to a trickle.

She snatched the white cloths from his hands. "I can wrap this. It isn't that bad. Damn bullet ricocheted off that trough. If it had hit me direct I'd probably be dead. That bastard your brother?"

"Tobias Varney, one of the jailers I mentioned to you. My brother is with him."

Elijah ripped the side of her dress. "You're right. This isn't too bad."

He started wrapping.

"Damn it all to hell, I passed out from the pain. That's a bruise to my pride, I don't mind telling you. When my little finger got crushed—" she held up her right hand and the deformed finger, "—that should have hurt like blazes and made me pass out. But it didn't." Once he'd finished her side, she gestured at his bloodied head. "Slow down, boy. We've got to clean this out. *Slow down.*"

"I cannot. They have my Mary Jane." Fear slammed him like another rifle shot. He sank down on the couch next to her. "Every minute longer she gets another mile father away from me. I have to find her *now.*"

The old woman's gnarly hand pressed over his fingers where the blood dried. "I understand. But tarnation, if you get a fever you won't be able to help Mary Jane or yourself. Get that waistcoat and shirt off while I find another one for you. Go rinse your head under the pump outside and get all that blood outta your hair and off your neck."

Wanting to curse the heavens, he worked quickly to remove the waistcoat and shirt. His trousers had blood on them, but he didn't care. Once outside, he made haste to the pump and splashed icy water over his head. He gasped as cold and pain pierced him, but by the time he finished, he felt more clear-headed and the nausea roiling in his stomach disappeared. He hurried back into the house and found Mrs. Connor sitting on the couch with poultice and bandages.

"Here, young man. There's the new shirt. Don't have a waistcoat for you, but there's a big coat that used to belong to my husband. It'll take care of you in bad weather."

Realizing it would be foolhardy to leave without her dressing his wound, Elijah settled on the couch. Working fast, she applied the smelly poultice to the side of his head and assured him the smell meant it worked mighty fine. "Old Allegheny recipe. Keeps infection away. Leave it as long as you can. We'll pack more poultice and bandages for you."

After she finished tending to his wound, he asked, "What about you?"

"I can wash it later, and it's already stopped bleeding. Right now we need to get you on your way and find your wife." She stalked to one corner and picked up her rifle. "Here, you take this."

"What about your protection?"

"Don't you worry none. There's more where that came from stored in a space below the floorboards of this cabin."

While he donned another shirt and threw on her husband's big, brown leather coat, she collected more bandages and poultices. In record time, he jumped into the saddle of her old mare, saddlebags packed with fresh ammunition, a rifle, more food, water and Mrs. Connor's blessing.

She stood nearby, her eyes glistening with pain, tears, or maybe both. "God speed, Elijah. You come on back now, you hear?" Mrs. Connor's voice cracked. "You both come on back someday so I know you made it all right."

He nodded, his throat tight with a grief that surpassed what he'd felt when he found Maureen lying in her own blood. He once thought he understood pain and sorrow and desperation, but this ran far deeper.

Voice hoarse with emotion, he managed to grind out a few words. "I will, Mrs. Connor."

To see Mary Jane again, to have her in his arms again was worth any sacrifice. Any cost.

"I'll bring her back." His voice sounded worn to his own ears. "I'll bring her back or die trying."

As he rode away, desperation threatened to swallow him in fear. What if he couldn't find her? What if she was already dead? Dread twisted his stomach and nausea threatened to double him up. He pressed one hand to his midsection and prayed for strength, for whatever it would take to see this through. He wouldn't fail Mary Jane. Once before he'd made a vow based on a pure hate and need for revenge.

Now he vowed to find Amos based on another emotion he thought he would never feel again.

Love.

If he could hold Mary Jane in his arms once more, he could live with anything that might happen next.

In less time than he imagined, he rode into the forest as if the devil chased him out of hell.

Mary Jane sucked in a pained breath as Amos McKinnon kept one powerful arm around her waist. They had ridden for several miles, though she had no idea where they headed. She could not think, her mind and heart consumed by a grief so profound she wished she could die.

Elijah is dead, and the sun will never shine for me again.

If she must kill Amos to escape, to show him one bit of the pain he caused Elijah, she would do it. Such a thought a few days ago would have horrified her.

No more.

"You shouldn't have taken the wench." Varney's voice was choked with his anger and perhaps physical pain. "She's dead weight. You should've killed her."

She stiffened. Amos tightened his grip around her waist again, and it hurt. At this rate he would break her ribs.

"She's mine to do with what I want," Amos said. "I had his other woman, and I aim to do the same with this one."

Mary Ann shuddered with revulsion. She knew Amos felt her reaction. He aimed to have her? Pure horror threatened to overtake her anger, but she clung to her rage.

"Oh, yeah. You have a powerful hunger you ain't filled in a while, eh?" Varney asked.

Amos said nothing, though she could almost hear his mind running through appalling possibilities.

She glanced over at the man Amos called Varney—the bastard overseer at Eastern State Penitentiary. Varney's weather worn face blanched, and he grimaced. Crimson soaked clean through his coat. As far as evil men went—or what she assumed evil men must look like—he seemed almost too ordinary. She tried to keep her gaze away from him, half convinced if she refused to acknowledge him, he could not exist.

Amos, now, he was another danger all together. He drew a profound picture in her mind of depravity. Now that she had seen him, she understood that he was not a mere caricature but the man who ruined hopes and dreams for Elijah.

Elijah would never have the chance to fulfill those dreams because of his brother. For that alone she wanted to kill Amos.

"What's a matter with you, little girl?" Amos's voice, a deep, uncannily rich tone, sounded too beautiful to belong to a killer.

How many women had he seduced with that voice? How many lies had he told?

He leaned forward and whispered in her ear. "You're too quiet, missy. What's your name?"

"Mary Jane Mc—" She gulped. "Lawson."

"What did you almost say?" Amos asked.

"I do not know what you mean."

"You almost said a different name."

"My last name is Lawson."

"You married?"

"No."

"Why do you wear a ring on your left hand, then? Trying to keep men away? Well, it won't do you any good. Because we found you."

He laughed, and if Mary Jane closed her eyes she could almost hear Elijah's laugh overlying Amos's. Oh, what she wouldn't give for Elijah to hold her again, to laugh until the sound echoed through the forest.

She decided silence would work far better than arguing with a lunatic.

Varney coughed violently, and when she glanced over, she saw the blood staining his chin. He wiped his mouth on his sleeve.

"We gotta stop soon." Varney's voice turned raspy, harder to hear. "I gotta wrap this wound."

"You stop if you want. We're going as far as we can tonight. Catch up when you can," Amos's cold voice said.

Varney coughed again. "We stop here, or I shoot you and leave you for dead."

Amos's pulled back on the reins, and she looked over at Varney's rifle pointed straight at them. Alarm stiffened her spine. Varney's eyes went glassy, and before he could make good on the threat, he tumbled from his saddle and fell on his side. He lay still. Amos stared at the fallen man.

Part of her not yet lost to hatred almost insisted they help the man. Before she could speak, Amos left the horse. For an instant she considered riding off. Instinct warned her not to try. He would either shoot her or catch her. She must concoct a plan to make him feel confident that he could trust her. Her stomach roiled. She knew he planned rape at the very least. What could she do to prevent it? Would such a fate prove worse than death?

She thought of Elijah and wished they had consummated their relationship. She would have that small peace to hold close to her heart. *Oh, Elijah.*

Amos leaned over Varney and checked his pulse in his neck. A dark smile crossed his face. His gaze flicked upward to her. "Get off the horse."

Her stomach dropped. "Why?"

"Don't question me. Get off the horse." She eased from the horse's back, and he gestured for her to come forward. "You'll ride his horse from now on."

"He's dead?"

"As a train rail, honey."

He grunted as he searched through the man's pockets, retrieved a pistol and money. A large wad of money. Amos grabbed the man's rifle from the saddle and anchored it to his own saddle. "He won't be needing this anymore."

She waited, unwilling to make any move he might consider threatening. Eventually he looked up, his icy glare sending new chills through her heart. "What you waiting for? Get on the horse."

She struggled to mount the smaller mare. At least she would not suffer Amos's touch riding this horse. Once seated, she trained her gaze away from Amos and the dead man.

Amos's grin held condescension. "Damn, but you're a pretty girl. I can see why my brother wanted you. Did he break you in for me?"

She refused to answer.

He laughed. "Well, I'll find out, won't I?"

Not if I can stop you. Once more her stomach pitched, and for a few seconds nausea threatened.

"I know a place we can stop for the night, girl. We'll camp there. It's real cozy." He remounted his horse and rode over to her. He grabbed the reins and led the way. "You try and run from me, girl, and you'll regret it."

She had no doubt he spoke the truth.

Time crawled as they rode onward and the sun settled lower in the sky. From what she could tell, they progressed west. How far were they away from Portage or other civilization? Though at first her mind reeled from all that happened, Mary Jane clung to the emotions she recognized. Without fury, grief would have made her pliant. A plan formed in her mind, and nothing would stop her from executing it.

What happened to her after that, she simply did not care.

Mary Jane jerked to awareness as her horse whinnied. Fear bit into her with talon-like sharpness. She could not believe she had fallen asleep. Trees threw intimidating shadows over the ground as Amos stopped the horses. Nothing around her looked comforting. Civilization seemed far away, and they had ridden for what seemed hours.

Amos dismounted. "We camp here."

Her body ached as she swung down from her animal and tried not to tangle in her skirts. Her left leg gave way, and she tumbled on her butt to the ground with a surprised cry. Tears filled her eyes. *I hate this. I hate him.* Struggling for control, she stood. No matter what happened now, she could not falter.

Amos's hands came under her armpits and hauled her upward unceremoniously. She forced a laugh to her lips and leaned against him, pressing her breasts against his chest. His arm came around her for a moment, then he shoved her away.

Disgust filled his face. "Get to work unsaddling that horse."

Surprised, she assessed him. Perhaps conversation would change his mood. As she did as she was told, Mary Jane asked, "May I ask a question?"

He grunted. "You can ask. Don't mean I'll answer."

"Where are we?"

"You don't need to know."

She abandoned questions while she worked. It took her considerable time to undo the saddle, and she tore a fingernail in the process.

"Damn it woman, what's taking you so long?" He pushed

her away. "If you can't do this right maybe you can cook. That pack has beans and utensils. Get to work making a fire."

"I do not... I do not know how to make a fire."

Amos swung around and glared. "Figured as much. You a city woman?"

"I live in Pittsburgh."

A slow grin didn't improve his looks. Though any woman would acknowledge his attractiveness, and his resemblance to Elijah proved disturbing, his soul made him repulsive beyond repair. "Guess I'll have to do that much for you. You cook?"

As she'd revealed to Mrs. Connor, she did not, but she could lie. "Yes."

"Good. At least you're of some use. Gather kindling, and don't think you can run off into the woods. You do and you die."

She knew he meant it. After all, what could she do in the forest without supplies or any idea of which direction to run? Dependence on Amos made her angry, but she had no choice.

He set to making a fire, and as he worked, her mind raced despite exhaustion.

"Someone will see the fire, will they not?" she asked.

His head jerked up. "Someone?"

"Well, yes. I assume someone from the train will look for me. Especially after..." She swallowed hard around the grief threatening to tighten her throat. "...especially after they find Elijah's body and the old woman."

Amos's laugh held genuine mirth. "Well, if that doesn't beat all. And why would you care if it were true? Don't you want someone to find you? Aren't you planning to escape?"

His question stalled her for a few seconds, but she recovered quickly. "Why would I try to escape?" She walked closer to the fire. "Elijah told me all about you. I am fascinated."

He squatted by the fire pit and watched flames dance. "Girl, I'm sure he hated my innards. Why would anything he told you make you fascinated with me?"

Though loathing threatened to derail her acting, she pressed onward with her plan. She moved nearer to the fire. Shivers racked her body as night temperatures encroached. "Because I was starting to find your brother...uninteresting. I like a man with an..." she fumbled for words, "...edge of violence."

"You're quite the adventuress?"

"Yes."

"Don't believe you."

She crossed her arms as fear coiled in her belly for what she might have to say and do in the next few moments. "Do you think I would have acted as Elijah's wife all this time if I was not the adventurous woman? What proper woman does that?"

His eyes went as flat as the icy surface of a winter pond. "You said you weren't married. Did you marry him?"

"No. Your hired men Claypool and Hoop threatened me. Elijah offered his protection. I could only accept if we pretended to be man and wife."

"Then you lost your virtue to him? Or was it already gone when you met him?"

Her mind reeled with how to answer. She laughed and hoped she sounded convincing. "Would a virtuous woman tell you? I think not. I lost my virginity long ago."

"How old are you?"

"Twenty-two."

"And not hitched yet. I'll be. If Elijah was so Joe fired gentlemanly to you, why did you stay with him? You said you like a man with an edge."

His intelligent questions threw her. Though he was Elijah's brother, she expected a man of low comprehension. Now that she knew otherwise, she must take care.

She sat close to him, even though the action made every muscle within her stiffen in repulsion. "Elijah was in jail. That gives him all the disreputable quality he needed to attract my

234

notice. Then I realized he was not as unsavory and sinful as I had hoped."

Amos gazed into the fire. Wind blew against the flames and caused them to dance and crackle. In the distance an animal howled in horrible pain, adding a surreal ambiance. Her skin prickled as nature around her turned eerie and haunted. What sort of creature inhabited this wood that would make such a sound? What dangers lurked in the dark?

She scooted closer. "What was that?"

He glanced down at her, his eyes sparking with a strange fire in the disappearing light. "Don't get too close to me, girl. Unless you're offering something you don't mind giving."

She stayed put.

Amos returned to his work. "Probably a mountain lion attacking a deer or some such."

A kind man would have reassured her that fire would keep animals at bay, but Mary Jane knew Amos wouldn't bother and he certainly wasn't kind.

Amos fixed their entire meal of beans, jerky and coffee, even though she had told him she could cook. Odd. They ate in silence, and when her stomach growled and asked for more, she reached into the pot to ladle more beans. For a long time, her mind whirled around morbid possibilities. She could show her real feelings about this man, but then he would remain on guard. So she would stay the course with her plan and hope she did not live to regret it.

She eventually asked, "What do you plan to do with me, Amos?"

He took a sip of coffee from a tankard. "What do you think I should do with you, girl?"

"You could let me go. I will only slow you down."

"Too late for that. I let you go and you die in the wilderness. You best resign yourself to staying with me."

Despite Amos's calm, his temper must be avoided at all

costs. "Why do you hate Elijah so much?"

"Because he is who he is."

"What does that mean?"

Amos snorted. "He's always been the lily white son in the family. Damn boy took care of puppies instead of drowning them when our Da said he should. He always did what Ma told him and worked hard. Never did a thing wrong even when I tried to drag him along for the trouble. A boy like that is way too good."

Amos's odd take on Elijah did not surprise her. "You hate him because he saved dogs from drowning?"

He sneered. "There was plenty he did that I hated. I'm not going to make a list for you."

He lapsed into silence until they finished eating, then he made her clean the dishes in a creek nearby. Before long he made a bedroll of blankets for them both. He put them close, and she recoiled when contemplating what he might attempt in the night. Though Mary Jane thought she had considered every angle of her plan, when the very last rays of sun disappeared through the trees, dread stalked her. Yet she feared no animal as much as she did Amos.

Perhaps if she took this slow and acted friendly, perhaps Amos would show some vulnerability. A way she could exploit that weakness. She almost smiled. Here she sat, in many ways defenseless, and plotted this man's downfall as callously as he once plotted Elijah's demise.

Well, well. Mother would have something to say about that. She waited, but the normal mental dialogue with the specter of her aunt did not materialize. Anything that happened from this point forward, she relied on herself. Listening to an angel on her shoulder had no merit in this situation if Mary Jane planned to survive. She could almost hear Elijah's voice urging her onward. *Do whatever you must to survive, darlin'. Whatever you must.*

Inside, Elijah's death created a hollow within her weary heart. One moment she felt strong, the next weaker than a newborn. How could she do this? How could she find the right way?

Though she clutched a blanket around her, comfort diminished under the odor. The rough fabric smelled like horse and leather and sweat. She wrinkled her nose. She ached for Elijah's enveloping and comforting warmth, and the protection she had taken for granted in the short time they knew each other. She swallowed hard and fought the desire to moan with a terrible agony that refused to ebb. She forced it back and drew on reserves of strength. If she wanted to live through this, no matter how horrible things might become, she must move past the grief threatening to rip her into shreds.

Amos smiled, his mouth crooked and sarcastic. "You're one of those fine city women."

"I am from the city, yes. Like I told you."

An epiphany came to her. "Elijah said you and Zeke and your father went into the wilderness in Ireland and learned how to survive."

Amos lay on his side and angled away from her so he could lean on one elbow on his blanket. "That's right. Elijah told you the truth on that one." Amos slipped a flask from his waistcoat and after opening it, tipped a portion of liquid into steaming coffee. "Whiskey. Give me your coffee."

She wanted to refuse, but at the same time, she could not ignore his request and make progress in gaining his trust. *Trust.* She would never trust him, but he did not have to know that. If she could make him believe she would not run, would attempt no retaliation...

She handed him her tankard. After he tipped whiskey into her tankard, then a bit more, he returned her cup.

She took a healthy swallow. The liquid made her gasp and cough as the drink raced hot and fast through her body. So this was the deceitful and sinful drink that drove men mad. If she planned to dance with wild men, she would have to drink their liquor and understand them. With that logic, she felt better.

One of his dark eyebrows winged upward, the sneer of contempt on his face clear. "Good?"

She nodded. The watchful look in his eyes made her nerves jumpy. Fear battled with curiosity about this man who came from the same womb as Elijah.

"You want to know why I killed her, don't you?" His eyes glinted. "Why I took her from Elijah's arms?"

She knew the answer but asked, "Who?"

"Elijah's whore."

No. No. Do not tell me. "Maureen?"

"Yeah."

Did she want to hear this too? His twisted statements, his meandering desires? "Tell me, then."

Amos tilted his head to the side, his gaze filled with curiosity and a mean gleam. "You aren't anything like Maureen. You're darker and more exotic looking. Maybe Elijah thought if he was going to bed down with a woman he might as well pick one that looks less the angel and more of the whore."

That stung, and she snapped back, "I am not a whore, Amos McKinnon."

He chuckled. "You're a sultry piece. You simmer and burn at just the right temperature. A man knows that underneath there's substance." He smiled, but it did not add up to more than a grin of ugly satisfaction. "Maureen had red hair and freckles across her nose. She was small. You're a hearty sort. Not large, just not as breakable as her. You see, I get that about a woman. I understand women better than Elijah. I know which ones are real and which ones play with men."

"How can you tell?"

"'Cause men are basically stupid, see. Women like Maureen...she was real young and impulsive. As full of heat as her hair. She had a side Elijah didn't see. She didn't want him to know."

Mary Jane encouraged him, eager to learn more in her

search for an angle through this man's skin. "Tell me more."

He smiled. "She liked rough sex."

He waited, that smile growing bigger, as if he wanted her to soak in the information.

"She was a virgin when she met Elijah," Mary Jane said.

"That what he told you, girl? He thought she was this sweet thing with no experience under a man's cock. He was dead wrong."

She tried to keep her face even despite his crude expressions, and he continued.

"I remember the first time I had her. You see, I had her before she even met Elijah. She wasn't as white and tender as he imagined, what with her needs and wants. She liked when a man beat on her...begged for it as a matter of fact. Sick isn't it, girl? Anyway, I always thought my Da was a first rate bastard beating on all of us, but when she asked me for it and said she'd tried it once—hell, she said it made sex more exciting. I decided to try it. So I slapped her around. Maureen was right."

Mary Jane did not know what to believe, appalled and yet eager to understand the story.

He laughed softly. "Every time I hit her, no matter where I hit her, it felt...it felt good. Better than anything I did before. She screamed, but it was a good scream. A scream full of pleasure."

Horrified, Mary Jane struggled to keep the disgust out of her face. "If she was bruised surely someone would notice."

"Nah, I never hit her where anyone would see. We did it in hotels where a woman could scream and no one would ever ask a question." His eyes danced with memory, filled with a delight both stomach-turning and fascinating. "But you see, it didn't stop there. Once I found out how good it felt, I knew I wanted it again." Wicked delight left his eyes, replaced by pure anger. "It didn't stop with her, though. I had plenty of other women, some that didn't like getting hit. I didn't care. You see, I needed it then. And I hated that because Maureen made me like it. It was all her fault."

Anger blindsided Mary Jane with its ferociousness before she could temper her response. "Her fault because you hit her? I have never heard anything so absurd."

He sat up, and Mary Jane flinched. "Well, believe it. She made me want it. But I know how pristine ol' Elijah was. He didn't know any better because he was too innocent himself to know what evil shite that woman had in her heart."

Mary Jane licked her dry lips and took another swig of liquor-laced coffee. "Then what happened?"

"She turned her back on me after I broke her in for my little brother. That's when I realized no real woman would like the things I did to her. So she must be a whore. A whore who thought she could fool me." Amos got on his knees and then sat back. He pointed at his chest with his thumb. "Damned bitch thought she could make this Irishman a fool."

"Did she fool Elijah?"

He snorted. "Yep. She made him think she was the sun and moon and the bleedin' stars at night. Believed every last word. She roped his hide but Elijah isn't as holy as you think. Hate can fuel a man's revenge. I'll bet he wanted to kill me too."

She could not argue with that.

Stunned by the twisted insight coming from Amos, she soaked in the disturbing quiet.

"That does not explain why you killed her," she finally said. "If you despised her you could have left her alone."

Amos didn't twitch an eyebrow over her disgust. "I didn't start off intending to kill her. Maybe hurt her, yeah. When she came to me and asked me to take her away, I thought I might actually do it. She said didn't want to marry Elijah because living with a man who wouldn't beat her didn't appeal."

"That is the most awful thing I have heard."

"Yeah, you lily white girls always think men are swine with base natures that need taming. But you see, it isn't always that way. Sometimes women are just as base and evil as any man thought of being. That was Maureen. When she came to me outside the tavern and said she wanted to run away with me, she started to cry and said she didn't love him. That she was carrying my child and wanted to marry me. That's when I understood she would probably betray me someday if I married her instead of Elijah. She was no good." His eyes flashed as the flames from their fire started to sputter and lose height. His hands clenched into fists on his thighs, his mouth a grimace. "I knew the good book was right about this type of woman. She was a whore brought up from the dens of hell, and I couldn't let her get a hold on me. I pulled out my knife and cleansed her."

Fear shot high inside Mary Jane, an insidious monster more terrifying than nighttime tales told by parents to scare children into compliance. She wished right now that their campfire would transform into a bad dream. She would awaken in Elijah's arms, free from grief. Tears welled. The truth, if Amos told it, was as hideous as any scenario she could have imagined.

He finished his drink with one gulp. He threw the tankard down by the fire. Leftover droplets went into the flames and hissed.

Disbelief hovered under the surface. "You certainly twist things to fit your needs, Mr. McKinnon."

So much for her attempt to win his favor.

His eyes hardened even more with a darkness in their depths that made her wonder how he possibly could have been born from the same mother as Elijah.

"That I do, Miss Lawson. That I do. I'm as evil and dark as Maureen ever thought of being. Unlike some I never claim to be anything else. That's why I recognized an evil whore when I saw one." He tapped his temple. "But Elijah got off easy when he went to prison. It kept him safe from the temptations that have wrecked me. If I went to Eastern State it wouldn't fix me. It would make me more evil than I already am. No good would come of that."

"When you heard Zeke succeeded in getting Elijah pardoned...that threw your plans into chaos."

"It did. I figured Elijah would have twenty or more years in that place before he got out and started looking for me. Me...well, I'd be dead by then for sure. Satan would long since carry my soul away."

"Instead you heard Elijah intended to hunt you down."

"I did."

Reasoning in the conventional way would not work with this man, and she now understood this. "You could let me go. I will not tell the authorities what you did. All I want is to return to my family. You will never hear of me again."

"No, that won't do, girl. You'll tell the authorities because you want to see justice done for your man. I can't have that."

Mary Jane almost did not ask the question, the one where she dreaded the answer. "What do you intend to do with me?"

He smiled and the coldness she saw there made her blood freeze. "Girl, that's a problem I'll have to ponder. Best you get some sleep." Amos nodded towards the bedroll. "We have a ways to go in the morning."

Exhaustion beckoned. She settled onto the bedroll, apprehension tightening her every nerve to within inches of snapping. Eerie darkness pressed on their campsite. She drew the heavy wool blanket closer around her shoulders. Sleep would elude her this night.

He lay down on his bedroll so close to hers, his rifle crossed over his stomach. As if he could read her mind, he said, "Don't even think about trying anything, girly."

Amos's calm statement sounded more deadly than Hoop or Claypool's most descriptive threat. She lay down on the bedroll. Her heart ached, her mind racing with ideas on what she could or should do next. Mary Jane wanted to remain strong, but her heart ached for Elijah. She covered her mouth with one hand to hold back sobs as tears rained down her face.

Chapter Sixteen

Elijah saw the man lying under the tree and at first didn't recognize him. Elijah retrieved his pistol, glad for additional ammunition supplied by Mrs. Connor. Shooting Varney had used the last of his bullets. Within a short piece, Elijah stopped the mare near the man. Matted hair and beard growth hid the man's face, but Elijah identified the jailer easily. Varney.

Elijah got down from the horse and cautiously moved towards Varney's prone figure. Varney's waistcoat was covered in blood. Too much blood. Elijah kept his weapon at the ready and turned the man over.

A groan issued from the man's throat. Elijah jerked to a standing position and stepped back. Varney's eyes fluttered open, their glassy surface unfocused. His hand reached up, as if searching for comfort or forgiveness.

Elijah swallowed hard, and emotion swelled in his throat. He didn't expect this. Varney was a stone cold bugger, and yet Elijah couldn't hate the man.

Elijah didn't get any closer. "Varney, can you hear me?"

Varney's eyelids fluttered, and he turned his head to the right. He cleared his throat and his breath grew raspy. "That you, McKinnon?"

"Elijah McKinnon."

"Can't see much. Thought I was dead."

"The devil has seen fit to keep you alive."

Varney coughed, and a spasm of pain filled his face. "Must be the devil, since God won't have me."

Words left Elijah's throat without him taking a second to think. "Maybe God will have you if you tell me where Amos has taken Mary Jane."

Varney managed a half smile, his lips reddened with blood. He swallowed hard, his breath coming harder, as if he'd run a race. "Maybe God would. Look, McKinnon, I know I don't have much time. Since I don't, I'll tell you where that asshole is taking her."

Elijah wondered if it could be that easy.

"But you got to do me a favor," Varney said.

"Why should I?"

"'Cause you're a damned sight more decent a man than your brother. He's a tad crazy, he is. Plus, he left me to die. I don't owe him nothin'."

"What do you want?"

"After I tell you where he's goin' with her..." He coughed, body wracked with a long shudder from head to toe. "You got to kill me. Shoot me in the head. Send me on to my maker or the devil, whichever one will claim me. It hurts, McKinnon. It hurts like the black depths of hell."

Elijah's eyes watered, and now it was his turn to swallow hard. It wasn't as if he'd never seen anyone die or seen a dead body. But he'd never had a man like this ask for mercy. He could do what his brother had and leave Varney here to writhe in agony for however long it took.

"I could leave you for the bears or big cats," Elijah said.

"You could. But you won't."

Feck him. The bastard was right. "Where is he taking her?"

"Promise me you'll shoot me, man."

"I promise."

Varney licked his lips and grimaced, another groan leaving the man's lips. Elijah feared Varney would die before he told him what he needed to know.

Elijah drew his weapon up and held it with both hands. "Tell me, damn it, and I'll put you out of your misery."

"Like a lame horse, eh, McKinnon."

"Tell me!"

"There's another cabin up the way. Up towards that ridge beyond the trees. It's just outside of Portage. I don't know what he plans to do to her. He thinks your Irish ass is dead."

That was news to Elijah.

Varney clutched at his bloody side, his breath now coming in pants. "I didn't know if your hide was dead, but that's what I told him. He's all-fired crazier than a bug, that McKinnon. All-fired crazy. Should have known he'd be mad at me when I told him I killed you. He wanted to kill you himself."

"And you were afraid of him."

Varney didn't speak, his eyes glazing with a far away look. "I'm in this condition because of you, McKinnon. From the moment I met Amos I figured a McKinnon would be the death of me. Just not you. Now I've told you where he's taken—"

"That's not enough." Elijah's temper rose. "What's the cabin look like?"

Varney gave him a decent enough description. "Shoot me, McKinnon. Shoot me, damn it. You shot me once. You can do it again."

Elijah walked a few steps closer, his forehead itching under the bandage and his stomach cramping. His breathing accelerated.

He brought the gun to aim at Varney's head. "Close your eyes, Varney."

Elijah's hands started shaking.

He counted in his head. *One. Two. Three.*

Ready to pull the trigger.

Varney's eyes stayed blank and open, staring into the great beyond. He couldn't shoot a defenseless man in the head with the bastard staring at him. He couldn't.

Wait. Elijah lowered his weapon, his whole body trembling. Varney didn't move. Not one breath. Not one blink of an eye. He crouched down and felt for a pulse in the man's throat. Nothing. With a tentative hand, Elijah closed the man's eyes.

Elijah stood and backed away, his gaze stuck on the dead man. "Thank you Jesus or the devil."

Relief made his knees weak. Shaking inside, Elijah mounted his horse. Under the bandage his head pounded a steady drum. After taking a healthy swallow from his water canteen, he wiped his nose with his sleeve as sweat trickled down his face. Under his hat, the sun beat down.

Time to move.

He rode for what seemed forever through the fading daylight. He paused in a slight clearing, keeping his mind open to possibilities, looking for signs.

He smiled as another sign appeared near a lone tree stump. "Good girl."

He left his horse and retrieved a piece of brown material from a woman's dress. The dress Mrs. Connor had given Mary Jane. *Keep dropping those clues, darlin'.* He didn't know how she did it without alerting his brother, but Elijah was damn glad she did.

Still, the night approached, and in his gut he knew he had a long way to catch up with Amos and Mary Jane. He took his time, half afraid if he came upon them without staying quiet, he would bugger the situation. One thing he didn't like, among *all* the things he didn't like, was the fact Amos could track better than him. That's why it seemed mighty strange Amos didn't notice that Mary Jane had dropped pieces of dress along the way. Elijah gathered the material and rubbed it between his fingers.

Unless, in his lunatic way, Amos *wanted* Elijah to find him.

It would fit in the sickening game of cat and mouse they now played.

He scanned the forest and listened. Birdsong drifted through the air. Earthy scents reached his nose. Over the rustling treetops high, puffy clouds darkened the day. More rain would come and hamper his efforts. Armed with new determination, he tucked his weapon into his waistcoat and rode into the trees.

Mary Jane woke, groggy and cold. She'd huddled on her bedroll, her blankets wrapped around her securely. She sat up and suppressed a groan. Her body ached.

Amos was gone. His horse was there, his bedroll lying nearby, rumbled and empty. Also to her amazement, the fire crackled, burning steady as if someone had just stoked it into life. The aroma of coffee reached her nose. It smelled like heaven. Still, where had Amos gone? It crossed her mind, in a quick jump, that she could run now. Could jump on her horse and make for the hills. No. That direction lay death. She didn't know how to survive out here alone and didn't have enough supplies on her own to make it in the wilderness. She had no weapon in case she ran into man or beast. Mary Jane sighed. What she wouldn't have given to be a mountain man at that moment.

Her mind turned to Elijah again, as it seemed to do every five minutes or so. Heartache astonished Mary Jane with its force. She had thought her grief for her father bad enough, but this...this could not be ignored no matter how hard she tried. Sorrow thumped inside her like a drumbeat, an insidious pain she hadn't imagined before. She wondered if women who suffered from a broken heart died this way, their pain excruciating, their minds wrapped around obsessive thoughts the entire day until it became unbearable. She sucked in a breath.

She must stick with her plan to gain Amos's trust if she planned to leave this wilderness in one piece.

She closed her eyes and drifted into a fantasy world where

her diary lay open on her desk at home. She would lift her pen, dip it in ink and start writing.

Dear Diary,

Something most horrible happened yesterday. So very horrible I almost cannot write the words. Elijah's brother found us and one of his friends killed Elijah. My dear Elijah, who I loved so much, was taken from me. And poor Mrs. Connor. Such a dear woman. She was killed too. Though I knew both of them for a short time, I feel as if knowing them has altered my life forever. Despite the peril I find myself enduring, I cannot regret having met either of them.

Especially Elijah.

Many might ask how I could love a man so quickly. I do not know, only that it happened so swiftly I was defenseless against it. He was nothing like Thaddeus or my father with their airs and pretensions and desires to control what I thought and did. Elijah brought me...freedom. He was so protective, but there was also a loving heart with him. He hid his heart well, but when I saw it flare like the sun in the morning, I knew how bright he could shine. Though prison may have hardened him with a fierce desire for revenge, I cannot rebuke Elijah. For I understand what once made no sense to me—why his revenge drove him to hunt his brother. How five years of speaking little and reflecting so much compelled him to kill. How such terrible emotions could force a man's hand in such an appalling direction.

Right now I cannot bear to say how Elijah died or why. The pain is too great.

Now that he is gone, the hollow inside me yawns like a cavern. I do not know how I will ever fill it again. It is unthinkable. What lesson does this situation leave inside me? I am brittle but not broken. Amos has taken me prisoner and my fate may be, in time, a dreadful one. Not, however, if I can find a clever way to escape. I must press on, find a way to forget this crushing pain that will never leave me.

"Did you think I'd left you?"

She gasped and whirled around. Amos stood a few feet away, his rifle tucked in the crook of one arm.

"You would not leave without your horse."

He chuckled and strode past her. "You are a mighty clear thinking woman."

"A practical one."

He propped his rifle on a large boulder and reached for the coffee. He poured one tankard and then another.

"Figured you'd want some of this to wake you up this morning." He handed her one tankard. "I suppose if I was southern I could whip up some chitlins."

Disgust wrinkled her nose. "That sounds about as appealing as calf's head."

He smiled again, the resemblance to Elijah's warm grin barely a skeleton. Gooseflesh covered her arms. "Or maybe bullock's heart?"

She sipped, and when he brought out hard tack and jerky, her stomach rumbled. When Amos laughed, she ignored his amusement. She polished off the jerky and coffee before he did, surprised by ravenousness when her life hung in a balance. Maybe living on the edge of disaster had toughened her.

She stood and allowed the blanket to slip from her shoulders. She folded it. "Where do we go from here?"

"Wherever the wind blows, girly. First, we'll spend some time out here. Then in a few days we'll head to another state far away. I have a price on my head now. It'll take us a damn long time traveling, but it has to be that way."

"No, I cannot. My family is in Pittsburgh, and they will be distressed when I do not arrive. They may already know something is wrong."

He scratched his chin. "I doubt that. The train robbery was about three days ago." He rubbed the back of his neck. "Then

249

again, news might've reached Pittsburgh." He shrugged. "Hard to say."

He finished his coffee, rinsed the tankard with water, and stood. "You think I give a damn about what you or your family wants? I got a price on my head, and that means we aren't staying here. Besides, I want to get back to a city where no one cares who or what I am. Once I get to that city, I might let you go. Or I might keep you for my whore." He shrugged. He glanced at the reticule, which she kept around her wrist come rain or shine. "Give me that purse. Surprised Hoop or Claypool didn't take it from you."

"They figured they were delivering me to you. Maybe they thought you would not take kindly to them robbing me."

He tossed her a dubious look. "You mocking me? You're giving me too much credit. Remember, I don't have a soft side."

"Oh? If that is true, why am I still alive?"

"You asked me that before."

"I am just trying to understand you."

"Don't try. You won't like what you find."

"I already do not like what I see."

He leaned over, grabbed the collar of her dress and yanked her up to him with bruising force. She cried out in surprise and fear. Eyes glittering with anger, he rasped into her face, "Give me that purse."

She relented, holding the reticule out to him, reluctant and concerned. He released her. "I need money when we arrive in whatever city you plan to dump me. You would not be cruel enough to leave me without funds."

He snatched the bag and rummaged through it. "Hmm. Money. Comb. Pretty much nothing but crap."

He took the money and shoved it in his trouser pocket.

His contempt drove her anger. "What do you care if I have...crap as you call it, in my reticule?"

"I don't." He threw the bag and it landed in the dirt in front of her.

She retrieved her reticule and placed it in her lap. She wanted to curse the high heavens as fresh pain sliced her open. Determination had not left her, but it felt blunt and worn. She forced a neutral expression, devoid of fright that threatened to erupt from inside. Struggling with her emotions, she drew in a deep breath.

"Come on," he said, "pack up."

Before long they headed away from their camp. The morning had dawned pretty and cool, without threat of rain. She wondered how nature could feel this pretty and lush, the forest around them breathtaking, when her heart burned like it might erupt with pain. She hated this. Hated it with more passion. Tears surged into her eyes and fell even as she tried in vain to hold them at bay. She gave up, allowing them to trickle down her cheeks unchecked. Maybe they would cleanse the ache that never seemed to end.

"What you crying for?"

"For Elijah. For me." Her throat burned. "For what might happen next."

Despite the pain, she decided to show her vulnerability in full. After all, he would think her extraordinarily weak and broken down. She would lead him astray. She failed earlier to convince him that she desired an evil man.

What did it matter? A man like this did not care what she thought or what she wanted. Her anger amused him as much as compliance. It did not take much to allow the sobs to come. Not much at all. She bawled. Cried like a baby as the horses moved through the remaining forest towards another rustic cabin below a ridge. This one perched nearby some boulders. Smaller than Mrs. Connor's abode, it appeared newer.

"We're staying here," he said.

"But we have not gone that far."

"Doesn't matter. We are homesteading here until I say."

Anger burst from her. "We could have stayed in a cabin last

night?"

Calm as a breeze, he said, "I wanted to see what you were like out in the woods in the dark and cold. That tells a lot about a man, but it tells even more about a bitch. You know, girl, I think that you believe I'm a stupid man. Well, I am not. I saw you dropping bits and pieces of your dress here and there. Why did you do that? Who do you think is looking for you?"

Elijah saw the cabin and waited. As he crouched down along the ridge, he wondered if old timers built cabins below ridges for a reason. This scene reminded him too much of coming upon Mrs. Connor's abode. He'd followed the trail to the campfire and Mary Jane's signs. Apprehension held him immobile. He cocked the rifle and waited for the right time to approach. Night would do it, he figured. That meant he would stay on this ridge for quite a few hours. Or he could think of another way.

His thoughts wrestled with possibilities until his head ached again. He'd changed the dressing as best he could last night, then rode in the moonlight, hoping to come upon Mary Jane and Amos. What he'd do when he found them had gathered strength as he moved through the trees last evening. His plan, fully formed, promised to break when he recognized its fatal flaws.

One thing didn't falter.

His overwhelming desire to get Mary Jane back.

He needed Mary Jane, and maybe if things went his way, she would need him, too. He wanted to have another chance to show her what she meant to him. Knowing that, he'd act on the plan, imperfect or not. His gut burned thinking about what his brother might have already done to Mary Jane.

If he'd touched her...

If he'd raped her...

Damn you, Amos. I will feckin' kill you. I will feckin' kill you.

Knowing Amos the way he did, Elijah had no doubt Mary

Jane must have already suffered greatly at his brother's hands. Self reproach piled upon the fear in Elijah's heart.

I didn't keep Mary Jane safe. I've let her down.

No matter now. His brother would die one way or the other, and Elijah would have his revenge.

Hours went by under a hot sun, and storm clouds rose over the mountains and threatened towards late afternoon. He worked his way down the way he had come. He would have to find a way to the boulders nearby the cabin without Amos seeing him. He'd left his horse near a tree, out of sight.

Time crept by as Elijah worked his way to the boulders. They looked insignificant from the ridge, but they towered over him by a good twenty feet. He wormed his way between two rock formations until he spied the back of the cabin. He heard a sound that made his heart stop. A laugh. His brother's cold, dark laugh. *Damn him all to hell.*

Blood rushed through Elijah's system as his heart raced into action, his muscles tightening with the need to spring. Yep, Amos must think he was dead, otherwise he would have high-tailed it out of the area far faster.

Step by step Elijah cased the cabin. He drew alongside one of the windows in the back and when he took a swift glance, he absorbed the entire situation in a heartbeat. The situation confronting him made rage inside rush forth like a huge wave threatening a beach. It crashed in upon Elijah, and without further hesitation, he made his move.

Mary Jane twisted in the bonds that held her wrists to the bedposts. She wanted to scream, but no one would hear her. Amos sat on the edge of the bed as he finished the last knot in tie holding her left wrist to the bedpost.

"There. That ought to hold you while I hunt up some game."

She tugged on her left wrist, but it only made the material tighten. "Please, let me go. What if something happens to you out there? I will be stuck here. Defenseless and...I could die."

He nodded. "You? Defenseless? See, that's where I think you made your first mistake. Thinking that I'd believe you're defenseless. Nope. I've seen too many women like you manipulating a man. I know the signs."

She almost screamed in his face. Mary Jane hated him as much as she could hate anyone, a feeling she once believed she could never have.

In desperation she growled her next words, so incensed she wouldn't have been surprised to see flames shooting from her own mouth. "So help me God, Amos McKinnon, I am going to kill you myself."

A loud laugh burst from his throat, and he started out the front door. "I'll be back, don't you worry your pretty head."

She screamed again, this time high-pitched and filled with impotent wrath.

Amos stepped out the front door, and after a short while all sounds of his presence ceased. She struggled against the bonds, drained from her outburst, half tempted to cry again. She breathed deeply through her nose, let it out slowly, and started once more. Her heartbeat had started to cease its frantic thumping when the back door opened. She jerked in shock as she saw who stood there with a rifle at his side.

He could not be real.

He simply could not.

Shock assaulted her, and she gasped. Perhaps he was a ghost. A very roughed up, dangerous-looking ghost with a dirty face, hair sticking up everywhere, and a bandaged head. He stared at her as if she were the apparition, his lips parted and chest heaving up and down with emotion. He held a rifle in one hand.

Joy crashed in on her with crushing force. "Elijah."

He rushed towards her, placing the gun on the small bed long enough to work frantically at the restraints.

"Darlin', are you hurt?" His voice roughened with worry.

"N-no. I—you—" She choked on the words, breathless. "I thought you were dead."

"An inch to the left and I would've been. Good thing Varney wasn't a good shot and I run fast. No time to explain. We're getting out of here."

He cursed as he ran to the other bedpost and undid the tie around her wrist. Within seconds he freed her. He grabbed her hand, pulled her off the bed, and headed out the back door.

They barely made it outside when she heard footsteps come around the side of the cabin. Her heart banged, her pulse rushing in her ears as they came face to face with Amos.

Elijah's rifle came up.

Amos did the same.

With a sinking heart, Mary Jane didn't have time to feel more fear as the inevitable rolled up and seized them by the throat like a rabid dog.

Chapter Seventeen

"Well, look what we got here." Amos's voice held contempt as he snapped out his words. "It's my baby brother."

Mary Jane dared look at Elijah. His mouth thinned into a grim line, eyes piercing as he kept his attention on the other man. The air crackled with electricity, and thunder rumbled. Clouds hung low over the ridge, dark and roiling, threatening a different sort of violence.

"Let her get on a horse and ride out of here, Amos. This is between you and me."

Amos's glance darted from Elijah to Mary Jane and back. "You got her mixed up in this, baby brother. How you going to get her out?"

How, indeed? She had believed she could extract herself from the situation, had made plans, but now things turned from bad to worse. Terror threatened, ripping at her control.

"Let her go. *Now.*" Elijah's demand bit out strong and hard.

Amos shook his head. "She takes a step away, and I shoot her. Hear that girl? Run and you're dead."

"Why would you do that, Amos?" She kept her voice modulated and calm. "I will go with you, Amos. Let us leave now."

His gaze darted to hers. Held a few tension-filled seconds. "You must think I'm mighty stupid and whipped. There isn't a thing you can do or say to make me think you're stuck on me, girl. Not a thing. Wasn't more than a few minutes ago you were shrieking like a banshee at me." His voice thickened a little, his Irish heritage breaking through. "And she's a fine prize, baby brother. Varney is a horrible liar, and I knew you weren't dead."

"You knew all this time?" she asked, surprised. "But even *I* thought he was dead."

Amos's eyes stayed cadaver cold even as his mouth curved in a wide smile. "You don't know Elijah that well if you think a man shooting at him would be enough to kill him. No, it would take a passel more than that. I figure if a man can make it through five years in that prison, he can make it through a bullet. Isn't that right, brother? You see my baby brother has larceny in his heart, even if he doesn't show it to a woman. If he didn't, he wouldn't be trying to murder me now."

"Wouldn't be murder." Elijah's voice snarled low with contempt. "It would be justice."

"For taking your woman? You could beat me up for that and leave me to the bears. Kill me now and you'll end up right back in the pen. This time you'll stay in there twenty-one years for certain. No governor will pardon your arse this time."

"Who says? Maybe they'll give me a medal for wiping your ugly face from the earth."

Mary Jane tensed as their words grew sharper with hate, and thunder rumbling in the clouds grew nearer by the minute.

Amos's smile held icy confidence. "No, I don't think you're as all-fired sure on killing me as you say. I don't think you want this pretty woman here seeing you at a necktie social."

She shuddered at Amos's slang for a hanging.

"That so?" Elijah said. "Did you make off with everyone's money from the train? Or were you more intent on killing me and forgot to?"

Amos frowned and his eyes flashed. "You could say that. Screw Claypool and Hoop for making this a damn sight complicated."

"So you're out of money and on the run. How far do you think you'll get without funds, Amos?"

"Who said I'm without money? The pretty lady here gave me hers. You trying to stall me? Won't make any difference. One of us is dead sure as shite."

Elijah drew in a slow breath, and she watched him exhale. "Yeah. Yeah, that's right. So what are doing now, Amos? We going to stand here all day? Or are you begging for you life?"

Amos's sharp gaze, so like Elijah's, sent a shiver through her. They hung on an abyss. And the fall, when it happened, would be cruel and long.

Amos moved enough to make her flinch. "I'll make you a deal, baby brother. Your life for hers. I promise I won't kill her. I'll take her to Portage and let her go."

No. Oh God, no, Elijah. She couldn't lose him again. She would rather die herself. Right then she made a determination. Another plan.

If worse came to worse, she would die for *him*.

Elijah blinked, then blinked again, but his expression never changed. The rifle in his hands did not budge. "What guarantee do I have you won't hurt her?"

"My word as your brother."

"You bastard, you aren't my brother." Elijah's voice thickened with Ireland, emotion tight and charged as the thunderstorm threatening above. "You were some changeling. Our poor mother must have taken you in."

Amos's chuckle sounded real, filled with condescension and mirth. "Living in that cell must have turned you mad. Pretty little Mary Jane here would be better off with me."

Elijah's voice hissed with fury, his eyes narrowed, his lips curled with loathing. "You're *not* going to touch her ever again. I'll lie down and die like a dog first, do you hear me, Amos? You'll have to shoot my head off."

She had never seen Elijah this incensed, and her blood ran cold.

"Ooohooo." Amos's voice crooned. "Damn, but you have

learned a few things in jail, haven't you?"

"I learned to hate you more than anything or anyone. I learned to despise you as much as you hated me all my life."

Amos grunted, the noise a clear dismissal. "You know, I confessed all to this girl here. Tell him what I told you, Mary Jane. Tell him why I had to kill Maureen."

She stared at Amos in disbelief. "No—I—no."

Amos lifted his rifle a tad higher. "Tell him now, or I shoot him."

She put up a hand in panic. "No. Please. I will tell him. Do not do anything rash."

"Then turn towards him and tell him everything."

She turned slowly, facing Elijah. But Elijah kept his rifle sighted on Amos and his body still.

Panicky and feeling weak she said, "He thinks that Maureen was…in the wrong." She swallowed hard.

"Get the story right, girl."

Amos's remonstration sent a wave of courage through her. She would tell Elijah, and that would give her and Elijah time to think how to escape the situation.

She cleared her throat and started with a stronger voice. Sweat dotted her face, and the wind increased, sending a cold breeze over her body. A flash of lightning brightened the sky to the northwest. "He said that Maureen was not a virgin when she met you. That she had…"

"Spit it out for him, girl."

"That she had relations with him of her own free will. That she came to him the morning she died and asked him to run away with him." As her words flowed, she watched a muscle twitch in Elijah's jaw, but he never took his gaze off his brother. "She was not the woman you believed. He killed her because he wanted to and because he believes she was sent by the devil to lure him into hell."

Amos made an indignant sound. "That's the short version

of the tale, Elijah, but she's got it mostly right."

Elijah's jaw continued to clench and release, then his voice purred out with lethal intensity. "Even if all that were true—and it isn't—Maureen didn't deserve to die. No one deserves what you did to her, you filthy serpent." Amos started to speak, but Elijah cut him off. "From the first day I entered Eastern State, I lived day by day knowing that when I left that cell twenty-one years later, I would hunt you down and kill you for what you did to Maureen." Elijah took a deep breath and let it out, some of the heat leaving his eyes, his shoulders less tense, his voice not as rough. "But I'm making a vow, Amos. I'll lay down my rifle if you will."

Thunder punctuated his statement, and then all she heard was the wind tossing in the trees, gathering strength. Amazement held her silent and immobile.

Amos kept his rifle pointed on his brother, his own eyes reflecting surprise. "What?"

"I said, I'll lay my weapon down if you will. We walk away from this alive. Both of us. Because nothing is more important to me than being with Mary Jane. And I can't have that if I'm dead or in jail."

Her heart swelled, her eyes watering. She wiped at her face as tears spilled onto her cheeks for what seemed the hundredth time in the last three days.

Amos's rifle lowered slightly. "You would do that? After everything?"

"I would."

She saw one second of softening in Amos's eyes. One smidgen of regret. Then it disappeared like a wisp of fog.

"Elijah, you willing to die for Mary Jane? Lie down and die like a dog?"

Without hesitation Elijah said, "I would. I'd die for her."

Amos smirked. "Well then, I guess you got me, brother. I'll put my rifle down real slow."

Elijah nodded, and started to lower his as well.

Amos stooped, his rifle now touching the ground. He reached for his waist holster, jerking a pistol free and aiming the business end under his own chin. "Ah, feck this. Goodbye, brother."

Elijah moved. "No! No!"

A pistol blast assaulted her ears, and Mary Jane saw Amos's face dissolve in a splatter of blood. Stunned, she put her hands over her face, "Oh my God. Oh God."

"Jesus." Elijah's voice ached with horror, breaking as he said, "Ah Jesus."

Silence blanketed them. Mary Jane dared drop her hands to her sides, but she did not look at Amos crumpled on the ground. Instead, she turned towards Elijah. He stared at his dead brother, his face wiped clean of expression, his eyes glazed.

"Elijah."

When he did not speak, she moved towards him. She stood in front of him and cupped his face. "Do not look at him, Elijah."

As if broken from the spell, he gasped. "Damn you to hell, Amos McKinnon."

He looked down at her, sorrow etched in his features.

"Elijah..." What else could she say, her body and soul numb from what had happened?

She released him, and he walked slowly towards his brother. When he reached Amos, he knelt beside the fallen man. He heaved a shuddering sigh, then hung his head. He stood and walked back towards Mary Jane until he met her halfway.

He tugged her close, his gaze searching, as stunned and haunted as she felt. "He's gone, Mary Jane. He can't hurt you again. I just wish..." His voice broke, and tears filled his eyes. "I...I didn't want to kill him anymore, Mary Jane." Ragged and aching, his voice cracked and tears spilled from his eyes. "I was going to tie him up for the authorities. He could have faced justice."

"Why did he kill himself? I do not understand."

"He wanted the last word, darlin'. He wanted to take my revenge away from me. The sick bastard wanted the last word no matter what."

"That is where he was wrong, Elijah. He could not take from you what was already gone."

He buried his face in her hair, gathering her tight to his body. As he released his grief, she clasped his head and pressed him close. "It is all right, it is all right." She murmured reassurances, her heart breaking along with his. "You did all you could. You tried to save him."

He leaned back enough so she could his face. Her thumbs grazed his wet cheeks. "When he took you, nothing mattered to me anymore but finding you. Nothing."

His words, rasping in his husky, rumbling voice, cradled her heart. "I thought you were dead, Elijah. I thought..."

Tears on her own cheeks showed him her feelings. Feelings too deep and raw to share easily.

Elijah crushed her against his chest as his mouth came down over hers. Immediately his touch gentled, his light, cherishing kisses soothing rather than passion filled. Shaken to the core, the terror of the hours in Amos's presence crashed in on her. A sob escaped her lips. She knew her face was screwed up in a type of anguish she could not express any other way. Grabbing his shirt and hanging on, she buried her face in his shoulder. She allowed the terror she had experienced to erupt.

Sobs shook her shoulders as he whispered words of comfort. "Easy now, darlin'. It's all right. You are safe. He can't hurt you. You are safe."

His fingers tangled in the hair that tumbled about her shoulders. His soothed her with as he palmed her back, rubbing life and connection into his embrace. Her eyes burned as she released each pent up emotion. It seemed forever, but she finally calmed. Quiet descended around them but for the forest birds chirping and a rumble of thunder overhead. Sunlight disappeared under clouds.

He drew back a bit, eyes ridden with apprehension. "Did he... Amos didn't touch you?"

She pressed her fingers over his mouth. "He slapped me once, but he did not touch me inappropriately. I feared he might, but he did not."

He leaned his forehead against hers, a sigh of relief gusting from his lungs. "Thank God."

A cracking noise nearby caused them both to jerk. Elijah released her and shoved her behind him as he snatched his rifle from the ground. Fear arched through her until she saw what caused the noise.

One of the O'Gannon twins stood outside the tree line, rifle raised. "Someone want to tell me what the hell is goin' on here?"

Elijah kept his weapon trained on the other man. "That depends on whether you're friend or foe, O'Gannon."

O'Gannon lowered his rifle and held his other hand up. "A friend to you, McKinnon." He reached into his pocket and held up a shiny badge. "I'm U.S. Marshal Seamus O'Gannon at your service. My brother and I were having some time off when all this happened. Looks like we walked right into some mighty bad blood without even trying. Are you both all right?"

As O'Gannon walked towards them, Elijah's shoulders lost tension and he lowered his weapon as well. "We've been better. What the hell are you doing here?"

The other man approached Amos's body, took a glance, then came towards them. "Been tracking this mess for a couple of days after the train robbery. It's long story, but it looks like you and your wife need some help."

"Thank you, Mr. O'Gannon." Mary Jane snuggled into Elijah as he put his arm around her waist. "Is Robert all right?"

O'Gannon nodded. "He was when I left him." He smiled.

"He's got quite a temper, and he told me if I didn't get out there and kick some ass, he'd kick mine. Looks like you've taken care of everything for me, McKinnon."

Elijah shook his head and then pressed a kiss to Mary Jane's temple. "Amos took care of himself."

O'Gannon nodded as he scanned their battered appearances. "You both look like you need a doctor. There will be considerable explaining to do when we get to civilization."

Mary Jane saw the resignation in Elijah's face. "I expect so, Marshal. I expect so."

But as Mary Jane leaned her head against Elijah's shoulder and sighed, she realized the nightmare had truly ended.

Portage

Mary Jane sighed as she sank onto the edge of the hotel room bed, relief threading through her body after her bath. She considered dressing in the unmentionables and clothes given to her by the hotel owner's wife...including the corset and crinoline. Instead she pulled the quilt, blankets, and sheets down and crawled naked into bed. She huddled into the coverings and hissed as the cold sheets prickled her skin. A warm bath had felt wonderful, but she needed more. She needed calm thoughts and sleep. Precious sleep. She closed her eyes, thoughts of Elijah dominating. Nothing mattered for now but that he was safe.

O'Gannon had accompanied them into Portage, which turned out to be only ten miles away from where they had the showdown with Amos. There they met with the sheriff and told their stories a couple of times. Mary Jane rejoiced when she realized no charges would be filed against Elijah for Claypool, nor did the authorities wish to jail her for saving herself from Hoop. Though the whole process had taken hours, O'Gannon had spoken up for them as well and that shortened the time they spent explaining nightmarish events.

Everyone else on the train had fared well and testified that

Elijah and Mary Jane had acted bravely in the face of the train robbery.

Now all Mary Jane wanted was to snuggle in this bed with Elijah. Thoughts of what might happen when he returned from purchasing food filled her mind. She ached to hold him, to connect in a deeper way. To show him how much she loved him.

He had not mentioned love, but she knew he did love her. His actions told her everything she needed to know.

When the door unlocked and opened, she jerked from a half sleep and clutched the sheets to her chest. Elijah stepped in and closed and locked the door. Relief regulated her heart.

"Goodness, Elijah, you scared me."

He smiled, some of the old Irish charm back in his eyes. "Sorry, darlin'. It might take you a while to calm down. I know I'm still edgy. Did you have a nice bath?"

"I did."

He placed his purchases down on a table. "Why don't you rest while I take a bath?"

"All right. How is your head?"

"Doesn't even ache."

When he started to disrobe, she sighed and enjoyed watching him. A doctor had examined his head and the wound showed no sign of infection. A small bandage covered the bullet's graze.

For the first time in what seemed ages, she relaxed, her body releasing ravaging fear. With that she found she could not keep her eyes open. Tiredness caused her to drift, lovely sounds of him sloshing around in the big tub music to her ears. Some time later she awakened, and felt his arms slip around her. Sleep, though, refused to relinquish Mary Jane. She sank into a cloud of fluffy comfort, cradled in strong arms and the delicious contentment of total safety.

What seemed an infinite time later, she awoke, much more

alert. Elijah's arms held her against his chest. One of her thighs nestled between both of his hard, muscular legs. She pressed to his side, her right hand cradled in his as he held her palm to his chest. He secured her in a protective grip. For a few moments she breathed deeply, drinking in his clean, wholly masculine scent. A swirl of delicious need pulsed to life inside, demanding she shift and rub against his warm skin.

"Awake, darlin'?" His question rumbled, and as she looked up at his bristle-covered chin, he tightened his arms in a gentle squeeze.

"Yes. Did you sleep?"

"Some."

Despite the comfort and rightness she experienced in his embrace, it hit her that she had never been pressed to him *quite* like this. Yes, they had sat naked together in Mrs. Connor's bathtub, but now the air felt more intense, as bright as the lightning that had burst over Portage not long ago. She had never felt as vulnerable as now. It thrilled her, but it also sent apprehension through her. Now they were in Portage and had survived the authority's interrogation—what would happen to them? Between them?

Disturbed, she sat up. She held the sheets over her breasts, unwilling to relinquish all modesty. It was too late to be embarrassed that she had lain completely naked with him.

Elijah stretched and yawned. His muscles rippled and bunched in his arms and chest. Every inch of her tingled as she watched the sheets slide low on his hips. She may have seen him naked before, and she had taken a bath with him and touched him intimately. She shared things with him she'd never told another person. That didn't stop Mary Jane from admiring his blatant masculinity, the power she felt coiled in his body. Her gaze roamed over his muscled chest and followed the hair that curled there and trailed over his stomach.

His eyes narrowed. "What's wrong?"

She tried for a smile, but it failed. "We survived. We are

alive."

His eyebrows went up. "That is a good thing, right?"

"Yes. I—I just feel as if now we are in Portage and the trip is almost complete, we will go back to our lives. We..." She drifted, unable to verbalize her fears. "There is so much I want to say, Elijah. So much feeling inside me I do not know where to start."

His sad eyes stared into hers. Would he tell her they could not pursue a relationship? She dreaded the possibility.

"I am sorry about Amos," she said. "I mean... I am not sorry that he is dead, but he *was* your brother."

Emotion raced across his face. He shifted and then sat up, turning away from her as he climbed out of bed. "I planned and plotted and seethed with anger for five years, Mary Jane. Up until I faced off with him rifle to rifle, I planned to kill him. Then I couldn't do it. That's why I offered to put down my rifle. But before that I couldn't think of anything but killing him. What kind of man does that make me? Why aren't you afraid to be with me knowing what I'm capable of? Why aren't you on the next train to Pittsburgh and running as far away from me as you can?"

Hurting for him, for the self-contempt she heard in his voice, she stared at his naked strength. "Damn it, Elijah, do not tell me you are anything like your brother or that you somehow deserve punishment for what he chose to do. You are such a beautiful, handsome man. But not just in form, but in mind. I know that about you. I think I must have known, somehow, from the first time I saw you. I could not have trusted you otherwise."

His turned back towards her, a slight smile on his face. "Is that a curse I heard, darlin'?"

She smiled. "Yes, it is. If you are corrupted, then I am as well. I might as well start with cursing."

He laughed, but the mirth was short lived. "You trusted me from the beginning?"

She lowered her gaze to his hard chest, fascinated with his

dusky nipples, the broad muscled planes. "Do you think I could have been as intimate with you as I have been if I had not trusted you?"

As he watched her, she slipped from the bed and stood in front of him, completely naked. She thrilled to the way his gaze raked over her. Pure, masculine hunger filled his eyes, a steady, burning desire that flared. Renewed need, simmering steady beneath the surface, settled low in her stomach and fluttered to life. Unashamed, but feeling shy, she allowed her gaze to slide down to his waist and lower.

Oh my. Oh indeed. His cock lay semi-erect, large and thick and fascinating within a nest of dark curls. Below that proof of his desire hung twin globes.

She jerked her gaze back to his face. "When I thought you were dead, I did not care about anything but taking my own revenge. I wanted to avenge *you*, Elijah. I plotted to trick Amos. To make him trust me. Then, I would do the unthinkable. I would kill him."

His eyes widened for a mere second, then he reached for her shoulders. "You what?"

"I wanted to kill him, Elijah. I finally understood, really understood, what you felt when Maureen was killed. Other than staying alive, I made it my mission to find a way to kill him."

He stared at her for a long time, his eyes showing confusion and growing belief. "You put your life in danger."

She shook her head. "In any more danger than I already was? No. My life did not mean much, because you were no longer in it. You see, Elijah, you are not the monster you think you are. Because if you are evil, then so am I."

"No." His voice was a harsh whisper. "You could never be anything but the most beautiful..." His voice broke a little. "Beloved woman I have ever known."

Her heart soared with heady happiness. "Beloved?"

"When I woke up after Varney shot me and realized they had taken you..." He swallowed hard, his eyes blazing with anger, with sorrow. "When I realized that you could be hurt, could be taken from me forever, I knew nothing mattered beyond finding you. Telling you how I feel. Showing you how much you mean to me." He kissed her forehead and her nose. "Maybe I did go mad when I was in Eastern State those five years. Then you gave me my life back. You showed me gentleness and respect and understanding. You wore away at the hate inside me."

She smiled. "Even when I was arguing with you in the rain?"

One corner of his mouth turned up. "Even then."

She pressed into his body and clung to his shoulders. "Perhaps I just reminded you of what was already inside you. It was just hiding, Elijah. Just hiding."

With a low groan he gathered her to his chest, cupping the back of her neck as he covered her mouth with us. His kiss did not cajole her into passion, but hurtled her straight into the fire. Something new exploded between them, refusing and denying restraint. She wanted this. She wanted him more than anything she wanted before. Even her need for revenge had not topped this growing, wonderful desire to love and be loved.

He drew back with a gasp, his chest heaving up and down, his eyes simmering with a barely banked heat. "Darlin', tell me to stop if you don't want this. Tell me to stop right now."

His erection pressed hard, a masculine invader. She wanted to give him pleasure. "I want to know what you feel like inside me. Show me how you feel, Elijah. Show me."

He plunged his fingers into her hair. "God, yes."

With a whisper soft kiss, he tempered his passion for a single moment. His lips feathered over hers, sweet and light, and kindled an exquisite burn low in her stomach. He lingered over her top lip and then her bottom, each caress driving her mad with need. She shimmied, and her nipples brushed the hair on his chest, and her belly brushed the hard press of his cock.

With another groan, his kiss angled this way and that, exploring and tasting with ravenous hunger. Tongue against tongue, he tutored Mary Jane in how to kiss, what he wanted and needed. Her tongue coiled with his, then she licked deep into his mouth, and he groaned in obvious approval. She had never felt this free or powerful in her life, and she gave in to the desire, the wanton and wild that yearned to explode. Her hunger to know and explore him surprised her, but she reveled in it with freedom. She'd never felt this out of control.

All doubts vanished.

All worry escaped.

Her world came alive under his touch.

Sensations exploded into brilliant life as Elijah cupped her breasts. His lips traced over her ear, his tongue stealing inside, his hot breath stirring shivers of delight. The stubble on his jaw tickled her neck as he pressed hot kisses along her skin. As his thumbs swept over her nipples, she gasped. Writhed in his hold. Before she knew it his lips were there, sucking and teasing, his tongue flicking over one nipple and then the other with relentless licks. He ravished her breasts over and over until the heat and want between her thighs ached. Whimpering in delight, she clutched his head to her breasts and arched. Down, down his lips wandered. She pressed her legs together to try and remove the ache. His hands caressed her small ribcage and along her stomach. She moaned and shivered as her skin came alive, so sensitive under exploration. He knelt on the floor in front of her and stared at the fluff of dark hair between her thighs.

Her cheeks heated. "What are you...?"

He kissed his way across her stomach then back up, every sweet, tender kiss a revelation.

When he reached her lips, he whispered against them, his voice a carnal, fervent tone. "I need you. God, how I need you."

Her heart soared. "And I need you."

Seconds flowed into minutes as his touch learned her body.

Though she knew he tried to be gentle, the urgency of his touch, the rasping of his breath told her how much he wanted her. With sweet and delicious attention, he caressed her back and cupped her buttocks, drawing her up so her feet left the floor. Instinctively she wrapped her legs around his waist as he carried her to the bed. He fell backwards onto the surface, and she sprawled on top of him. Feeling awkward and unsure what to do, she hesitated, falling into the startling intensity of his eyes.

"Touch me," he whispered. "Touch me anywhere you want. However you want."

His eagerness to allow her exploration gave her freedom. Joy touched her soul as she sat up and straddled his thighs. She ran her hands over his chest, delighting in the crisp rasp of his hair, his nipples drawn into tight points. She wondered if Elijah felt the same exciting jolt when he was kissed or touched there. She decided to find out, and leaned over to swirl her tongue over his right nipple.

He hissed in a breath, his groan a testament to how much he liked it. "Yes."

Emboldened, she worked his nipples with her lips and tongue. He stuffed his fingers through her hair as she tasted his ribcage, then worked her way down to ridged stomach muscles. So much power. So much...male. The hungry ache between her legs increased. She didn't understand how she would appease this unremitting desire, but eager to discover the answer, she continued exploring. Over and over her lips and tongue journeyed across one muscle then another. She skipped over his erection, still too shy to even look at it closely. Instead she caressed and kneaded his thighs, finding the perfect symmetry and strength more arousing than she expected. The rough hair on his thighs and calves even thrilled her. His feet, big and well made, delighted her need to discover.

When her hands swept over his toes, he jerked. He propped up on his elbows, his chest rising and falling, his eyes filled with raw heat. He watched as she made her way back up his legs, touching, kissing, learning what made him groan and move restlessly. When she reached his cock, which stood hard and upright, Elijah gripped it in one fist and stroked.

A bolt of heat charged through her as she stared. *Oh my. My. This is indecent. This is...wonderful. Exciting.* That excitement coiled in her belly with a force that made her squirm.

Before she could reach for him, he whispered, "Come up here, darlin'."

She crawled up his body, and he enveloped her in his arms. His mouth found hers, and her mind went blank. With each velvet thrust of his tongue, her eagerness heightened, her desire a raging storm that needed to break. She slid her arms about his neck and rode out the thunder, showing with equal force how much she wanted whatever happened next. One of his thighs slipped between hers, then his fingers were there...touching...brushing the secrets he brought to ecstasy back in Mrs. Connor's cabin.

She moaned against his lips as he plied her swollen folds, then concentrated on touching that one spot. One so, so sensitive spot. She gasped. Writhed as his lips closed over one nipple and his fingers brushed across the other nipple.

A rhythm began. His tongue brushed and licked and tormented her nipples, while his hand strayed between her legs and explored with shocking intimacy. Higher and higher the bliss grew until her breath panted, her thighs trembled, her body went tight. But the bliss wouldn't come.

"Take it, darlin'. Feel it." Then he slipped a finger inside her, and she almost yelped as the brush of his finger over aroused tissues felt so wonderful.

A glorious heaven hovered near and she reached for it. She trembled on the brink. His mouth closed over hers, his tongue pumping into her mouth as his thumb caressed her pleasure button over and over. Seconds later the ecstasy rushed through her body, her fingers tightening on his shoulders, her body contracting and releasing over the finger buried inside her. She heard whimpering moans turn to a scream, muffled by his lips and realized she had flown off the edge of the world.

Elijah shifted, parting her thighs with his hips. The broad tip of his cock, so smooth and hard, touched her. He pushed slightly and entered. She gasped in delight as his thick, broad flesh parted tissues aching for yet another release.

"All right?" He kissed her forehead, her nose. "Am I hurting you?"

"No. It feels..."

"Yes?"

"So right."

Braced on his elbows, he gazed down at her, his eyes bright with feral hunger, his voice raw. "Do you want this, sweet Mary Jane?" His hips moved and his cock left her. She moaned and he brushed the length of his flesh over her wet folds, teasing and testing. "Do you want me deep inside you?"

As he continued to tease her, the ache in her body rose. Her hips arched into his and enjoyed the slick slide of heat between her folds.

She barely managed the words, caught up in a daze. "Please, Elijah."

"Hold tight to me."

As his lips covered hers, he thrust again, then back. Each slow intrusion tested her tightness, stretched and glided until with a harder thrust he sank deep. She gasped into his mouth, and he pulled back, sliding out of her. She moaned with disappointment and arched her hips again.

His eyes narrowed, concern plain to see. "Did I hurt you? You're so tight."

"No, you did not hurt me." A small smile touched her mouth. "Do it again."

A broad grin broke over his lips, and when he entered this time, her gasp held the wonder of a woman discovering physical love for the first time. What little she understood about sex after Thaddeus had taken her, had not prepared her for the heat, the thickness and hardness of Elijah's body as he slid full and deep. His hips came flush against hers. He could go no deeper. She felt stretched, but a delicious, growing ache filled her center where Elijah rested.

She clenched and released over his thickness, and now it was his turn to gasp. "Mary Jane."

His hips started to move, each slow, silken thrust parting her flesh, caressing.

"Oh, I... Oh, Elijah, what is happening?"

"I'm loving you. Just loving you."

With those words, the steady excitement escalated. She never knew anything as wonderful as these sensations could exist. The motion, the heat, the fullness combined. Moans parted her lips as her hand glided over his hard body, exploring with frantic need. He thrust with long, deep strokes until the pace quickened and their panting breath filled the night. Ragged breaths tore from her throat as the pleasure grew. She needed more but did not know how to ask for it. He sucked one nipple into his mouth, swirling his tongue. He touched a place high up inside her that felt so wonderful Mary Jane let out a whimpering cry.

Elijah opened his eyes and watched her, trying to leash his passion. He wanted to draw this out, to rein in the seething pleasure that ached in his cock and balls. He rested inside her, pressing down hard, and her eyes widened. Five years of celibacy threatened to unravel him. His arms shook as he braced above her, his breath shuddering as his body screamed for completion. Mary Jane was a light he never knew could exist in his world, a beauty that illuminated the darkness that had taken root in his soul. With her there could be nothing but light and comfort, and a thousand brilliant days and nights.

He stared down at her rosy, parted lips, her eyes glazed

with pleasure. Wonder filled him, and shocking happiness he had abandoned long ago. Sheathed in her heat, he knew only the deepest contentment, the rightness of being a part of her. Her body clenched and released around him, tiny whimpers escaping her throat.

"Please, Elijah. It feels..."

"What does if feel like, darlin'?" The aching question barely made it past his throat.

"So wonderful." The amazement on her face said it all.

Any worries about hurting her vanished as her hips squirmed against him, and her hands cupped his buttocks. He returned to long, slow thrusts, determined she'd know ecstasy before he found his.

Savage need gripped him. *Mine. She is mine.*

Mary Jane caught his rhythm, moving to the tantalizing strokes that pushed his thick length in and out. A tingling sensation started in her middle, and she centered upon it. Boldly she explored his body until her hands clutched at him in desperation. Back and forth his hips swayed, slowed to a pace that maddened her. Blood rushed in her ears as hot pleasure stoked between her legs and expanded to the little button he'd teased so unmercifully. He buried his hands in her hair, his face in her neck. His breath gusted against her skin as his hips started to move faster. His thrusts increased in intensity, each deep plunge sending such sweet bliss through her. The bed creaked beneath them, and even the sound of it increased her pleasure.

Then wild heat blossomed and exploded in her loins, and she cried out again and again as the bliss tore her apart, and she writhed in his arms. As she shivered in delight, his strokes quickened to a hard beat until he stilled, stiffened and growled. His hips jerked and his entire body quaked as he growled again and again, and she felt hot spurts bathe her inside. His seed. She was taking his seed, and the thought sent more sweet shivers through her body.

He raised his head and in the gathering dusk she could still see the deep green of his eyes, and a melting expression that proved his feelings. "I love you, Mary Jane. I love you."

She smiled as her heart expanded with a new joy, and she could say without hesitation, "And I love you, Elijah."

As their breathing slowed, he slipped to the side and drew her tight to him. A warm contentment flowed within and without, a sense that what they experienced transitioned from darkness into light. She knew somehow before the dawn came, she would feel renewed in body and soul. Their connection had brought her the greatest happiness she had ever known.

Chapter Eighteen

Mary Jane awakened in the early morning with Elijah's arms wrapped around her as she lay on her right side. His hands drew her back against him. He teased her nipple, fingers compressing until an arousing sting made her gasp and arch her back. Her buttocks pressed into his erection, and she realized her body wanted him already.

"I want you." His hot breath stole over her ear, his words coaxing her. "I want you."

He lifted her thigh and his thickness pushed into her folds and parted sensitive tissue, sliding slowly but deeply until he filled her as far as he could go. He pressed and retreated, thrust and drew back, the pace an intoxicating blend of sensuality and invasion. As his touch teased her nipples, he feathered and stroked her pleasure center. Sensations heightened, flowing and ebbing until she did not know where she started and where he began. As the excitement surged to a furious buildup, she heard her own groans and did not restrain them. Ecstasy culminated in great waves, surging and shifting until she fell back to earth with a sigh.

Elijah felt her flesh pulse as her cry echoed in the small room. Need rose, and he closed his eyes and fell into the bliss.

He'd awakened with his arms around her, his body absorbing the softness and heat, his craving for her a live thing beyond control. Jesus, Mary and Joseph, she was soft and wet and tight, tightening around him as he kept his thrusts slow. Every time he entered, her breath would hitch. More than animal needs coursed through his body. As he pushed deep inside, and Mary Jane's heat and wetness clenched his hardness, he thought he'd die right there. Nothing had every felt as beautiful as sinking into her body, as pouring his seed into her womb. A primitive desire surged into his blood. He wanted her mad with desire, writhing on his cock until she begged him for more, to bring her to an edge she'd never experienced. He thrust hard, pounding into her until he grunted with each motion.

He flattened his hand over her belly, his voice thick in her ear as he made demands. "God, darlin', you feel so good."

And as her muscles clamped down and shivered around him, he shoved hard and bliss released his seed. He gasped, a groan of soul-melting ecstasy escaping his throat.

He finally stilled and listened to their breaths panting in the otherwise quiet room. Nestled together perfectly, their hearts thumped as one.

"You all right, darlin'?"

She rolled towards him, and in the dim light he saw her smile. "I am more than all right, sir. I do not think anything could have prepared me for...this."

"This?"

"Our...marital relations."

He chuckled and kissed her quickly. "I meant what I said last night. I love you."

She cupped his face, and even in the low light he saw her beautiful smile. "And I meant what I said. What I feel with you and the love right here in my heart is more than I can express, Elijah Jonas McKinnon."

He swept his fingers through the long curls that covered one breast. No, not quite all of her breast. A nipple peeked out and tempted him. He brushed his tongue over the hard tip and she gasped. Then he couldn't stop. She was life and love and tasted better than any desert. His mouth painted kisses down, down, down until he parted her thighs and inhaled her musky arousal.

His tongue flicked over her folds and their creamy essence. She gasped. "Elijah. Oh, what...?"

"Shhh. Lie back and enjoy."

As his mouth and tongue worshipped her, he drank in her taste, her gasps and sighs. She clutched at his head, and urged onward, he learned what made her cry out, what made her pleasure build to the highest point. Discovering her secrets one by one gave him an equal joy, and he desired nothing more than filling her with shattering ecstasy as often as he could. Her breath caught as Elijah smoothed his tongue over the top of her sex. Her musk tasted delicious, her perfume a heady elixir he wanted to feast upon for hours. Soon she twisted and begged and he slipped a finger within and added a new rhythm to match his tongue. She shook and gasped, her body quivering as he took her over the edge.

"Oh my," she said softly. "That was... I never..."

"Until now." He laughed softly. He slid up her body and rested beside her. After brushing a long length of hair from her eyes, he smiled. Her beauty stunned him.

Her eyes held a wonderment and love he'd never hoped to see again in a woman's face. "Sure, and I must be the luckiest bastard that ever once lived in Ireland, Mary Jane."

She cupped his face, and that single touch sent his heart soaring. When she'd witnessed his tears without ridicule, without calling him less than a man, he knew Mary Jane belonged in his heart.

"No more nightmares, Elijah?" Her eyes searched his.

He smiled. "Not a one, my darlin'. Not a one. All I can do is hope they don't come back."

After a short silence, tiny frown lines appeared between her pretty eyes. "We are not married, Elijah."

Panic returned to his thoughts and threatened to diminish

the security he acknowledged moments before. Could it be she didn't wish to marry him?

He clasped her left hand and looked at the ring. "You're saying you don't want to marry me?"

Her mouth popped open, eyes filled with denial. "Of course I do. I love you so much."

Warmth encased his heart. She loved him. Oh God, how wonderful that felt.

"What of your family?" he asked.

Her mouth drew tight with doubt. "They shall be scandalized, but I am finished with pleasing them. With trying to pretend I am something I am not."

Gratified, he smiled. "What type of wedding would you care for, darlin'? One of those fancy to-dos?"

Her frown deepened. "Any way I can marry you, I will." Her eyes brightened. "Let it be here, in Portage."

"Without your family?"

She propped on her elbow and looked down at him. "There is good possibility they will reject the idea of us marrying. If we do not want a scene, we could marry before we arrive in Pittsburgh."

"Where we marry or how is of no consequence to me, Mary Jane. Having you for my own is all I care about." Other concerns started to bombard him. "Damn. Damn."

"What is it?"

"I have no money, no possessions except for that ring. Nothing to offer you."

Her frown grew as wide as a river, and she sat up. As coverings fell to her waist, he was treated to a blatant display of beautiful breasts. He fixated there for a moment, then forced his attention back to the unhappiness on her face.

"Nothing to offer me, Elijah McKinnon?" She sighed again. "Maybe two weeks ago I would have agreed. Would have said an Irishman would never have my heart. But now...now I could live a pauper's life as long as you were in it. You could go back to blacksmithing if you like, or any number of occupations. I do not care about any of it except for being with you."

He scrubbed one hand over his face. "It's a fine thought, but you must be sure. I want you to have a comfortable life."

She rolled her gaze to the ceiling, then sighed. "A fine, comfortable life is well and good, Elijah, but without love I doubt it is worth it. I could marry the richest man in the world tomorrow and it would mean nothing to me. Do you know why?"

He dared ask. "Why?"

She ruffled his hair. "Because he would not be you. Get that through your thick Irish skull, McKinnon. The thought of leaving you, no matter how long... I cannot do it. I do not want to. If you want me to return to Philadelphia, I would follow you."

Pleasure and amazement filled him. "You would do that?"

She nodded emphatically. "Without a doubt."

A smile spread over his face and extended to his heart. "Then let us go to Pittsburgh and your family. Even if they hate me, it won't matter. We will do what we want and choose what we want."

She tilted her head to the side and pursed her lips. "Scandalous."

Wonderment replaced worry as he drew her back into his arms. "I can't believe you would give up crinolines and corsets for me."

She elbowed him gently. "Who said I plan to give up crinolines and corsets?"

He clasped one of her butt cheeks and squeezed, then slapped it gently. She squealed in surprise. He chuckled as she blushed. "Crinolines can't disappear too soon for me, darlin'. I prefer you naked."

She grinned. "Do you?"

He pressed the rising evidence of his desire into the folds

between her legs, teasing her with his promise. "I do." When he kissed her to demonstrate, another thought invaded, and with it, another confession. "Mary Jane, I owe my life to you."

She brushed her palm over his hair, then slid her fingers into the thick strands. "Are you certain it is not the other way around?"

He nodded, the movement emphatic. "My mind was once consumed by one thought—revenge. Because of you, I'm changed forever."

Pittsburgh

Two months later

Mary Jane reached for a glass of wine and sipped the drink with relish. Her throat was parched, and the reception was in full tilt with fifty people in attendance. Certainly not the size of a society wedding...a wedding to a wealthy man would have garnered more adulation. Yet Mary Jane would have it no other way. Would want no other man but Elijah Jonas McKinnon. As she watched over the crowd, she caught sight of Elijah's brother Zeke and his lovely wife and their baby daughter chatting amiably with two other guests. She knew Elijah was elated that they had ventured to Pittsburgh for the wedding.

"He is a fine, fine man, Mary Jane," Mary Jane's sister, Faith, said as they mingled with the small crowd after the wedding.

Mary Jane, who wore a beautiful ecru dress her mother had paid for, smiled with gratification. "I am so glad you think so. I know I do."

Her family had started off scandalized, just as she thought they would be. But, when they saw she refused to back down, they retreated from their position. When they also learned that Elijah had saved her life, that he risked everything for her, their concern about him eased into admiration.

Mary Jane found it immensely pleasing that she no longer cared what society felt, and that she embraced her true self once more.

Faith pushed a curly length of golden wheat hair from her eyes, clearly angered at the recalcitrant hair. "I do have to admire you for...well, telling Mother the wedding would happen with or without a trousseau, with or without money. You were very persuasive."

Mary Jane gazed at her petite sister, so in contrast with herself, and so much more feminine. Yet even Faith had changed. Mary Jane did not know why or how, but it might have something to do with her recent announcement that she, too, planned to wed. A very stuffy, older gentleman she claimed to love. Mary Jane doubted it.

Faith had gone from sunny disposition to staid old matron in a heartbeat. Mary Jane aimed to discover why as soon as the wedding finished.

Her mother now sat next to Elijah on the couch in the family parlor, her expression as welcoming as sunshine from the heavens. Elijah had charmed all the women in the house.

"It is too bad it was not a bigger wedding. You certainly deserved one," said Mary Jane's older sister, Cora, said.

Cora, with her tall and rather thin frame, was as dark as Faith was blond. Mary Jane, being in the middle with coloring, wondered off and on if her sisters could possibly be offspring from different fathers.

Not that she would say as much. *Heavens, no.*

Cora looked down on Mary Jane and sighed. "Elijah is wonderful. Now that he has that job with the newspaper here, he will bring in a decent living and not just be a proper but poor husband."

Leave it up to Cora to speak about money and its necessity.

The only thing Mary Jane regretted was that Elijah's nightmares had not left him forever. Sometimes he still awakened in the middle of the night with his past invading his dreams. But demons haunted his mind less and less. He assured Mary Jane that with her by his side, those dreams would someday disappear forever.

She knew in her heart this was true.

Faith used her fan to cool herself and tilted her small nose up in obvious dislike. "That man is staring this way again."

"Robert O'Gannon?" Mary Jane asked, amused. "Or Seamus O'Gannon?"

Faith shrugged. "I do not know which one he is. Both of them are rather rough around the edges."

Mary Jane quirked one eyebrow. "They are both handsome."

Cora tossed a meaningful look at Faith. "More handsome than your fiancé, Faith. And much younger. How old do you suppose they are?"

Faith glared. "Handsome and young is not a requirement for a good husband."

Mary Jane almost laughed, but held back. "Perhaps you have an admirer, Faith."

Cora snorted. "The other brother is...taller, is he not? They are quite the same except for that."

Mary Jane wasn't certain, but then she did not obsess with the brothers, who had become good friends with Elijah. Mary Jane found it amusing that Seamus and Robert kept darting intrigued glances at her sisters. Cora and Faith, whether they would admit it or not, obviously found the O'Gannons equally interesting.

Mrs. Connor, who attended the wedding in a dress she had purchased with a stockpile of money she had kept under the floorboards of her old cabin, looked elegant enough to compete with any woman in the room. Of course, Mrs. Connor's plain speaking gave her away, and Mary Jane's mother found the woman far too coarse to abide.

Mary Jane smiled at Mrs. Connor and waved. In typical Peg Connor fashion she waved and hooted, causing other people in the room to stare at her.

A surge of pure happiness hit Mary Jane as her handsome groom walked towards her in a dark waistcoat with crisp white shirt, elegantly pressed trousers, and an overall polished appearance. Yes, her Irishman was most assuredly the handsomest man in the room.

A grin curved those sinful lips, and when he reached her he wasted no time asking to speak with her privately.

As they left by way of the back garden door, she clasped his arm. "I hope nothing is wrong, Elijah."

With a quick movement of his left arm, he swept her into a secluded area around the corner of some bushes. In the late afternoon the area was shady and secret. The perfect place for a rendezvous. When his lips met hers, it lasted a long time. Heat and warmth and excitement shot through her.

"My beautiful wife, nothing can ever be wrong again."

"And my family loves you now. I never expected it to be this easy."

"Well, they did oppose it at first."

"For all of two days." She plucked a fallen leaf from his hair. "I think this wedding was good for another reason."

He dived in to nibble her ear, and she shivered in delight. "What is that?"

She moaned as his tongue traced a path along sensitive nerves in her neck. "The O'Gannon brothers seem to have made conquests."

"Your sisters? I noticed that too. It will never work." Elijah shook his head in stern denial, but the amusement in his eyes gave him away. "They are rough country men and your sisters are refined and delicate."

She gave an unladylike snort equal to anything Mrs. Conner might make. "Honestly, sir, I would think you would have learned after meeting me, that delicate is not something that runs in my family. Whether my sisters know it or not, I do not think they are as proper as they believe."

He tilted his head to the side. "I suppose I should know better, but I don't see Robert or Seamus dropping their positions as U.S. Marshals to marry society ladies."

She rolled her gaze to the night sky and sighed. "Well, never underestimate the power of an Irishman to seduce a fine and proper lady to another way of thinking."

He chuckled. "I think it was the other way around, darlin'. I was a rough grain of sand until you smoothed my edges."

In a most scandalous fashion his hand came up and cupped her breast. She had not worn a corset or a crinoline, and when his thumb brushed over her nipple, sweet arousal bolted straight through her. She gasped. "Oh, sir...I think you were mistaken. It was my rough edges that were worn down."

He cupped the back of her neck and brought her close for a kiss, whispering against her lips. "Darlin', I was drowning. Before the dawn, I didn't know how far into the dark I had fallen. Your love saved me."

About the Author

Suspenseful, erotic, edgy, thrilling, romantic, adventurous. All these words describe Denise A. Agnew's award-winning novels. Romantic Times Book Review Magazine called her romantic suspense novels "top-notch" and her erotic romance *Primordial* received a TOP PICK from Romantic Times Book Review Magazine. Denise's record proves that with paranormal, time travel, romantic comedy, contemporary, historical, erotic romance, and romantic suspense novels under her belt, she enjoys writing about a diverse range of subjects. The fact she has lived in Colorado, Hawaii and the United Kingdom has given her a lifetime of ideas. Her experiences with archaeology and archery have crept into her work, as well as numerous travels through the U.K. and Ireland. Denise lives in Arizona with her real-life hero, her husband. Visit Denise's web site at www.deniseagnew.com

It's all about the story...

HORROR

www.samhainpublishing.com

CPSIA information can be obtained at www.ICGtesting.com
Printed in the USA
LVOW041523090412

276823LV00002B/12/P